MW00681899

Ms. Conception

Ms. Conception

Dagmar
To my wonderful
Garfield neighbour.
xo Jen

Jen Cumming

Tryst Books

Tryst Books
720 Bathurst Street, Suite 303
Toronto, ON M5S 2R5

This is a work of fiction. Names, places, and incidents either are the product of the author's imagination or are used fictitiously. Any resemblance to actual people, living or dead, events, or locations is entirely coincidental.

Copyright © 2015 Jen Cumming

All rights reserved. No part of this publication may be reproduced, stored in a retrieval system, or transmitted, in any form or by any means (except brief passages for purposes of review) without the prior permission of the author or publisher.

Cover design: Two Dots Design (Thisistwodots.com)
Interior design: Meghan Behse
Author photo: Anna Prior Photography 2014

Library and Archive Canada Cataloguing in Publication

Cumming, Jen, 1974-, author
    Ms. Conception / Jen Cumming.

 Issued in print and electronic formats.
ISBN 978-0-9940297-1-3 (pbk.).--ISBN 978-0-9940297-2-0 (epub).--
ISBN 978-0-9940297-3-7 (kindle)

    I. Title.

PS8605.U444M7 2015   C813'.6   C2015-902220-7
                                             C2015-902221-5

This is the original print edition of *Ms. Conception*.

To Sydney and Travis, who bring me joy every day.

To the egg and sperm that finally got together –
with a little help.

1

A PROCREATION VACATION? What the hell is that? The first email is from my best friend, Jules, one of the few people who know Jack and I are struggling to have a baby. I ignore the rest of my inbox and start Google searching.

There are hotels in the Caribbean that offer fertility vacations? *Seriously?* Powder white sand beaches, private infinity pools, couples massages with fertility-boosting kelp wraps and reflexology, all to supposedly stimulate semen production. After three years of unsuccessful pregnancy attempts, I've found fertility utopia.

Wait, hold on; there's something here about drinking sea moss elixirs. That doesn't sound overly appetizing. I read a quote from a successful vacationer: "I conceived as soon as I got home." With rising excitement, I check out the menu, knowing Jack loves a great meal. Darn, there's a lot of tofu – this might not fly. My husband Jack is many things, but tofu lover is not on that list.

I click on another link and find the Fertile Turtle vacation package. Apparently sea turtles are symbols of fertility. "You can watch sea turtles hatch while trying to fertilize your own egg." My cheeks flame. I couldn't have sex with anyone watching, even poor sea turtles. Jules is definitely yanking my chain. Hitting reply to her email, I type, "The poor turtles. You bitch!"

This is what my life has come to. The ongoing struggle to have a baby has spilled over into desperate Internet searches, sexy lingerie purchases, and my ovulation cycle scheduled into our iPhones. Oh god, sexy lingerie purchases. My face flames brighter at the memory. I thought spicing up our sex life might help, but in my crazy one-track baby-on-the-brain mind, I'd stupidly put the office address in the "ship to" box. That was a *really* fun day in the office. Pressing my hands against the heat of my cheeks, I sigh and turn back to my computer. Another day begins for me, Abigail Nichols, marketing maven by day, fertility-obsessed sex fiend by night.

"You okay, Abby?" My assistant, Scott, is hovering in the doorway. Cheeks betraying me, I quickly close my browser, hiding evidence of my infertility desperation. He is the best assistant I've ever had, anticipating my needs before I have a chance to articulate them, right down to keeping a spare pair of panty hose in his drawer in case of emergency, and for all that, I can forgive his office gossiping. He crosses the room gracefully, and sinks into my spare chair with a sheaf of papers requiring my review or signature. I smile tightly, mentally telling my hot cheeks to cool it, and reach for Scott's pile. He pulls back out of reach.

"Spill it, lady." Scott looks huffy. He knows something is up, and not being a part of it is maddening for him.

It's not really Scott I'm worried about. I don't need my bosses, both "guys' guys," to find out their hard-working director of client services is eyeing a maternity leave. Granted they can't sack me for trying to have a baby, but they can make my life miserable. Marketing agency life, particularly at small boutique shops like ours, can be brutal. It's all about the bottom line. Well, and the profit line for the partners. I have yet to make partner, but don't want to jeopardize the possibility.

"Is Production finished with the promotional package for Saber?" I ask, hoping the change in subject will throw Scott off the scent. Saber, a high-end furniture manufacturer, is one of my clients, and we are creating a new marketing strategy and corporate identity.

"Not yet. They got backed up with a design for Marco. You're next in the queue." Scott isn't remotely British but is always trying to work in words like "queue" and "flat" to sound more cultured.

"Damn him; probably a new logo for his effing bowling team." Marco is one of our two partners, and constantly uses work resources for personal gain. He cultivates a four-season tan, blond-enhanced wavy hair, and smoldering gray eyes. Some women are drawn to his Euro fashions, others to his BMW, and me to nothing about him. Charlie is our other partner. His name is actually Norman, but we all refer to him as Charlie, as in *Charlie's Angels*. He mainly communicates with the senior staff via email, voice mail, or notes on our desks and is rarely spotted in person. I am positive he sneaks into the office at night to review our work because, despite his absence, he seems up to date on all our latest projects. Charlie and Marco bonded (strangely, because they are like oil and water), began working at an advertising agency together, and took what they learned, along with a few choice clients, and started up our agency. Charlie, the senior partner, is the brains of the operation, and Marco is its face.

Many of the other females who have worked in our office, though, have landed the job because they were "shagging" Marco, as Scott would say. They are all young, buxom, and sorely lacking in intelligence or skill, at least in office matters. When Marco bores with one of his conquests, he breaks up with her by giving her a job and leaves it to me to fire her.

When I first joined the firm, it was rumored throughout the building that I was his latest blonde, but soon it was clear I lacked the credentials: too much brain, too-small breasts. When he hits a dry spell, he tends to focus his flirting energies in my direction, but he's pretty much harmless. There are days when our working relationship feels more like mother and delinquent child, not employee and boss.

Scott and I finish reviewing the production schedule and move on to my calendar.

"You've got yourself booked out at one o'clock today?" I can hear the curiosity in his voice.

"Doctor's appointment."

"Didn't you have one last week?"

"Follow-up. Totally routine." I'm not a very good liar. The truth is in my iPhone. I'm ovulating, and Jack and I are meeting up for a quickie, but there is no way in hell I'll let Scott know that. The desperation kicked up a notch when Jack and I celebrated our third anniversary two months ago. I'm thirty-one and Jack is forty. Our relaxed, wait-and-see approach is no longer working.

"Hmm..." He doesn't sound convinced. "You should really think about getting your hair colored. I think I see a gray or two," and with that he twirls, nose in the air, and flounces out of my office. *Ouch.* Cringing, I reach for my compact to check out my hair. When I can't spot a single gray hair in my blonde chin-length bob, I realize he's just being petty. He knows I'm holding out on him. Standing, I smooth down my navy blue skirt, shrug into my suit jacket, and head downstairs. Hounding Production to drop Marco's latest personal project takes up most of the morning, so I text a quick reminder to Jack as I get ready to sneak home.

To Jack: *C u in 20 mins. Xo Abbs*

To Abby: *2day not good. 2nite work? Xo Jack*

To Jack: *ovul8ing – NOW.*

No answer.

To Jack: *Just wham bam thank u ma'am – no 4play, quick, I promise. x*

To Abby: *fine. 30 mins.*

Great. I need a willing partner in this venture and he's already grumbling. Jack has been having trouble with our baby-making plan. I know he desperately wants to be a dad, but he finds the pressure of trying to get pregnant seriously affects his performance. Truthfully, turning forty hasn't helped in that department either. He worries about being an old dad. That's why racy lingerie and illicit "nooners" were high on the list of ways to spice up our sex life. The challenge, he tells me, is that he still knows it's a command performance. My ovulation window is only open for so long, so it's do-or-die time. This quickie is going to take a little extra effort on my part.

I jog to the subway station, which is quite a feat in my heels. I'm slightly ahead of schedule, but I'll need to take a little extra time primping, to help Jack along. Good thing there is all that newly acquired lingerie in my closet. The chime sounds to warn of the subway's imminent departure just as I dash on board. I plop into a seat and notice a young woman with a stroller. My uterus instantly contracts. Gasping, I close my eyes. I don't hear any actual ticking from a biological clock, but my body reminds me of my childless state every time I see a baby.

I open my eyes as the subway lurches forward and watch as a little bootie drops from the stroller. Balancing myself against the swaying of the cars, I scoop up the boot and hand it back to the young mother.

"Oh, thank you, she's always kicking them off," she says with a mix of exasperation and pride.

I smile and sneak a look into the depths of the stroller. My breath catches and my uterus throbs. "She's gorgeous. How old is she?" My voice sounds breathy.

"Six months," she answers as she gathers up her things, preparing to leave at the next station. She waves good-bye as the doors slide open, and I slump back into my seat, close my eyes again, and cup my belly protectively with my hands. I picture myself as a mom; pushing a stroller through Toronto, playing in the park, coming home from work and seeing the joy that "Mommy's home." I want all of that. Taking a deep breath, I mentally chant my mantra, as my hippie mother has suggested.

"I will get pregnant, I will have a baby, I will be a mom." I continue to repeat this as the subway rumbles across the Bloor Viaduct, and by the time we pull into Broadview Station, I am feeling calm. I am feeling fertile. I know this will work.

Making it to our tiny two-story house on Ellerbeck Street in record time, I scan the street but don't see Jack's car. Perfect. I drop my keys on the front hall table and dash upstairs to the bathroom. This is the next room on our to-do list, but after three years, we still have yet to tackle it. The tacky seventies tile with its gaudy orange flowers mocks me as I rummage through the drawers for makeup, hairbrush, and perfume.

I hear Jack's key in the door as I fluff my hair one last time and adjust the sexy but abrasive black-lace teddy. A man must have invented these damn things. There is certainly no way on earth the creator has ever tried one on. I sprawl across the twisted sheets of our unmade bed and listen for Jack's footfalls on the stairs.

"Abbs, I don't want to sound like a jerk, but can we hurry this along? Traffic is awful and I left in the middle of a meeting with a potential new client and ... wow. Wow." Jack appears in the doorway, looking rushed – his navy tie slightly askew against his blue pinstripe shirt. He is momentarily speechless and runs his hands through his brown hair, then lights up in a huge smile, blue eyes widening and his twinkle turning to a hungry glint as he catches sight of me. Knowing time is precious, Jack strips down, tossing his clothes in a heap.

"You're going to look all wrinkly and everyone will know what you've been up to."

"They'll be jealous." Jack kisses my neck, which sends shivers up and down my body, goose bumps appearing everywhere. I catch sight of my watch and realize we need to speed things along if I'm going to make it back to the office in time for my senior staff meeting. I get Jack to roll over and I straddle him, running my hands over his chest. We move together and Jack utters a low groan.

"Wait baby, let me get you going," he breathes into my ear. I pause, trying to find the sexiest way to say, "I just need your swimmers; don't worry about me." These encounters have little to do with me and my pleasure – god, how sad is that? I curse the friends who never told me how unromantic trying to have a baby really is.

"I'm almost there. Let's come together." I cross my fingers – a leftover superstition from my childhood – and lie. The safest route is just to fake it.

"Oh god, here I come," he says through clenched teeth. I put on an orgasm imitation that would do Meg Ryan proud and match in stride. At that very moment, our bedroom door opens and we hear a shriek.

Is that–? No. It couldn't be.

I hear another scream and realize this time it's me.

"Mom, what the hell are you doing here?" Jack barks as we both fumble helplessly for the sheets that are knotted underneath us to cover our nakedness – well, Jack's nakedness and my crotch-less black teddy.

"Oh my, I'm sorry," Marilyn stammers.

"Mom, get out," Jack screams as his mom hurriedly closes the door. He leaps up, grabs his clothes, and starts to put them on, while I pull the sheet over my head and curl into the fetal position. Part of me wants to laugh, but the other part is furious with Marilyn for intruding in our home.

"Abbs, I'm so sorry." Jack is stomping into his black pants, the waves of anger and embarrassment radiating off his body.

"Why is she here? How the hell did she get in? Did you give her a key?" I pull the sheet down and sit up. The urge to laugh is gone. My mind plays a movie of all of the meddling and interfering Marilyn has done over the years. "Please tell me you didn't give her a key?" Jack's silence gives me the answer.

"Abby, she's my mom. I'm all she's got." Jack tucks in his shirt, which is totally rumpled, and shoots me a pathetic look. "I'll just go and see if she's okay." He heads for the door.

Oh sure, I think; *go see if* she's *okay. Make sure* she's *fine after she broke into our house and walked in on us.* I cringe, the humiliation building to the sort of climax I wish I'd had a few minutes earlier. I shudder and lie back. Shoving a pillow under my butt to lift my pelvis, I put my legs in the air, feet pointing to the ceiling. On the bright side, I have Jack's swimmers inside me. I squeeze my legs together for my allotted twenty minutes, close my eyes, and begin to chant.

"I will get pregnant, I will have a baby, I will be a mom."

2

I ALTERNATE BETWEEN humiliation and rage as I ride the subway back to work, my earlier inner peace and mantra eluding me. I try to visualize Jack's sperm moving upstream, but the calming breathing exercises my mother taught me are of no help. I keep seeing Marilyn's horrified face, Jack leaping up and rushing to see if his mother was okay, and me, legs in the air like an idiot. Ideally, I should be feeling buoyed and satisfied, even a little bit wanton, from an illicit quickie, but as I trudge up the stairs from the subway station, weariness takes over. At a coffee shop near the office, I order a chai latte, the smell of cinnamon and spices soothing me. I hide at a small table in the back and pull out my phone. Jules answers on the first ring.

"Hey, it's me."

"What's going on? You don't sound like yourself." Even though we live miles apart, Jules can always tell when something is wrong. Some nights when we chat on the phone, each of us knocking back the better part of a bottle of pinot grigio, it's like she's beside me on the couch. We have passed many evenings like this, dishing on our jobs – she's in sales – men, money, and anything else that comes up.

"You could say that," I say, rolling my eyes skyward as I whisper the events of the last hour into the phone, hoping no one overhears me.

"Abby, you can't stand for this. That woman is unbelievable." I smile for the first time in an hour. Jules's outrage justifies my own. "I love Jack, you know I do, but this is getting crazy. I would crucify Liam if he gave his mother a key to our house. What did he say?"

"Not much. I mean, a lot of apologies, but that's about it." I sigh. Jack can't stand up to his mother – that's my problem, and I know it.

"You should change the locks."

"Think about it, Jules. I'd have to give Jack a key and inevitably he'd give one to Marilyn. Believe me, I've already thought of that."

"Do you want me to talk to him?" she asks, tentatively.

"I love you for offering, but no. I already have a meddlesome mother-in-law. I don't want him to think I have a meddlesome friend."

"What are you going to do?"

"I don't know. It's like our wedding all over again. She can't keep her nose out of our business. Remember the dresses?" Jules laughs as we both recall the horrible pink chiffon "thing" she pushed to have my bridesmaids wear. Jack and I had many heated discussions about the proper role of the mother of the groom.

"Don't forget her toast to you. Remember she went on and on about Jack's ex?"

I don't need Jules to remind me. The memory still burns.

"I guess I have to let it go. I want a baby, and walking around like a stress case isn't healthy. It won't help anything to rehash this again with Jack. I already know all of Marilyn's excuses. He's so protective of her, which on some level I love about him. I only hope I have kids who love me that much. Besides, it's not like my mom is staying out of our business. She tried to talk to me about different sexual positions that can effect conception. Why can't I have normal relatives?" Exhaling loudly, I slouch back in the chair and take stock. My tea is cold, my afternoon meetings are beckoning, six missed calls and fifteen emails flash on my phone, there's a stain on my skirt, and I'm exhausted. "But I cut up that bloody teddy Jack liked so much."

That brings a laugh from Jules, and I smile ruefully at the memory of me fumbling in my bedside table and taking a tiny pair of nail scissors to the teddy as I lay with my feet in the air.

"Well done. Those things are such a pain. Have a drink tonight, honey. Relax, put your feet up, and remember today may have been more productive than you think."

"Thanks, Jules. I've gotta run." We hang up, and I sit for a few more minutes before I rouse myself from my fog and head back to the office. As I open the smoky glass front doors to our one-story black-stuccoed building in the trendy fashion district, Scott pounces on me.

"Why are you back so early? Did you get interrupted?" His words stop me in my tracks.

"What did you just say?" I ask, madly trying to figure out how Scott would know Marilyn interrupted us. Damn, maybe someone was at the coffee shop?

"You're back earlier than I thought. Your doctor's appointments normally take longer. What's with you?" he asks, staring at me. I can feel my cheeks tingling, signaling their intent to turn beet red, and turn quickly toward my office, refuge in sight.

"It was just a *quick* visit." Tripping over the word "quick," I duck inside my door, face aflame.

The afternoon passes slowly. We have our typically boring staff meeting, and then the day seems to move even slower as I robotically answer my emails and push paper around my desk, doing my best to keep busy while I try to take my mind off Jack and Marilyn. Every time they creep into my consciousness, bile rises in my throat. Jack calls me twice, but I ignore him, sending his calls to voice mail. When I play them back at the end of the day, I can hear the worry in his voice. He promises me a wonderful dinner and a quiet evening. It all sounds lovely, but feels a bit hollow.

"Got a minute?" Marco asks as he walks right into my office, disregarding the fact that I'm on the phone and papers are strewn over my desk. When I shake my head, he gives me a "wrap it up" signal and leans back out the door, returning with a well-dressed gray-haired woman in her late forties. Her charcoal gray pantsuit looks more expensive than anything in my closet, and I catch a glimpse of pricey shoes – ones I'm sure I've seen in the window of Holt Renfrew. Her deep brown eyes widen as she takes in the state of my desk, and I self-consciously run one hand through my hair and attempt to tidy my desk with the other. Marco cocks his head to the side and glares at me. Remembering the phone tucked between my ear and shoulder, I delete Jack's messages and hang up the phone.

"Abby, I'd like to introduce you to Linda Lester. Linda, this is Abigail Nichols." I lean across the desk, hand extended, and knock over a teetering pile of papers. Watching paper flutter to the floor like confetti at a wedding, I feel my stomach sinking. I have no idea who this woman is, but I'm certainly not winning any first impression contests.

"Um, nice to meet you," I say, waving away the mess on the floor. Linda eyes me up and down, my Banana Republic outfit suddenly feeling rather cheap.

"It's nice to meet you too – Abby, is it?" Her voice is hard, like someone who is used to issuing commands that are instantly obeyed. I nod, feeling a little intimidated. "I'm looking forward to working with you."

What? Attempting to keep a smile plastered on my face, I feel my brow crease in confusion and turn toward Marco.

"Linda is joining our team here at Axis. We managed to woo her over from the Cooper Group." Marco pats her shoulder and quickly pulls his hand back when her head snaps in his direction and the light glints off her whitened teeth. Did she just snarl at him? Marco looks unnerved and shoves his hands in his pockets. I hear a small noise from the hallway and realize Scott must be lurking, listening for the latest office gossip. Stealing a senior account person from a major agency is certainly big news. She wouldn't have crossed enemy lines for chump change. Given her penchant for high-end clothing stores, Charlie and Marco must be shelling out a lot for her defection. Shaking my head to clear my thoughts, I try to follow the conversation.

"She'll be our new director of sponsorship. We'll have to put our heads together to figure out how to divide up our resources. I'm putting Linda in the office beside you, so it probably makes the most sense to share Scott as well." A muffled gasp comes from the hallway, but no one else seems to notice. "Linda's bringing a big client with her. I need you to walk her through the account team profiles and figure out who will move over to her project, given our current workload." My head dips a little and Marco beams, taking my head bob as an affirmative. This is my team, the team I hired and trained, and now I have to give some of them up?

"I'll let you girls—" Marco flinches as Linda's head snaps sharply in his direction. "Linda, I'll be back to finish the tour, but you're in good hands with Abby." I cringe as Linda turns toward the mess on the floor and stares pointedly back at me. Grabbing briefcase and purse from my spare chair, I usher her toward the now vacated seat and stoop to grab a handful of papers from the floor. Shoving them into my desk drawer, I pull at the bottom of my floral blouse, which was cute when I donned it this morning but now feels loud and shapeless in the wake of Linda's power suit. When our eyes meet, I realize she's been watching me fidget and adjust myself. The silence feels as uncomfortable as my top.

"So, Linda, I must say this is a bit of a surprise, but I'm sure you'll feel at home here—"

"Look, Abby, no offense, but I'm not here to make best friends. I was stuck waiting to make partner, and this should get me there faster. Once I get that, I can move on to bigger and *better* things." She looks around the room, wrinkling her nose as if she's smelled something offensive.

Without meaning to, my mouth opens. "Well, look, Linda, no offense either, but I'm not here for best friends either. You're going to have to wait a little longer, I'm afraid. I'm at the front of the partnership line." I hold myself rigid, hoping I exude confidence, and even intimidation.

"Really?" The scorn is heavy in her voice. "I don't think you should feel too confident. After all, I just got here, and I've brought in the biggest client this company as ever had. Seems to me like it's an easy choice." Before I can respond, Marco reappears at the door. On her way out, Linda reaches down, picks up a lone paper from the floor, and puts it on my desk. "It will be a real pleasure to work with you, Abby," she says, and Marco smiles widely, happy to see us getting along so well. I force the

corners of my mouth up, trying to match Linda's performance,
but slump into my chair the minute they're gone from view and
sigh loudly. Scott is beside me in an instant, worry stamped on
his face, carrying Tylenol and a bottle of water.

"She's a piece of work," I say, rubbing my temple, feeling
the pressure of a headache building. Scott shakes out two
tablets and passes me the water. He perches on the side of my
desk, watching me swallow. I close my eyes and pinch the
bridge of my nose, willing the medicine to kick in. "Do you
think they've promised her partner?" I ask in a tiny voice.
Scott's silence gives me my answer.

⌒

On the subway going home, I check out my fellow passengers
in an effort to get my mind off of Linda and my mother-in-law.
There is always such an interesting mix of people on my daily
trip through Toronto. First the Bay Street types, sheathed in
bespoke suits. On the morning commute, the requisite jewel-
tone tie is perfect; on the ride home, it has been loosened a
little and sits slightly askew. They've always got the leather
briefcase and a Globe and Mail tucked under one arm as they
madly hunt and peck on the tiny keyboards of their handheld
devices, squeezing in productive minutes.

Today, there is also a pack of teenagers riding together.
The girls, heavily made-up, eye the boys across the aisle. They
each wear headphones that blare music, and I feel old when I
realize that, like my mother, I want to warn them that they
might go deaf. I also shudder when I see the girls budding into
puberty, walking around in short shorts and spaghetti-strap tank
tops. Baggy clothes were in when I was a teenager. I'm sure
my parents were thrilled that we were all covered up. I find
myself hoping that trend comes back for my kids.

Across from me sits a family. Maybe Mom and Dad both
work downtown and have managed to find a day care near their
offices. It's close to seven o'clock and the poor little kid is
asleep on his mother's lap. I catch the mother's eye and smile,
feeling mild contractions in my uterus. She gives me a tired
half-smile and turns away.

The father is reading one of the free daily papers, and I scan the headlines as he holds it open. The new subway development plan is delayed; unrest in the Middle East continues, as does the latest on Will and Kate; and the chief of police is promising a crackdown on the recent spate of burglaries that have plagued various upscale neighborhoods.

As the subway pulls into my station, I stand patiently till the train stops and the doors slide open, then head up two flights of stairs, pushing through the turnstile and exiting onto Broadview Avenue for the second time today. I make my way toward my favorite fruit and flower stand on Danforth Avenue, hoping the Korean shopkeeper there has fresh tulips for sale. I need something pretty and colorful to help me get out of my funk.

One store away from the fruit stand I see a hardware store, and the solution to my Marilyn problem dawns on me: a security chain for the front door. It's not perfect – I mean, what's to stop her from entering when I'm not around – but at least when I'm home I can keep her out. With renewed vigor – one problem solved – an armful of fresh-cut tulips, and my new security chain, I hum happily home.

The aroma of garlic cooked in butter assails me as I open the door.

"Hey Abbs, is that you?" Jack hollers from behind the closed kitchen door. It's his standard greeting when I come home later than him, and I've always thought it was cute – who else would it be? Well, today's events have made me realize that he is actually asking.

"I'll be there in a minute," I yell back. Depositing the flowers on the dining room table, I hang up my coat and pull our measly collection of tools out of the bottom of the hall closet. Scanning the back of the security chain to see what's needed, I find the right screwdriver and make quick work of the security chain. I didn't buy the top-of-the-line model, but it's not a burglar I'm worried about. I can't possibly see Marilyn expending the energy necessary to force open our door, but then again…

Jack arrives just as I tighten the last screw.

"What's with the chain?" He's wiping his hands on a blue and white kitchen towel and has a perplexed expression and a smudge of flour on his face. "Is this because of my mom?"

"What? No. I've been meaning to get one for a while. There have been break-ins lately; haven't you read about them in the paper? I would just feel safer, you know, when I'm here by myself." I hold my breath, hoping the helpless-female approach will work. The last thing I want is another confrontation today. Jack looks skeptical, but he doesn't challenge me. I quietly exhale. "So, what smells so divine?" I ask, changing the focus, brushing his cheek clean.

"I hope you're hungry, I got a little carried away." He smiles at me, and I know the Marilyn tension has abated for now. Grabbing my flowers, I follow him into the kitchen, noting his shirt still shows signs of our earlier tryst. The Chianti has been decanted, candles are lit on the eat-in counter, a decadent cream sauce is bubbling away in a pot, and steaming penne is draining in a colander.

"This looks amazing. Thank you," I say sincerely, knowing he's trying to make amends with my favorite penne à la vodka, and there is nothing sexier in my books than a man who cooks. I busy myself with the tulips, cutting the stems and arranging them in a vase. Jack wraps his arms around my waist and kisses my neck.

"So, is that window still open?" He breathes into my ear, goose bumps forming on my arms and legs.

"Really?" I turn toward him in surprise. He's not normally up for on-ovulation-demand sex. He tugs at my arm and leads me from the kitchen. "What about dinner?" I gesture toward the cooling pasta.

"It'll keep. This won't." Jack reaches over and turns off the stove. He grabs my hand and, grinning like an idiot, leads me toward the stairs. I reach out and secure my safety chain and grin idiotically to myself. I follow Jack upstairs, and my throat catches when I get a glimpse of our bedroom. The challenges at work melt away as I see the bed is made, candles are lit, and rose petals are strewn over the duvet. I look at Jack, tears forming in my eyes. He leads me to the bed.

"I love you, Abbs."

"I love you too."

Later that night, Jack snores softly beside me, satiated – from both food and sex. I chant my mantra.

"I will get pregnant, I will have a baby, I will be a mom."

Maybe it will work this time.

3

"HELLO?" JULES ANSWERS on the first ring. I attempt to speak, but sobs overtake me. I'm lying on the bathroom floor, my five-foot-eight body tightly curled up on the tiny blue bath mat, gripping the phone like it's a life preserver. There are a box of tissues and a box of tampons on the counter.

"Abby, honey, are you okay? Talk to me. It came, didn't it?" Jules knows my period is due.

"Why ... why ... What's wrong with me? Why won't this work?" I stutter between sobs. "My dad ... hell, that was the whole birds and the bees talk. 'Abby, your mother and I only had to be in the same room. Look out.'" Thinking of that uncomfortable conversation with my dad brings fresh tears. All the years I spent worrying I might get pregnant if a guy even looked at me, and for what?

"You will be a mom, it will happen." Jules lapses into silence and lets me cry it out. Exactly two weeks after our "quickie interruptus," I had woken up a little nauseous and rushed to check for my period. When I didn't see anything, I started hoping my luck might have changed. Two hours later, I was greeted by the sight of blood in my underwear and collapsed on the bathroom floor.

"I just want this so, so, so badly," I hiccup. "I've always wanted to be a mom. I just don't know what to do. What if we can't have a baby?"

"Abby, you guys are meant to be parents, I know that. But, maybe you need to start thinking of other ways."

"I should go, I just heard Jack come home." He jogs every Saturday morning. I know he will head directly upstairs, with a chai tea for me, a strong black coffee for him, and the Saturday paper to share in bed. I don't want him to find me on the floor. I know he'll be disappointed that I'm not pregnant, but he doesn't like to see me upset every month. I mentally calculate that this will be the twenty-sixth month we've been unsuccessful. This does not help me collect myself.

"Okay, sweetie. I love you. Get riotously drunk tonight and call me tomorrow." Jules's answer to every setback in life is to get riotously drunk. Actually, it does work sometimes.

Jack stops short when he sees my face as I emerge from the bathroom. His broad shoulders slump and for an instant the glimmer leaves his eyes. I smile through my tears and bite my lip as I get back into bed. He places our drinks on the bedside table, drops the heavy Saturday paper on the floor with a thud, and climbs into bed to hold me. We lie very still, barely breathing.

"Next month, baby," he whispers. On some level I'm sure this is getting to him too, but outwardly he's never very upset. I know how badly I want this. Does he?

෨

Jack and I beg off dinner plans with friends that evening, order in a feast from a local Thai restaurant, and open an expensive bottle of amarone, my favorite red wine and one we usually save for celebrations. Snuggling back into our navy blue leather couch, a throwback to Jack's bachelor days, we settle into our dinner, a movie, and at least one bottle of wine.

"My mom still really wants to apologize." He waits until I'm two glasses in before bringing up his mother. When I don't respond, he dives right in. "She wanted to surprise us with new curtains and came in to measure. I only gave her the key in case of emergencies. She promises not to come back without letting one of us know." Jack has attempted several times to explain his mother's behavior over the last two weeks, but I've shut him down.

When we were first dating, I found the ways he looked after his mother and involved her in his life endearing. In the five years that Jack and I have been together, I've come to realize that their relationship is not very healthy.

Jack is an only child, and his father left them for another woman when Jack was ten, after which Jack wanted nothing to do with him. He grew up fast, becoming Marilyn's "Little Man," and she was not happy about us getting together. I don't think she'd be happy with anyone scooping up her Little Man. She gets pleasure out of pointing out my faults, especially in front of Jack. He, on the other hand, never calls her on anything and lets her walk all over him. She's the only subject we cannot agree on.

I nod in Jack's direction, even though I expect she was breaking in to see if the laundry had been done properly and if Jack had any clean underwear. I make a mental note to hide my lingerie in case Marilyn tries another unsupervised visit, when the chain isn't on. Refilling my glass, I focus on the TV. We are watching *When Harry Met Sally* for the tenth time. By the time we get to the diner scene, I can smile.

∽

"Somebody better be dead," Jack murmurs from his side of the bed, his tongue sounding thick in his mouth. It's early Sunday morning and the phone is shrilling from the bedside table. I grapple for it, hoping to stop the noise, which in my hungover state sounds more like an air horn. Moving hurts, but the ringing is killing me. Damn Jules and her advice.

"Hello?"

"Abby, it's me, Cassie. Did I wake you?" She doesn't wait for an answer, but I'm not sure I could have formulated one. Jack moans. "Mom and I have been researching fertility websites and natural pregnancy-boosting herbs. It says here that you should carry three hazelnuts with you at all times and Jack needs to have a piece of mandrake root. Only thing is, mandrake root is extremely poisonous, so make sure he wraps it well. But it's a powerful fertility symbol."

When Jack and I first met, he thought I was kidding when I described my crazy family. My father is a professor of archeology and my mother is a yoga instructor. They met in India after university. My dad was on a dig and my mom got lost on her way to an ashram. Apparently, it was love at first sight. In their wedding picture, my mother, dressed in a caftan, is holding a goat and my father is holding a ceremonial mask. A local Brahmin performed the ceremony. With no marriage certificate to back it up, my dad jokes that their union is not legally binding but he's pretty sure my mom owns the goat. I do love them dearly, but I came out, sadly for them, normal. Somehow I missed the hippie gene.

My younger sister, Cassie, is more complicated. She's an investment advisor at a big firm downtown and has been working her way up the corporate ladder at a rapid pace. Despite a successful financial career, she is far more like my parents and definitely has the hippie genetic markers. Her latest hobby is Internet-doctoring, specifically traditional Chinese medicine – much to my chagrin, although my mother is thrilled. While I don't confide all the details of my life, they are all well aware that Jack and I are having trouble conceiving. My mom's solution for everything is to "go natural" – and I do mean everything. Cassie is slightly more reserved, but only slightly.

Physically, Cassie and I are opposites. I have blonde hair, while her hair is almost black. I get my height from my father's side, but Cassie and my mom barely reach my chin. As a kid, she wanted to save the world with my parents, and I just wanted to be adopted by a "normal" family. It was hard to make friends when my family was protesting against consumerism outside the local Walmart while I was a cashier inside. They adopted countless injured raccoons and held hunger strikes at the table. My parents would sigh deeply at my lack of interest and wonder how they had raised such a mainstream kid. I did go through a brief Goth stage in my teens, but with my dark eye makeup I looked more like the raccoons Cassie was saving. Now, she's blabbing on about wild yam and chaste tree supporting the production of progesterone in the body, but it's too early and my head feels like it's going to explode.

"Cassie, do you have any idea what time it is? I've told you many times not to call first thing in the morning."

"Abby, I'm just trying to help here." I can hear the whine in her voice.

"I'm sorry. It's just that you woke me up and I'm not quite myself." I swat Jack to stop his moaning.

"Are you hungover? I've told you before that drinking too much will seriously affect your fertility, not to mention Jack's sperm."

"I know, I know, his guys won't be able to swim in a straight line. Jesus, Cass, I'll eat your bloody wild yams and whatever else, just give me a break." Our conversations are always quick and go this way: her whiney and me defensive.

"Abby honey, I think you should see a naturopath." My mother's voice replaces Cassie's in my ear.

"Seriously, you're both up at this hour?" I'd shake my head in disbelief, but it hurts too much.

"Of course we are. We're off to my hot yoga class. Oh, do you want to join us?"

"No, Mom, I'm limber enough this morning. Maybe next time."

"I'm holding you to that. And Abby, I am serious, you should see a naturopath. In fact, mine works not far from you and she's fabulous. Jack should get his sperm tested. If the problem is on his side, it's faster to find out and far less invasive."

"Sure, whatever. Email me the details." I hang up, cringing at having sperm-related chats with my mother.

Jack mutters from under his pillow, "Are we having yams for dinner?"

"No. And you need to get your sperm tested."

4

SCOTT IS BEAMING when I arrive at the office on Monday morning, which can only mean trouble for me.

"I can tell I'm not going to like this," I say. Scott is rubbing his hands together, as if he's hatched an evil plan to take over the world.

"You have a new hire." He is practically vibrating. Fabulous, just what I need – one of Marco's playmates to babysit. My eyes automatically turn upwards, and I wonder who I've pissed off up there to deserve this. "The F&F sheet is ready at my desk and, as usual, you can't place any bets. I've got a great one this time."

What began as a drinking game in our production department two years ago has become a gambling game based on when and why Marco's conquests will get the axe. Production came up with the name "Fucked & Fired," a list of the top five reasons why the women might be fired. I'm outraged as a woman, but I have to admit that reading up on the alleged reasons for firing can be pretty funny. As the lucky executioner, though, I'm not allowed to place any bets.

"Fine, you know the drill. When she gets here, whenever that is, give her a tour of the building. Stay away from Marco's office in case he has photos of a new girlfriend out, and show her the production suite." I used to kid-glove these girls in the early days, but now I just throw them to the wolves. Plus, I have other pressing work and non-work to get to today.

When Scott leaves, I turn my attention to the flashing message light on my phone and my email inbox. The usual spam promising indestructible watches that are practically free and ways to enhance the size of my manhood pop up first. Delete, delete, delete. Where do these things come from? How is it no firewall can keep this crap out? Buried within the broken promises are emails from Jules checking up on my mental state, naturopath information from my mother, and one without a subject line from Marilyn, asking me to call her. It just gets better and better.

I pick up the phone and take a deep cleansing breath. As I dial her number, I wonder if it's too early for a drink. Probably.

"Please don't pick up, please don't pick up," I pray.

"Hello?"

"Oh, hi Marilyn, it's Abby. You wanted to talk to me?"

"Abigail." It's always Abigail with her, never Abby. "I was out yesterday with Jane and Arthur Cranston, you remember them." No, I don't, but she doesn't stop. "Anyway, their son David just announced that he and his wife are pregnant. Isn't that great news? Jane's been waiting *forever* to become a grandmother. It's so hard, you know, all that waiting. They were asking if I was going to be joining the grandmother club soon, but I told them how busy and into your career you are." She peters off waiting for me to say something. I picture her sitting primly on her couch – sorry, *settee;* lord knows I've been corrected enough – her feet crossed at the ankles, in her matching cashmere twinset and perfectly pressed pants. She is probably filling the silence by picking imaginary lint off her pants and flicking it away with her manicured fingers.

"You're right, Marilyn, I am extremely busy. Actually, I need to dash. Is there anything else?" I glance down at my own hands and realize I've been biting my nails again.

"Well, Jane suggested you might want to get your tubes checked, dear. You know, to be sure you can have children. A lot of women have problems."

"What?" I sputter. "Get my tubes checked?" I can feel my blood boiling, and I try to speak as calmly as possible. "Actually, Jack is going to get his sperm tested. The testing is far less invasive for men," I say, spouting off my newfound knowledge.

"Abigail, it's hardly an issue with Jacky. He's successful in everything he does. He practically oozes virility. At least that's what his ex-girlfriends always said. Anyhoo, just a thought. Talk soon, dear," and she's gone. It's a small miracle that with role models such as his mother and father, Jack wants to have children at all. Dejected, wishing I was home and could curl up under the covers, and knowing I would cry if I spoke, I type Jules a hurried email.

Marilyn has decided my tubes are the reason she can't join the elitist "Grandmother" club. I hate that woman! And it gets better: my mother wants to discuss Jack's sperm. On bright side, new F&F sheet circulating today – at least something to make me laugh (until I have to fire the poor girl). How goes the reno? Xo Abbs

Two minutes later, my email chimes with Jules's reply.

Abbs, Honey – M's a bitch. You are fabulous. Think of the sperm as a bonding moment. ;) Let me know who wins the bet. Tell Scott I cannot be bribed for insider info this time. Don't get me started, our contractor didn't show this week, so on the hunt for number two. Put plastic over the open holes where windows *should* be, and woke up to family of raccoons in TV room today. Liam's answer was to close the door and go to work – such a helpful husband. Is your sister still adopting animals?! Wish me luck. Xoxoxoxo J

I smile. Thank goodness for best friends. I place a call to Mom's naturopath and book an appointment for the following day, then I call Jack's doctor to schedule a sperm test – Marilyn be damned – but it turns out Jack has to provide a "sample" from home and drop it off at a medical testing building. Sounds easy enough. I pull up my file on fertility clinics, which I have been quietly researching over the last few months. After this last setback and Jules's advice, I think it's time to bring in the professionals.

I call the Hope Fertility Clinic and find out the earliest appointment I can get is in six months.

"Wow, you guys must be good if your waiting list is that long." I book it in my iPhone and work schedule. Yet another doctor's appointment for my bosses to see. At this rate, they are going to think I'm dying of some horrible disease. I'm not sure when I'll tell Jack about the fertility appointment, but I feel better for having taken some action. And now I can turn my mind to what I get paid to do.

Scott waves at me frantically from the doorway, gesturing at the phone, and mouths what I think is "Marco."

"Hi Marco–" I start, but he cuts me off instantly.

"Where the hell are you?" he hisses angrily.

"I'm in my office. What's going on?"

"Abigail." My full name twice in ten minutes; that doesn't bode well. "What the hell are you doing there? We are presenting to the senior VP at the bank today. You are twenty minutes late." The floor seems to open beneath me. Oh god, how could I have messed up a shot at new business, with some very high-powered bankers? I grip my desk with one hand, trying to get the room to stop spinning. Marco is still talking in an angry whisper. "You've been unfocused and absent a lot. I've cut you slack, but this is unacceptable." My stomach heaves and I clamp a hand over my mouth.

How could I have forgotten about this? That's easy: I've had baby-on-the-brain for so long, I'm falling apart. Good-bye partnership; I'll be lucky to keep my job.

"Marco, I'm so sorry. I can be there in twenty minutes." It sounds ridiculous as I say it.

"Abigail, we've already wasted twenty minutes, I'm not wasting another twenty waiting for you to get your ass over here. I'll see if I can reschedule. We are having a little chat when I get back." He hangs up, sounding flustered and angry. In these pitch meetings, we have great chemistry. Marco is fabulous at the small talk, as if at a country club trading golf scores and borderline sexist jokes, which still go over well with the banking crowd. I, on the other hand, am all business. I'm sure Marco's been filling the last twenty minutes with jokes and chitchat. He's probably run out of his best material.

I am so dead.

I put my head on my desk and berate myself.

∽

"My office. Now," Marco barks as he stomps past my door. I stand slowly, wiping my clammy hands on my pinstripe pants. As Scott peeks at me from behind his computer and crosses his fingers, I try to smile back confidently. I feel like a condemned prisoner, tapping lightly on Marco's door and slinking into his office. I wonder if there is an office pool on whether I get sacked.

"Marco, just let me say how sorry I am about this morning." The words come out in a rush – I'm trying my best to be contrite before he yells at me.

"Abigail." My full name instantly flashes me back to childhood, when my mother used it whenever she was mad. "I just don't understand what's going on with you. It's not like you to screw up that majorly. This was a big deal for us. Thankfully I managed some fancy footwork, and I think we'll be allowed another shot. I just have to know, are you with us here? You've always been my go-to gal, but recently, I just don't know..." He trails off. I bristle at the "go-to gal" comment. I'll never make partner with sexist attitudes like that, but today is not the day to call him out. Today is "Stroke Marco's Ego Day." Actually, today is "Abby Is an Idiot Day."

"Again, I'm so sorry. I know this was a big deal, and I'm glad you managed to get us another shot. I know I've been a little funny of late, but trust me, I'm here for the long haul." I hold my breath.

"This cannot happen again. You understand that, right?" Marco looks me right in the eye. I exhale quietly.

"I understand. Trust me, it won't." I meet his gaze and hold it. When he breaks contact first, I know I'm okay.

Back in my office, I collapse into my chair for a quick lecture-to-self. *Abigail Nichols, get your head screwed on tight. You'll never afford fertility treatments if you are unemployed.*

From now on, I'll focus only on work from nine to five, and everything else can take a backseat. Should be easy enough.

∞

I spend the rest of the day immersed in my job. It's after six-thirty when I head home, remembering to stop by a local clinic to pick up a sterilized specimen container. Walking slowly up Ellerbeck Street toward our house, I glimpse Jack sitting on our porch with a beer. I'm always amazed at how the sight of him makes my heart skip a beat. I never know quite how to describe him. He's very attractive and, well, manly, with broad shoulders, blue eyes, and sandy-brown hair that is just starting to show hints of gray, betraying his forty years.

He is relaxing in our yellow porch swing, eyes closed and rocking slowly back and forth. I quietly climb the front steps, drop my purse and briefcase, and time my descent onto the swing so as not to interrupt his rhythm. Jack smiles, but doesn't open his eyes. His hand closes over mine and we just sit, swinging, like a little old married couple.

When we were looking to buy a house just after our wedding, we fell in love with the area, but the porch was the reason we bought the house. Of course we liked the quiet one-way street and the multitude of families in the neighborhood, but we knew we could watch our children play and grow old together on the front porch. I cuddle closer to Jack.

I debate telling him about his mother's phone call, our upcoming fertility appointment, my anxiety over Linda, or my colossal screw-up, but decide not to spoil the moment. We sit quietly for almost an hour, Jack pumping the swing with his legs, and me, curled in his arms, answering emails.

As twilight dims, I gather my things. Jack gets up from the swing and leans against the porch railing, the lights from downtown glowing behind him. "My dad called today."

I scan Jack's face for his reaction. Phone calls from his father tend to leave him melancholy or irritable. "Oh. What's he up to?"

"Just the usual, checking in on his *boy*." Bitterness tinges Jack's words.

"You okay?"

With a startling intensity Jack answers. "I won't be anything like my dad. I'm going to be a good father, I promise. I won't let you or our kids down."

"Jack, you are going to be the best dad. Our kids will be so lucky to have you. You won't let us down, I know that." I drop everything and put my arms around him, my head resting under his chin. His heart beats in my ear and I can feel him relax in my embrace.

Later, as we prepare dinner together, I place the sample cup on the kitchen counter. Jack raises his eyebrow. "How is peeing in a cup going to check my sperm count?"

"It's not for urine, you dolt. You need to fill it with your swimmers." Honestly, guys can be so thick.

"You need me to fill that whole thing?" He sounds doubtful.

"No. Just as much as you can. You have to do it and then get it right to the lab, like pronto."

"Tell me you at least brought me some porn, you know, to help me out?"

"No way. Seriously, Jack, please do this. It's really important," I plead.

"Abbs, relax. I'm on it … or maybe I'm in it," he grins, ducking as I throw a dish towel at his head. "Look, I'm putting it in my phone. Seven a.m., spluge in cup; seven twenty, drop off at lab. See, we're all good."

Jesus, I think, first quickies, now spluging scheduled in our iPhones. I wonder if there's an app for that.

"Hey, did I tell you I landed that new client, rumpled clothes and all? It's gonna be great. This should put us on the map." Jack owns a small engineering firm and has been trying to grow his business over the past year.

"Congrats Jack, that's awesome."

"I know we've been pretty stretched for money lately, but this could be the beginning. I'm feeling really good about it. No promises, but maybe we can plan a vacation this year. What do you think?"

"Um, a vacation would be great, but maybe we should just start saving, you know, for the future."

Jacks looks startled. "Since when have you been so practical? I figured you'd jump at the vacation idea."

Normally I would, but the prices of various fertility treatments I've seen listed on the Hope Clinic's website are staggering. I have been worried about the cost, and expanding Jack's business has eaten up our savings. Maybe this money is the answer.

5

WE CARPOOL THE next morning and I wait in the car while Jack, smiling sheepishly, pops into the medical building to drop off his precious cargo. He reappears red-faced, mumbling something about a hot chick at reception. Ah, the glamor of baby-making.

Jack calls me frantically later in the day. I've been busy working on the bank pitch and trying desperately to finish off my to-do list before I slip out for my naturopath appointment. I can't seem to go one day without our baby plans encroaching on work.

"Abbs, my doctor's office called. Apparently the clinic called his office and they have flagged my file. He only wants to discuss the results in person. What does this mean?" He's panicking, and if that doesn't scream "problem," I don't know what does.

"Calm down. I'm sure it's fine. See if we can get in tomorrow."

I arrive at the naturopath's office on time, which can be a miracle some days in Toronto traffic. Her office is on the second floor of a nondescript low-rise in midtown. I climb the narrow, dimly lit stairwell, butterflies unsettling my stomach.

The smell of incense hits me like a brick wall as I reach the last step, and I immediately flash back to a teenage Cassie constantly burning patchouli in her room, while the rest of us complained of headaches. Later, my dorm room neighbor at university tried to mask the smell of his pot by burning incense all the time, too. God, I hate that smell. I hold my breath while I look at the office numbers, searching through the blue haze for 206.

Walking down the hallway, I notice the incense burner smoking away beside an open window. One quick look out the window shows nothing flammable or human below, and after a glance around to make sure no one is watching, I casually knock the incense and its wretched smell out the window. Feeling better, I straighten my shoulders and walk confidently to the end of the hallway. I nearly laugh out loud when I see a hand carved wooden plaque attached to number 206. Serenity LaFleur, Naturopath.

Okay, Abby, you can do this. I push the door open.

"Oh … my…" The room is painted with swirls of deep purple, and wispy lilac gauze flutters in the window. Lavender tickles my nose. The ceiling twinkles like the night sky and a large beanbag occupies one corner, with a clipboard resting on top. A huge, heavy purple curtain divides the room in half. God knows what's behind that. I feel as if I've walked onto the set of a seventies porn movie.

"I'll be right there. Please have a seat and fill out a form," says a voice floating out from behind the curtain.

"Um, okay." I look around. Sit down where? My eyes settle on the beanbag, which appears to be the only thing that can support a person. I don't remember the last time I tried to sit on a beanbag chair, but it was probably in grade school and I definitely wasn't wearing a pencil skirt and heels. I shift my legs in an attempt to shield the naturopath from an indecent view of my underwear and hear the distinctive sound of a ripping seam. I sigh and pray the tear is small enough that I can return to work without an emergency repair.

As I glance over the fairly standard medical questionnaire, I madly try to imprint every image and sense of the room so I can accurately retell it to Jack and Jules later. I make quick work of the form. History of infertility in the family? No. Major health issues? None. Any drug use? No way; total prude. Ever been pregnant before? I wish. Menstrual cycle? Here's the doozie: anywhere between eighteen to forty-two days. I flip to the second page and realize we are past the "standard" medical questions and into the frequency of bowel movements, description of cervical mucus, sexual positions used while attempting to conceive, days of the week we have sex, and how I feel during a full moon. Jack and Jules are never going to believe me.

My phone rings and I curse myself for not setting it on silent. I snatch it from my purse and whisper into it, "Abby Nichols?"

"Abby, hi, it's Andrew."

"Oh, hi." He's one of my high-maintenance clients – a great guy, but he needs handholding. We do a lot of business for his company, so I'm careful to stay in his good books.

"Is everything okay, Abby? You sound really quiet." I glance up, but Serenity has yet to make an appearance from behind the curtain.

"I'm great, just kind of in the middle of a meeting right now. Can I call you back when I can give you my undivided attention?" The "undivided attention" line is one I picked up from Jules. No one, not even high-maintenance Andrew, can resist the idea of having someone's complete attention.

"Of course. Give me a call when you're out of your meeting." I hang up, make a mental note to call Andrew back, and set my phone to silent.

The curtain parts and out plods a woman whom I can only assume is Serenity, wheeling an office chair. With a name like Serenity LaFleur, and knowing her chosen profession, I imagined a tall, willowy blonde woman dressed in a flowy handmade dress and Birkenstocks. I could not have been more wrong. Serenity is short and squat, with dishevelled cropped hair in a jarring shade of orange – clearly a home-job gone awry. She is sheathed in spandex from head to toe with Birkenstocks on her pigeon-toed feet. Okay, one point for the Birks. I struggle to control my nervous laughter.

"You must be Betty's daughter, Abby. I'm Dr. LaFleur, but you can call me Serenity." She takes the clipboard from my hand and gives my forms a cursory glance. "Tell me about your menstrual cycle," says Serenity as she transcribes my answers in her chicken scratch.

"Well, what's there to tell? I was a late bloomer. I got my first period when I was fifteen, and then I didn't get one again for over a year. After my third cycle in three years, my doctor put me on the pill to regulate me. I was on it until, well, our wedding, which was two and a half years ago." I remember making love on our wedding night with no protection, and then smile sadly when I recall how worried I was at the thought of getting pregnant that night and rushing into motherhood. "It's not very regular."

Reaching into my purse, I pull out a sheaf of papers. "I've been monitoring my cycle for the past eighteen months." I pass the pages to Serenity. She is delighted.

"Well, this is going to save us a lot of time. I see here you've been taking your temperature every morning and charting your cervical discharge. You know to look for the egg-white consistency as a sign of ovulation?" Another glamorous side of trying to get pregnant that no one ever talks about. As gross as it sounds to inspect your cervical discharge, it has become commonplace for me and I even keep an electronic diary.

"It looks like you have a kidney yang deficiency," Serenity says, gesturing to my cycle charts. She launches into a description of how we treat that, when I interrupt her.

"Um, what exactly is a kidney yang deficiency?" I ask.

"Sorry, I just assumed as Betty's daughter you'd understand." I try not to roll my eyes. "Let me back up. You understand the basics of a menstrual cycle, right? An average one is twenty-eight days. The first day of your cycle is actually the first day of your period. The estrogen builds up over the next fourteen days, which stimulates the ovaries to mature a follicle. Each follicle has one egg inside. The estrogen also stimulates the lining of the uterus to thicken, in preparation for hosting a fertilized egg." I nod and she continues. "Around day fourteen, one of your ovaries releases an egg. This egg makes the trip down the fallopian tube and into the uterus. This journey typically takes a few days.

"The second half of your cycle is the progesterone phase. Progesterone promotes the growth of the uterine lining, making your uterus hospitable to any fertilized eggs. A common reason for infertility can be a lack of progesterone. If we look at your charts, you can see that your temperature and cervical mucus peak around day fourteen, which is normal. What isn't normal is the length of your progesterone phase. In Chinese medicine, a progesterone deficiency is called a kidney yang deficiency. So that's what I feel we should treat."

"Great, let's try some progesterone," I feel surprisingly optimistic.

"I can't prescribe progesterone, but I have a wild yam cream we can try. I can also use acupuncture to stimulate your kidney yang. Why don't you come behind the curtain and hop up on the table. I'll get my needles ready." She gracefully rises from her chair and pulls back the curtain.

Wild yams. Where have I heard that?

I roll myself off the beanbag, briefly moving into the downward dog position, and finally struggle to my feet and try to take a glance at the damage to my skirt. I can't see much. I quickly check my phone. Five emails from the office. I am opening the first one when I hear Serenity clear her throat and, like a naughty child, I blush and drop the phone back in my bag.

"Sorry." I follow Serenity behind the curtain and am surprised to find no purple in view, just a plain office desk, an Ikea floor lamp, and a massage table. The room is painted muted gray and the glow of the lamp makes the room surprisingly warm. I climb up on the table and lie face up while Serenity mutters to herself and readies her equipment. I've never done acupuncture before, and the thought of being stuck with needles and letting them sit in me is making me sweat. "Does it hurt?" I ask in a small voice.

"Not a bit. You might feel one go in, but nothing more than a mosquito bite. I'm going to place the needles at your ankles, wrists, abdomen, and the center of your forehead. Acupuncture is about achieving balance in the body. Mostly I'm aligning with the kidney, liver, spleen, and heart meridians, but the one in the forehead is more for relieving stress." She swabs my body with what I hope is rubbing alcohol and takes the needles out of their packages. I stop paying attention somewhere between the spleen and the placement of the third needle.

I close my eyes, hold my breath, and brace for pain, figuring this is going to hurt way more than she is letting on. I am a total wimp when it comes to pain, and in my case, mosquitoes hurt when they bite.

"Okay, just lie totally still for twenty minutes."

I open my eyes. She can't possibly have put in any needles – I didn't feel a thing. I look down and can see wafer-thin needles sticking out of my body.

"Clear your mind of all excess thoughts and worries. Focus on your breathing. Imagine your uterus. Feel how welcoming it is to your husband's sperm and your egg. I will chant the ancient fertility chant for you." Serenity clears her throat and places one hand on her heart and the other on her belly. "My child, my body is open, my child, my mind is open, my child, my heart is open." I try not to snicker when I realize the tune is much like "My Bonnie Lies over the Ocean." I close my eyes and mentally chant my own mantra, hoping to drown out her performance, but Serenity's damn fertility chant sticks in my head and I find myself humming it all the way back to the office.

⁓

I slide through the front doors, hoping my absence has gone unnoticed and my stress levels continue to stay low.

"Well, it's nice of you to make an appearance today." Linda's haughty voice stops me.

"Excuse me?"

"You've been missing a lot of work lately." She taps her watch and eyes me up and down.

I take a deep breath and hold on to what little vestige of calmness still inhabits my body. "Linda, my whereabouts are hardly your concern. Is there something you needed from me?"

"Does Marco know how often you sneak out of here?" She leans closer, infringing on my personal space. "What is that smell?" She covers her nose and brushes past. I sniff my sleeves and realize I stink of incense.

Scott finds me a few minutes later in a state of undress in my office. Waving him in, I wad up my smelly blouse and shove it in a plastic bag.

"What on earth are you wearing?" Before I can answer, he wrinkles his nose. "You smell like a hemp store."

"This is the only thing I could find," I say as I zip up an orange exercise hoodie emblazoned with a client logo over my skirt. "Did anything come up while I was out?"

"Linda was looking for you." He drops his voice and starts to lean toward me until the smell hits him again, sending him upright. "She's been asking a lot of questions. Watch your back, Abby. She scares me."

6

JACK'S GP, DR. ANDERSON, is one of the only doctors I
know who is on time with his patients. Jack and I had driven to
work together knowing we would meet up after work for our
appointment regarding Jack's results.

"Well, Jack," he begins. "We might have found the problem.
It appears that you have no sperm."

"What? None, like zero? That's not possible. C'mon Doc,
look at me, I've got swimmers." Jack sounds defensive.

"Well, we can run the test again, but this time I want you to
go to a lab, not a medical clinic. Who knows, maybe someone
left your sample sitting out too long. I've seen that happen
before." Dr. Anderson scribbles off a referral and sends us on
our way. We sit quietly in the car, not bothering to turn it on.

"Abbs, I've got guys, I know it," Jack whimpers.

"I know, honey. I know," I say slowly. My mind is in
overdrive, though I mentally kick myself for not having
researched sperm banks and donors. I always thought the issue
was me, but maybe it's Jack. Maybe *I can* get pregnant. We
drive silently back to the house. I stare out the window and
marvel at the number of pregnant women I see walking around.
They are everywhere. Obviously their husbands have sperm.

∽

Jack is up early the next morning, ready to head to the lab. He is
wearing his "lucky" boxers under his clothes. He is obviously

nervous, but I'm thankful he doesn't want to talk, mostly because I'm not sure how to do a sperm-related pep talk. I haven't told him about Linda yet; I don't want to throw him off his game.

I head into the office early, determined to make up for time I've taken out of the office. I manage to clean out my inbox, saving Jules's response to my naturopath appointment for later in the day when I need a laugh. I make it halfway through the papers on my desk when my phone rings.

"Abby Nichols."

"It's me," says Jack.

"So, have you done the deed?"

"I'm in the car, almost there."

Jack continues to chat, but I barely pay attention, logging onto Facebook to update my status: "working hard."

"Okay, I'm here. I'll call you when I'm done," is the next thing I hear Jack say.

"Good luck." I'm not sure if that's the appropriate salutation when your husband is going to spluge in a cup, but "break a leg" doesn't sound any better. I hang up the phone and continue checking out what my friends are doing on Facebook.

My phone rings again and I see Jack's number pop up.

"What's wrong? Is the place closed? Are you at the wrong lab?" I ask, since only three or four minutes have passed since we hung up.

"Nope, I'm done."

"What?" I don't believe it. "Done? It's been like three minutes. What do you mean you're done?"

"I'm done. I even watched them pass the cup to the little lab guy in the white coat," he says proudly. "Gotta run, babe. Call you later." And with that, he's gone.

I hang up the phone slowly, stunned. Jack is a perfectionist. He takes his time in all things. Sex, even in the months and months of daily attempts to conceive, required at least a perfunctory amount of serious foreplay. How on earth could he have finished so quickly? I play out the last four minutes in my head: Get out of car. Walk in. Talk to the receptionist and explain what he needs. Get the cup. Walk to the sample room.

Close the door. Look around. Unzip... Seriously, how does one accomplish all that and get back in the car and on the phone in four, five minutes tops? As I laugh, the door pops open. It's Scott, like a puppy dog wanting to please his master. I can't let him in on the joke or it will be on his blog in five seconds, let alone five minutes.

∽

As I prepare dinner, Jack pours two glasses of wine and launches into a play-by-play of the sperm test.

"The receptionist was surprised that I hadn't brought a sample with me. She said everyone brings their sample from home. Ha! We know how that works out."

"Was she hot?" I am determined to get to the root cause of his speedy performance, surely deserving of an Olympic medal.

"Hardly," he snorts. "She gave me a cup and pointed me to a door. Abbs, I swear to God, the door was marked 'Janitor.' There were brooms and cleaning crap all over the place. Plus a couple of, well, let's just say well-used porn mags. I thought jerk-off rooms were supposed to be stocked with porn, you know – magazines, videos, comfy couch..." he trails off, probably dreaming of some jerk-off Mecca.

"I still don't understand how you did it so fast."

"I just wanted to get the hell out of there. I took care of things."

"Well, what did you, you know, think about?"

"I thought about my hot wife." Jack gives me a wink and turns to set the table. I have a funny feeling the receptionist was cuter than he let on.

∽

Going back to see Serenity is not high on my list of things to do. In fact, between the purple, the incense, the mocking from Jules and Jack, and the fact that I still have that damned fertility chant stuck in my head, I want nothing more to do with her. Unfortunately, my mom catches me at a weak moment.

"Abby, you can't just go once. Acupuncture needs to build up. Its effects are cumulative."

"I know. It just isn't, I mean Serenity wasn't really … I just don't think this will help me." How can I tell my mom I think Serenity is a flake without it reflecting on her as well?

"Just promise you'll try it one more time. Please."

"Fine. One time, but that's it." Later I make an appointment to meet Serenity after work. With Marco still miffed at me and Linda watching me, I'm not risking my job for a hippie.

At five thirty, cursing my mother, I trudge back up the stairs to Serenity's office and hold my breath as I hurry down the hall through the incense haze, noting the new incense holder. The curtain is pulled back to reveal the inner office and Serenity, in all her spandex glory.

"Abby, I'm just steeping some raspberry leaf tea. It's great for your uterus. Would you care for some?" I'd much rather have a Parisian Cosmopolitan, where the raspberries are in the vodka, but I nod and drop my briefcase and purse on the beanbag.

"I'm sure you know that a huge component of fertility is stress." She pours tea into what looks like a large thimble as she tells me that every patient with fertility issues she sees has major stress issues. "So a combination of acupuncture, herbs, and life balance helps calm the mind while we figure out the root cause. We should identify your major stressors and see if we can't remove them." I take a sip, nod, and wonder if banishing Marilyn or Linda is within her prescriptive abilities. Hey, a girl can dream.

Instead of chanting today, Serenity seems chatty and talks to me throughout my twenty minutes of needles. I'm feeling a little warmer toward her. For my progesterone deficiency, she tells me to eat organic meat, dairy, and eggs to avoid ingesting estrogen from animals treated with hormones. I also can't heat food in plastics and must drink filtered water. She prescribes a wild yam cream to apply to my inner thighs, inner arms, and stomach once a day.

Stopping at the Big Carrot, an organic market, on the way home, I spend three hundred dollars on organic groceries and then hide all of our Tupperware. Jack gives me grief when he gets home, but I'm determined to believe in anything that might help. Desperation does funny things to people.

Four days into the cream, an itchy, bright red rash-and-hives combination appears. It is everywhere and excruciating. Jack mumbles "voodoo medicine" under his breath as I hold cold compresses on the worst spots. I attempt an oatmeal bath to soothe my suffering, but at the end of the day I find myself, still scratching, at my doctor's, who prescribes a heavy cortisone cream and tells me to lay off the natural "stuff" for a while.

After I've left a voice mail message for Serenity, I email my mom in a shameless attempt to avoid confrontation and then I call Cassie.

"Hi Abby, what's up?"

"Cass, I gave it another shot with Serenity, but look, it's not working out. Maybe you can tell Mom?" I launch into my allergic reaction story, hoping that soothes the sting.

"That is so unusual. The Internet says people don't normally react to the wild yam cream. I can do some research and figure out an alternative for you," she says, eager to keep me in the naturopathic fold.

"I appreciate that, I do, but you're really busy with work, and to be honest, Jack and I have decided to take a break for a bit. You understand, right?" I hold my breath, waiting for her answer.

"Sure, sure, I get it. I know Mom will be disappointed it didn't work out."

"I tried, Cass, I really did. This stuff just doesn't seem to be working for me." Silence lengthens between us. "What about you and Roger, how are things with you guys? Are you going to start having kids soon?" I drum my fingers idly on my desk.

Roger is Cassie's husband. They started dating at university, and as a graduation present his parents – uber rich – gave them round-the-world plane tickets. I remember being insanely jealous of them at the time. Roger runs his family's charitable foundation, and both are seen regularly in the "Socialites" section of *Toronto Life* magazine.

"Oh, definitely not right now. I mean, kids ... well, look Abby, I know you're dying to have them, but truthfully, I'm not sure we will. I love my job and I don't want to lose my momentum." She pauses.

"Really? You don't want to have kids?" My sister never ceases to amaze me, but it dawns on me that my own dream has become so all-consuming, I can't help but assume everyone shares it. Which is clearly not the case.

"There are times when I can sense my body is ready, but I'm not sure it's what we want." She can *sense* her body's readiness? I look down at my stomach and think, *Hell, my body is ready; it's just not willing.* "And besides, who knows if it would even work? I mean, look at Mom and Dad, and then look at what you're going through."

"You really don't know until you try. I guess I just assumed you guys would have kids, at the very least to carry on the Ashfield line. Marilyn is dying for grandkids to bring her genes forth. I'm surprised Roger's parents aren't all over you two."

"Please don't say anything, Abby. You're right, they are fixed on the notion of grandkids, but – oh, I don't know." Our conversation dwindles. "I'd better run, my phone is lighting up like crazy and I have a few big trades to make. Bye." I hang up the phone and realize that for the first time probably ever, Cassie and I have had a grown-up conversation. Maybe this is the start of a better relationship between us.

I glance toward my office door to see if anyone is around, and seeing no one, I scratch my inner thighs. The cortisone cream is working, but my doctor warned me it would take a few days. Scott appears in my doorway, smiling devilishly until he notices what I'm doing.

"Isn't that man of yours taking care of those needs for you?"

"Piss off, it's this damned rash." Scott had seen me head to the ladies' room with my tube of cream and had later twenty-questioned me. I told him I had a reaction to a new skin cream, but knowing him, I'm sure he substituted "lubricant" for "skin cream." Either way, I know he'll give me constant grief. "What do you want?"

"Hot off the presses. Drum roll please. No wait, I can see your hands are busy. Here it is, the latest and greatest F&F list." Scott presents it to me with a flourish. Now I know why I couldn't find anyone in Production for the last few days. Valuable office time and resources were focused on Marco's latest cast-off firing list.

"Scott, for the record, as a woman I am morally outraged," I begin.

"Whatever, Abby. Have you seen this one?" Scott somehow manages to draw out the word "whatever" into five syllables. I actually haven't seen Ms. F&F, probably because I haven't been in the office very much. "Typical stuff: blonde, but not natural, tall, legs for days, size two, boobs out to here." His hands show me how well-endowed our lucky contestant is. "And no administrative skills." Well, that is typical too. "I don't know where Marco finds them, but if he could hook me up with the same type of men, I'd be in heaven."

"Oh come on, you don't need dumb blond guys. What's going on with you and..." Crap, I can't remember the name of Scott's latest fling. Is it Bill or Fred?

"Don't get me started. I went home last week to find Roberto had packed up and left." *Roberto*, of course – more exotic than Bill or Fred. "No note. You know what hurt the most? He cleaned out my fridge. Seriously, he left a tub of margarine. He never liked margarine."

"Gee, I'm really sorry. Are you okay?"

"Actually, I met the cutest guy on the streetcar today. We exchanged glances. I think this might be something. I'm hoping to meet him again tomorrow. Oh, I should get my hair done this afternoon. You don't mind if I scoot out a little early, do you?" Scott's ability to bounce back from heartbreak never ceases to amaze me. He leaves my office muttering about what he will wear to land Mr. Streetcar, and I am left alone with itchy inner thighs and the F&F list. I tuck it into my briefcase to read later and turn back to my real job.

∽

I feel like Wonder Woman on my way home. Okay, maybe I can't throw a golden lasso very well and I would have serious doubts about walking around in public in her outfit, but I, Abigail Nichols, am my own superhero. I walk to the subway thinking of how much I accomplished at work and how two of my clients called Marco at the end of the day to gush over what great jobs my team had done for them. After my major lapse last week, I need all of the gushing clients I can get. Now I'm looking ahead to a nice evening home alone with Jack, with maybe some bedroom fun after dinner. As I plan my seduction, my phone rings. Call display shows a blocked number.

"Abby Nichols."

"Hi, Abigail," a very cheery voice greets me. "This is the Hope Fertility Clinic calling. Dr. Greenberg has had a cancellation and was wondering if you and your husband could come in tomorrow at three o'clock?" Wow, my good luck is continuing.

"Of course, no problem. That's terrific news." I hang up, do a little happy dance, and stop quickly, realizing people are watching.

I bounce down the stairs and through the grimy subway turnstile, careful not to touch anything. I'd heard a radio report on the cleanliness of the subway handrails and turnstiles – crazy high levels of semen and excrement were found. Shuddering at the thought, I shove my hands in my pockets. The subway is waiting for me at the platform – another sign of my stars aligning.

I skip up our street, dying to tell Jack the news. I fling open the door and feel like bursting into "The Hills Are Alive" or "Oh What a Beautiful Morning," when my eyes come to rest upon Marilyn, sitting perfectly poised in my living room. I can see the dining room table just beyond and it's laid out for three.

"Abigail, darling, so good to see you." The instant killjoy is like walking into a brick wall. My good fortune and great news will now have to wait. There is no way I'm telling Marilyn we got into a fertility clinic or that my career is back on track. Taking a deep breath, I straighten my shoulders and paste a fake smile on my face.

"Marilyn. To what do we owe the pleasure?"

"Jacky suggested I join you for dinner. You don't mind, do you?" The question sounds benign, but I can feel the evil intent, as if she knows I want to be alone with Jack. And who calls their grown son "Jacky"?

"Of course I don't mind. It's always nice to spend time with family." I head into the kitchen, seeking out my husband, about whom I now have murderous thoughts.

"Hey, Abbs, I didn't hear you come in. Hope you don't mind, but Mom was sounding pretty lonely. I told her you'd be cool." He doesn't finish with "I'm all she's got," but I can see the cartoon thought bubble above his head. Marilyn loves to hold that over Jack.

"Sure," is all I say, shrugging out of my suit jacket and plopping my purse on the side counter, our catch-all area. I idly flip through the mail and check my phone, stalling for time away from Marilyn.

"Oh, before I forget," he said, lowering his voice a bit. "Dr. Anderson's office called. My test results came back and I'm all good." I look up, startled.

"Really? Your numbers are good?" I hold my breath, feeling hopeful.

"I've got lots of swimmers, and they can all swim in a straight line."

"That's great news, Jack." As I make a mental note to cross off researching sperm banks from my to-do list, gloom settles over me. If the problem is not with Jack, it must be me.

"So how was work?" Jack busies himself with getting supper ready and I climb up onto one of the high stools at our eat-in bar to watch him work. We usually prepare dinner together, but I'm content to sit on the sidelines tonight. "You okay, Abbs?" Before I can answer, Marilyn glides into the kitchen.

"Jacky, do you have any *good* wine?" I note the emphasis and I bite my tongue to stop from yelling "No, we only serve crap wine here." I roll my eyes toward Jack and fetch three wine glasses as he pulls out our best bottle, the really expensive one I was saving for a celebration. Hanging out with Marilyn hardly qualifies. I give him my best "Are you freaking kidding me" look, which he chooses to ignore.

The high I was feeling on the way home is totally gone. I can feel resentment flowing up from my toes like hot lava. Jack pours three generous glasses and I rush to take a gulp.

"A toast to you, Jacky, my little man." Marilyn pauses. That can't be it, I think; that is your toast? Marilyn turns toward me. "And of course to you, Abigail. May the fertility gods bless you, since we know Jack's sperm are fine. Drink up." I choke on my mouthful of wine as I watch Marilyn smile a snarl in my direction. Jack looks sheepish as I realize the real significance of her words. Jack told her about the sperm test. Has this family not heard of boundaries? The seething resentment is building into a full head of whoop ass, my only challenge being deciding which one to kill first. An old expression my grade four teacher used to say suddenly pops into my head: "If you have nothing nice to say, don't say anything at all." *Believe me, I have nothing nice to say.* I take another gulp of wine and glower at them.

When we sit down to eat, I go through the motions – please pass the pepper, great dinner dear. I hardly pay attention to the latest gossip at Marilyn's golf club, which centers around who's the newest grandparent, yet another zinger.

"Jacky, I ran into Sarah the other day at the grocery store." Sarah? I instantly pay attention. Sarah is Jack's ex-girlfriend, actually ex-fiancée. Jack's version of the "Sarah Story" is that she cheated on him and he broke it off. One night early in our relationship, and under the influence of some major alcohol, Jack's best friend Tyler told me that she broke his heart. Marilyn's twisted version is that they were perfect together, and I am constantly measured against Sarah, the "one that got away."

"That's nice, Mom."

"She looks great. She just got married and she's trying to have a baby too. Can you believe that? How great would it be if you both had babies at the same time?"

I stare wide-eyed at Jack, and he shifts uncomfortably in his chair. Is this woman serious? How great would it be to hang out with your husband's cheating ex-fiancée at some yummy-mummy class? I stab at my asparagus, channeling anger through my fork. Jack starts talking about business and I close my eyes, take a deep breath, and zone out again. The moment we have all finished eating, I rudely excuse myself and start to clean up the kitchen. Okay, truthfully, I slam cupboard doors as the most non-violent action I can think of. Marilyn pokes her head around the door into the kitchen.

"Good night, Abigail, always lovely to see you."

"Night." As the kitchen door closes, I bend at the waist, hands gripping the counter, and draw in deep shaky breaths to calm myself. I hear Jack walk his mom to the door and hear the murmuring of their good-byes. I pour myself a very large glass of wine, knowing I shouldn't on the eve of our big fertility meeting, but also knowing I need to. I hold up my hand when Jack re-enters the kitchen.

"Before you say anything, I have to ask, why does your mom know about your sperm test results? Why would you tell her before me? Jack, we're married, there are things in our lives that we need to work on together, and that means keeping people out sometimes. This is one of those times."

"Are you kidding me? Are you going to look me in the eye and tell me you aren't planning to tell Jules or Cassie or even your mom? Why can you share and I can't? How is that fair?" Jack slumps onto a stool, puts his elbows on the counter, and runs both hands through his hair.

"You know there's a difference. Jules and Cassie don't lord our faults over us like your mother does."

"I'd hardly say Mom *lords* it over you."

"Really? Who the hell makes a toast like that?" I put on my best Marilyn imitation. "'Here's hoping you are fertile, Abigail.' Come on! I have enough pressure on me already. I don't need your mother pointing out that I'm the one with problems."

"No one says you have problems. We both want to have a baby. I know this is hard on you, but my mom means well. She just doesn't execute well. She's actually on our side." Jack pulls me onto his lap and envelops me in a huge hug. "We can do this. Maybe we just need a little help," he whispers in my ear.

"Really?"

"Really."

"Well then, what are you doing tomorrow at three o'clock?"

7

I WAKE UP an hour before my alarm goes off. As I get ready, I find myself unable to decide on an outfit. I know, I know – it doesn't really matter what I wear and I'll be naked in front of this doctor, so why try to impress? Still, I take extra time to put myself together.

I also attempt to put in a full day's work before our three o'clock appointment. Marco has forgiven me, but there are times when I can feel his eyes on me. Tomorrow is our second chance at the bank pitch. I email Marco, informing him of my appointment and assuring him I will put the finishing touches on the presentation later tonight. With any luck, I'll be back at work in an hour. As I gather my things, Linda, passing my office, slows, looks pointedly at her watch and back at me, with my purse and jacket in hand, and raises an eyebrow. I smile, choking back an explanation, which I don't owe her. Brushing past her, I head out to the Hope Clinic, which is nearby, right downtown.

Jack meets me in the waiting room, which is deserted. We can't be the only ones who have this trouble – what a horrible thought. We settle in nervously and begin our wait, neither of us able to keep our eyes off Dr. Greenberg's receptionist. She is stunning: early twenties, long blonde hair, pouty pink lips, sparkling blue eyes, tall and very slim with huge breasts. She exudes fruitfulness.

I notice the nameplate on her desk reads MIRA. More like Hera, Goddess of Fertility. I lean over to Jack and jokingly whisper, "You wanna bet she's here for the guys to lust after in the jerk-off room?" Jack just nods and looks away quickly. I suddenly recall his fast "deposit" in the previous lab. *Aha.*

Two long hours later, with Jack checking the time every four minutes and muttering to himself, the nurse finally calls us. So much for getting back to the office. Dr. Greenberg might be the best in the world, but his time management sucks.

We are greeted by a large man – in girth, not height – sporting a monochromatic suit of dull gray. My breath catches as I stare at the thousands of photos of perfect babies papering his walls. I silently pray that these are real babies he has helped create, not a twisted way to decorate.

We spend the next hour and a half walking through our medical histories and discussing our failed attempts to get pregnant, and then Dr. Greenberg outlines our options. We can try "cycle monitoring" with a combination of fertility drugs or make the jump to in vitro fertilization, IVF.

"Of course there is a major price difference in the options. It is unfortunate that we don't all live in Finland, where the government covers the cost of IVF treatments for couples," says Dr. Greenberg, with a Santa-like chuckle. Jack and I look at each other, trying to figure out if moving to Finland in the next month might be a possibility.

"What kind of costs are we talking about here, Doc?" Jack asks, his foot tapping, a sign that he's anxious. I swallow with difficulty, remembering the prices on the website. Maybe I should have mentioned them before now.

"Well, the majority of the costs are related to the drugs, and that all depends on Abby's hormone levels. Some of our younger patients need only small doses, while our older patients typically need much stronger amounts. We'll have to run some tests to determine what kind of levels we are dealing with in your case."

"Can you give us a ballpark here? So we have some idea?"

"Let's see, given Abby's age and general good health, I'd say you'll most likely be on the lower end of the scale. Cycle monitoring can range from a few hundred dollars up to two thousand dollars, but again, it all depends on how much we need to boost your hormones." He nods in my direction and continues, "With IVF, I usually tell people to budget between twelve and fifteen thousand dollars." Jack makes a small choking sound and I feel his eyes on me. I stare straight ahead, afraid to meet his glance. I know what's in our bank account. There is no way we can afford IVF.

"Look, I know it's a lot to take in. While you think about your options, let's run some tests on both of you to see what we're dealing with." Dr. Greenberg smiles cautiously at us and we both nod.

After shaking hands with Dr. Greenberg, we quietly follow a beaming nurse to the blood lab. As reassuring as her constant smile is, my cheeks hurt just watching her. Jack offers to go first, sits in the chair, and gasps when he sees the male technician grab a handful of vials.

"You're gonna leave me some, right?" he asks nervously, his foot tapping like crazy. The tech barely looks up. He must have heard that one before.

Jack's veins make short work of the twelve vials, and then it's my turn. This time we both gasp – the tech has two handfuls of vials for me.

"You've gotta be kidding me," I say, dumbfounded.

I finish filling the vat of blood, and then we head into the procedure room for more fun. There, Dr. Greenberg attempts to explain the sonohysterogram that I'm about to undergo, although I'm not even sure if that's what it's called as I'm still reeling from the blood loss. The only words the doctor says that actually stick in my mind are, "This might be a little uncomfortable" – famous doctor words for, "This is going to hurt like hell."

Lying on my back with feet in stirrups, I do my best to brace myself, but I don't know what to brace for exactly. Turns out, they are trying to get a look at the inside of my uterus to see if there is scar tissue, growths, or anything that would impede a pregnancy.

After a few minutes, many of them very painful – "uncomfortable," my ass – I get the all-clear from the doctor and whimper as I change back into my clothes. So, we know my uterus is fine; one more thing to check off our list. I am to report to the hospital the following week for another test called a hysterosalpingogram. With the first six letters reminding me of "hysteria," I can't imagine I'll have a relaxing, pain-free experience.

"Does it hurt?" I ask the smiley nurse in a small voice. Jack has an incredibly high pain threshold; I, on the other hand, am a wimp.

We leave the office and enter a blast of sweltering August humidity. I try to take shallow breaths so the hot air doesn't scorch my lungs, while Jack, who not only loves the heat and humidity but hasn't been poked and prodded half as much as I have, leads the way as if we've just had a day in the park. The words of Smiley Nurse continue to ring in my ears.

"You'll probably find it a *little* more uncomfortable than today."

Oh shit.

∽

Okay, Abby, ignore the throbbing in your pelvic area and concentrate. Big presentation to the bankers; take a deep breath and smile. I will my grimace into a smile at the four suits around the oval boardroom table. They must all shop at the same store, or they have a standard uniform: dark navy suit, blue dress shirt, and diagonal-striped tie. Only one dares to rebel slightly, his tie striped in orange instead of the regulation red and navy. He looks late thirties, while his colleagues seem closer to retirement.

Walking the bankers through an extensive presentation on how best to reach a younger clientele, I show them our rough ideas for a new brand identity and how they can be seen as hip, instead of stodgy. Marco is nodding at me, his way of telling me I'm winning them over, and I hope no one noticed my squeak of pain when I knocked against one of the chairs. I end with a list of sponsorship opportunities that range from the national snowcross team to a concert series, each event hitting a younger and savvier audience.

"Can I ask where you do your banking?" one of the navy/red ties asks, looking over his reading glasses at me, his tone thick with condescension. Realizing there are two ways I can play this, I opt for the riskier venture.

"Not with you guys." I ignore Marco's sharp intake of air. "Basically for all of the reasons we've talked about today." I hurry on before they can hold a grudge. "Moving toward a younger demographic will open up a large untapped market for your organization. Truthfully, my parents and grandparents have always banked with you."

"Well, Abby, you've given us lots to think about." Mr. Orange Tie shakes my hand and looks down quickly, perhaps surprised by the firmness in my grasp. My mauve linen ruffle dress and heels gives them a false sense of what I'm capable of.

"You had me a little worried there at the end, but I think that probably sold them," Marco says as soon as we hit the lobby. "I mean it, Abby; good work."

∽

On the morning of the test, I'm nervous and make Jack come with me to the hospital, where we are second in line for the hysterosalpingogram test. I change into my open-backed sea-foam-green hospital gown and sit down on one of the vinyl chairs in the hallway to wait. Jack squeezes my arm and pulls out his phone. I have a book with me, but concentrating on the words is next to impossible. All I can think about is how much this is going to hurt. Tick, tick, tick, tick. The first hour of waiting passes slowly and I realize I am seeing a trend with Dr. Greenberg's punctuality. I also realize I'm probably flashing the couple across from me every time I shift in my seat.

After I've made three visits to the washroom with my nervous bladder, clutching at the back of my gown to keep some modesty, Dr. Greenberg comes huffing and puffing into the corridor and beckons the first woman inside, and her partner follows, rubbing her arm. She's in her mid-forties – at least the lines and hardness to her face say that. Her partner is older, or maybe life has just been tough on both of them. It's obviously her last chance to have a kid, and I'm thankful that I have some youth on my side. Even so, I'm wringing my hands and sweating. I pretend to stretch my arms, but really I surreptitiously sniff my armpits to make sure my deodorant hasn't crapped out on me.

Suddenly, screams emanate from inside the room. Oh god – I blanch and dive forward to put my head between my knees. Jack grabs for me and starts talking loudly about something, anything, desperately trying to take my attention from the tortured sounds within.

I'm sure only a few minutes pass, but it feels like eons until the door bursts open and the screamer staggers from the room in the arms of her partner. Peeling my bare legs off the vinyl, I stand, very shaky, very pale, and very terrified.

"Do you want me to come in with you?" whispers Jack.

"No, I'm good," I say hoarsely, and stagger through the doors.

Dr. Greenberg and the nurse are in full radiation protective gear, and I feel as though I have entered an episode of *The Twilight Zone*. They greet me at the table and I climb up and place my feet in the stirrups. The room looks like a standard X-ray room, with a windowed alcove off to one side. I must look awful, because they both ask if I'm okay. I barely nod, my mouth clenched shut, my lips surely bloodless and white. A bubble of hysterical laughter and a few tears try to escape. I will myself to hold it together.

"It's okay, dear; it's nothing to worry about," says the nurse.

Yeah right; explain the screaming. Tears course down my face, and I feel as if I'm going to either pass out or throw up as Dr. Greenberg explains the procedure: they're going to inject radioactive dye into my fallopian tubes and watch the X-ray for any blockages. Tube blockages would definitely explain why I can't get pregnant, although I can't imagine anything radioactive would help either.

"Okay, no problems on the right side. Let's try the left."

Having felt nothing, I look up at the screen, shocked. I'd thought he was still explaining the procedure. It didn't hurt – not even remotely. I bite my lip to keep from laughing and turn my attention to the screen, watching, fascinated, as the dye snakes its way through my left fallopian tube.

"Abby, left side looks great too. So I'll see you back in my office on day two of your next cycle. See, that wasn't so bad." And with that, Dr. Greenberg sweeps out of the room.

I lie there, stunned. What the hell was with the screaming woman? Then I remember Jack waiting nervously outside. Hopping off the table, I head out to the hallway.

"Are you okay?" Jack whispers, looking very white as he grabs me tightly.

"I'm fine. It didn't hurt a bit."

"Seriously? What about the other woman?"

"No idea. I've got good news and bad news. Good, my tubes aren't blocked. Bad, there must be something else wrong."

෧

The phone rings as we are finishing dinner, and Jack motions me out of the kitchen, knowing from the long-distance ring that it's bound to be Jules.

"Abby, how are you feeling? Did it hurt like hell?"

"Actually it wasn't bad," I start.

"Tell her about the screamer," Jack yells from the kitchen, and I fill Jules in on the whole ordeal.

"Well, honey," she pauses to take a sip of wine and I follow suit, "this is all good news. I know this will work for you."

"Thanks, Jules, but enough about us. How are things with you? Is Liam behaving himself? How's Victoria? Did you find another contractor? I feel like we haven't had a proper catch-up in ages." Liam is Jules's husband and I've always thought they made a nice balance: she is loud, outspoken, and has a "take-no-prisoners" approach to life, while Liam is soft-spoken, sweet, and still obviously in love with my best friend after fifteen years of marriage. Victoria is their ten-year-old daughter.

"The windows are finally in, but apparently the roof needs replacing. I'm living in a money pit, I swear. Victoria is great, ten going on twenty, which means some days I want to sell her. I am *not* looking forward to the teenage years. Oh, you would have loved this, the other day Liam had to change the motion-sensor light and he had Victoria out there jumping around, trying to get the damned thing to turn on. Wouldn't you know he forgot to turn on the switch. Typical Liam," she says with humor and love noticeable in her voice. We gab for another thirty minutes about work, life, and Marilyn – in code, so Jack won't catch on.

Ruffling Jack's hair, I head upstairs to get ready for bed. Later, lying in bed beside Jack, I realize I am filled with optimism. Work is going well, Jack and I are doing fine, my tubes and uterus are clear, and Jack has straight-line swimmers. This is definitely going to work.

8

I'M SITTING ON our yellow porch swing, wrapped in an old patchwork quilt of my grandmother's to keep the late September chill away. Regardless of temperature, my best thinking happens on the swing, and taking advantage of Marco's recent goodwill toward me, I've decided to work from home and review the initial design work for Saber, a client. Movement catches my eye and I see Cassie coming up our walk.

"Cass, what are you doing here?" I ask, surprised, piling my papers and notepad together to make room for her on the swing. I don't remember Cassie ever showing up unannounced before.

"I called you at the office, but Scott said you were 'working from home.'" She makes quote gestures in the air with her fingers. "I had to stop and pick up some supplies for Mom from Riverdale Homeopathics, so I thought I'd see if you really were here. In my office, 'working from home' is code for playing golf or visiting a strip club." Cassie starts picking at a loose thread from her Pink Tartan pants but doesn't make eye contact. Somewhere in the back of my head an alarm sounds quietly.

"Hey, is everything okay? You're a little pale." The alarm sounds louder.

"I'm just a little cold. Do you mind if we go inside? I'd love an herbal tea if you have some." She is still avoiding my gaze, so I collect my things and shove them into my briefcase as Cassie picks up the quilt and strokes a square of pink and purple.

"You are so lucky to have Nana's quilt. I love the colors." Cassie follows me through the house and into the kitchen. She pulls out a stool and cocoons herself in the quilt. I pull out my paltry selection of herbal teas, bought purely for her benefit, from the very back of the pantry, and wipe the dust off the box. Dropping a bag of mint tea in one mug, I toss a bag of regular tea in another. Cassie glances at my actions, but doesn't pronounce any judgment. Something must really be wrong.

"Everything okay with, um, you and Roger?" I ask tentatively.

"Abby," she starts and then stops. "I don't really know how to say this…" Again she trails off. The alarm in my head is going off like crazy. "I didn't– I mean, we didn't mean for this to happen. Actually, we didn't really *want* it to happen, right now that is."

"Cassie, what is going on?"

"I'm pregnant." Cassie says it in a rush and holds her breath, looking directly at me for the first time.

"What? But I thought … that doesn't make any sense. What?" The alarm has gone silent. I look around. I have never truly understood the expression "Turn your world upside down" until this moment. I will myself to breathe. *In and out; that's right, Abby.*

"It was an accident. I'm so sorry. Neither of us meant for this to happen. But it's true. I'm eight weeks pregnant."

"But … how? I thought you were on the pill." Mentally, I am slowly picking myself up from being hit by a Mack truck. Who gets pregnant accidentally these days? There are a zillion things on the market, most of them pretty darn effective.

"I haven't been on the pill in years. Synthetic hormones are so bad for you. We are usually really careful, but we had a few too many drinks at the Ashfield gala and, well, I guess…"

The conversation halts in an uneasy silence and I grip the counter, breathing slowly, trying to keep the waves of despair from engulfing me. Cassie sips her tea and I ignore mine, afraid I might choke on it. She is waiting, waiting for me to say the one thing she needs to hear, which is, "So, you're having a baby. This is big news. Congratulations."

I take one more deep breath. "I'm happy for you."

"Oh, Abby. Thank you so much. That really means a lot to me." She jumps off the stool and runs around the counter to throw her arms around me, gripping me in a patchouli hug. I hug back stiffly, trying not to gag on the wafts of incense embedded in her expensive clothes. Cassie doesn't seem to notice my discomfort. "I know how hard you've been trying to have a baby and I was so worried you'd be mad." She pulls back to look at my face.

I surely deserve an Oscar for my performance. "Mad? Why would I be mad?" Hysteria bubbles up and I do my best to clamp it down. "Truly, Cassie, I'm very happy for you, and of course, Roger." I can see myself at the podium, accepting my Oscar, *"I'd like to thank my crazy hippie family, who apparently don't believe in birth control, for this honor..."*

My award-winning performance is so convincing, she regales me with stories of morning sickness, tender boobs, and plans for a hemp and bamboo baby room.

"I've been doing some reading. Did you know you can toilet train a baby? It's called elimination communication. You look for the baby's signs and signals and then you give cue sounds that they learn to associate with going to the bathroom. It's so neat. No need for diapers."

I finally get her to leave by telling her I have to pick up Jack at work. I'm not entirely sure how long she stayed, but in dog years, I would have had to put her down. I wave good-bye, with a smile plastered to my face. Minutes later, Jack comes in, whistling.

"Hey, was that Cassie I just saw leaving?" Jack asks, as he drops his keys on the front hall table in the clamshell we found snorkeling on our honeymoon. I am standing still and rigid in the center of our living room. My mouth opens but the stress and heartbreak of the afternoon catch up to me and I crumble.

"Whoa." Jack manages to catch me before I hit the floor. I can't speak for sobbing. Jack grips me tightly.

"Abby, talk to me. Are you okay? What the hell is happening?"

"She's, she's, she's pregnant. My fucking sister got pregnant. By accident."

"Oh Christ."

∽

I make it to the office on time the next morning. Jack wanted me to call in sick, but with all of our fertility appointments I know I'd better put in some office time or I'll have bigger problems than my sister being pregnant. Just the thought of it makes me well up again.

"Abigail, pull yourself together. No blubbering in the office," I whisper severely to my emotional self.

In front of our agency building, I notice a gold-colored Hummer parked illegally at the curb. My heart rate quickens. It must be Charlie. I take a deep breath, mentally and physically straighten myself, and push open the front door. There is not a soul walking the halls or gossiping by the coffee room, yet the tension is palpable. Scott pokes his head out from under his desk – yes, he is actually *under* his desk – and flicks his head toward the end of the office. His wide, spooked-bunny eyes tell me Charlie is here. Scott darts into my office behind me and closes the door.

"He's been here all morning. What does this mean? He's never here so early. Oh my god, we're all getting fired. They are selling the agency and we all have to go. Maybe we've gone bankrupt. We'll all be on the streets, Abby, I can't live on the streets," Scott wails.

"Scott, pull it together. Don't make me slap you. I'm sure there's a perfectly good explanation. Go make some coffee and be useful." I'm not at Scott's freak-out level, but I am curious, and frankly a bit nervous. Missing work as often as I have been, I'm worried there might be a bull's-eye on my back.

Maybe it's my fatalistic mood, but I decide I have nothing to lose by not waiting around for my life to be determined for me. I boldly get up from my desk and stride to Charlie's office, armed with the theory that male bosses will shrivel when female employees explain that absences or tardiness are due to "female issues."

I knock and push open Charlie's door, but weirdly, he's not there. Maybe he and Marco are meeting in Marco's office? But no, Marco is at his desk, staring intently at his computer screen, as he does when he is surfing the net for porn and wants to pretend he is working. I check the boardroom: nothing. I make an entire circuit of the office and there's no Charlie. I notice the tension in the building seems to be gone, and when I check the street, sure enough, there's no Hummer. I walk back to my office a little dejectedly and smile when I realize I was gunning for a fight. My breath catches in my throat when I see a glass vase overflowing with yellow roses on my desk. I inhale their sweet perfume and reach for the card.

"Abby, great job landing the bankers. Keep up the good work. Norman."

Feeling better than I've felt in the last twenty-four hours, I push all thoughts of Cassie, babies, and fertility clinics from my mind and start to do the terrific work Charlie just praised me for.

↩

I collapse onto our battered leather couch, leaving Jack to pick up my coat. I watch him, vaguely recalling throwing my jacket in the general vicinity of our coat hooks and missing. Jack raises his eyebrows at me and I smile, realizing our roles have reversed – I'm usually picking up after him.

"Quite a day," he says as he retrieves two wine glasses, holds them up, and catches my eye. I nod and he heads off to open the wine.

"Quite a week," I say to his retreating back. Between Cassie's news and fertility testing, I'm exhausted. Rallying what little strength I have left, I reach for my briefcase, and as I pull out my laptop, a solitary piece of paper drops out. I pick it up, spy the auspicious F&F logo our production team no doubt spent good company time working on, and smile. The first time Scott showed it to me, I stared at the weird symbol for a few minutes and then declared defeat. Scott showed me that it was not a symbol, but rather two Fs, in the missionary position, the one on top holding a match. The team probably designed it on a cocktail napkin during a drunken evening. Luckily the logo isn't too obvious. I've caught Marco staring at it a few times and he seems oblivious. I'd forgotten about the list till now, and when Jack comes back, hands me my glass of Chardonnay, and settles on the couch, TV remote in hand, I consider putting it away, knowing I have so much work to catch up on. Dammit, though; I deserve a laugh. I smooth out the paper listing the top five reasons our latest contestant should, would, or might get fired.

1. Ms. F&F sends condolence email to top client on the death of their spouse. As a parting greeting, Ms. F&F thinks the short form of "lots of love" is "LOL."

2. Ms. F&F sends emails detailing Marco's boudoir routines, signed "anonymous," from her work email account.

3. Ms. F&F sleeps with client.

4. Client is sitting in waiting room. Ms. F&F comes out to greet. No extra chairs around, so she kneels beside him. He offers his chair, but she assures him that she is "great on her knees."

5. Team is assembled in boardroom for a "get to know you" meeting with new client. Everyone introduces themselves and reveals something personal. Example: I'm Lee, manager, and I'm a black belt in karate. I'm Jill, account exec, and I'm a black belt in cooking. I'm Ms. F&F, assistant, and I'm a black belt in ... bed. Seriously, I am.

I choke on my wine reading number five. This is a new one to me and it's perfect. I recognize number one, having lived through that unfortunate incident with the widow of one of our biggest clients. Number four makes me grin. I know it has to be Scott's entry thanks to Jules, who chats with Scott whenever she calls for me at the office. I'm sure she hasn't told Scott that the tale is autobiographical: not only did Jules not land that client, but it took her a while to get the guy to stop calling her.

I pass the list over to Jack. "So, when does the ax fall on this one?" he asks as he reads it. I'm about to answer when he laughs out loud, which makes me laugh with him. Jack has a wonderfully loud and infectious laugh. He startled me with it on our first date and has managed to keep me laughing with him ever since.

"I think I'm in love. Are you sure you have to fire her, Abbs?" He gives me his puppy-dog eyes.

"Shut up, Jack. None of this has really happened, yet. It's just the overactive and horny minds at work." I yank the list from him and open my laptop.

"But honey, a black belt in bed, what could be better? Maybe you could train for that." He yelps as I tweak his nipple, and he jumps off the couch. "I'm just saying." He ducks as a couch pillow flies at his head and is grinning as he retreats to the kitchen.

As usual, Jack is able to cheer me up. Years ago, I had a horrible business trip to Chicago that coincided with our first wedding anniversary. Everything seemed to go wrong – my flight was delayed, I was late for my meeting, the presentation file on my laptop was corrupted, and Jack hadn't acknowledged our anniversary. Needless to say, I was a wreck by the time I made it to the hotel and found my room key didn't work. I remember sliding down the door into a puddle of frustration and tears, when suddenly the door opened and I pitched backwards into the room.

Familiar arms caught my fall. It was Jack – romantic and sexy as hell. He had conspired with Scott to surprise me for our anniversary. We stayed through the weekend, snuggling in bed, ordering room service, laughing and wandering along the Magnificent Mile hand in hand. The stress and tension of my failed business trip melted away in Jack's company. Remembering that cozy weekend makes me smile, and I realize the funk has lifted.

9

DAY TWO OF my cycle arrives. Why is it that when you want your period to start, it takes forever, and when you don't want it to come, it's on time or even early? I head into the clinic at six thirty, before the sun is even up, determined to get in and out as quickly as possible, but when I arrive, I find my idea of being early is not unique. There are nine women in line ahead of me, stomping their feet against the cool, dark October morning air. The clinic doesn't even open for another twenty minutes. We mill around the doorway. I see a small, fragile-looking woman in scrubs heading to open the door. I look around, worried that the minute this little china doll opens the door, she'll be flattened by a stampede of women wanting their ovaries checked. I might hold back, but I'm worried I'll lose my number-ten status, since our numbers have now doubled. We probably look like picketers, minus placards and bullhorn. The china doll opens the door and smiles brilliantly.

"Good morning everyone, and how are we today?" She has the cheeriest voice I've ever heard. It's as if she is singing. I wait for the crush of bodies to mark the end of Cheery Nurse, but amazingly the mob is calm. We all file through the door in the order in which we arrived, nodding at Cheery Nurse. Number Eleven actually defers to me as I pause, trying to remember who I need to follow. The first ten of us file into the elevator, and no one else tries to push on; they just quietly let the doors close and wait for the next one. This is a place where everyone wants something so badly, they can taste it. Lord knows I can.

Music greets us as we enter the clinic and line up to add our names to the sign-in sheets. I sign on the blood test list and the ultrasound list, and in minutes I'm called to the blood lab. After I make my donation there, I head back to the waiting room, waving hello to the Goddess of Fertility now on her throne at the front counter, and then the ultrasound tech is calling for me. The process is moving so swiftly I should be out of here before seven thirty, with time for a latte and maybe an apple fritter before work.

The only ultrasound I know of is the kind on TV, with cold gel applied to your belly and a wand wafted over. I hop onto the table and expose my stomach. In hindsight, I probably should have noticed the stirrups on the table, but thoughts of a latte and a doughnut were fogging my early morning brain.

"Bottoms off, dear; feet here please," are the tech's only words as she pulls out a very large dildo-like thing attached to the monitor. My eyes widen in horror as she rips open a condom package and proceeds to roll it on. Surely it's too early in the morning to be so violated, and by something the size of a yardstick. I give her marks for fully lubricating, though, and with deft hands she guides the thing carefully inside me. I stare at the ceiling – I mean, where the hell else should I look? I barely know this woman. Actually, I don't know this woman at all. She moves the probe around, seemingly swinging it from side to side. I wince.

"You okay, honey?" she asks.

"Yep," I mutter through clenched teeth.

"I see from your chart that you're new here." I nod, focusing on the ceiling tiles. "Every time you come in, we'll see how many of your follicles inside each ovary are maturing. We will count them and measure their size."

"Really? You can see them? Aren't ovaries, like, the size of an almond? That's amazing." Finally, I look at her.

"It is pretty amazing. We basically watch them right up until one is released from the ovary at ovulation. I am also measuring the thickness of the lining of your uterus, to watch how it grows leading up to ovulation. Okay, Abby, we're done. You can get dressed and head back to the waiting room for Dr. Greenberg."

I walk gingerly to the waiting room, all too aware of what just occurred in my nether regions. I glance at my watch, feeling upbeat about getting to work on time. Blood test, check. Ultrasound, check. Just waiting on the doctor – how bad can that be? The clinic is really busy and there are not many empty chairs. I sit beside a short stocky woman and beam warmly as she catches my eye.

"So you must be new here. What's your issue?" she asks loudly.

"Excuse me?" I notice a few women glance in my direction. I can't quite place their common expression. It seems to be a mix of pity, humor, and pain. The alarm in my head usually reserved for Cassie sounds and I look around for an escape route.

"I had an abortion when I was eighteen and then picked up an STD from some damn one-night stand in my twenties. Spent the majority of my thirties chasing a loser I thought loved me, only to find out he was boinking my best friend on the side. Met Stan, the love of my life, and we've been trying to have a baby ever since. Three miscarriages so far, but I'm not giving up."

Here is this desperate woman unloading her very private and dirty laundry on me, a complete stranger, and I have no idea what to do or how the hell to make her stop. I keep nodding and making appropriate noises, or so I hope, but then two other women join in with their own tales. The next hour is excruciating as I am bombarded by one horrible heartbreak story after another.

"I've had eight miscarriages," a heavy-set woman chimes in.

"Oh my, I'm so sorry." I say, trying to imagine having motherhood ripped away that many times. My eyes tingle, tears threatening to form.

"I've had ovarian cancer," says another. I blink rapidly, hoping to keep from crying as she walks me through her chemotherapy treatments and subsequent pregnancy attempts.

My latte and apple fritter goal slips away. Maybe I shouldn't be here; after all, I've suffered nothing compared with these poor women.

Just when I'm about to run out of the clinic screaming, with a plan to tell Jack we will just be a happy, childless couple, Dr. Greenberg's nurse appears. All the women straighten and the nine lucky contestants ahead of me gather up their belongings. This must be "the sign" that Dr. Greenberg is finally here. We file behind her like cattle, but I am buoyed at being released from waiting room purgatory. A glance at my watch tells me it's nine o'clock. As I follow, patient number nine hangs back a bit to walk beside me.

"You okay?" she asks. I nod, terrified she'll unleash another desperate story.

"Next time, bring a book. He's always late. Oh, and watch who you sit beside."

"Thanks." I consider asking her to sit with me next time.

∽

"So Abigail, have you decided what you want to do this month?" asks Dr. Greenberg, when it's finally my turn. It is now nine thirty.

"I don't think we're ready to make the jump to IVF right away."

"I totally understand. We'll do a cycle with drugs to try and stimulate your ovaries. The goal will be to get each ovary to produce multiple follicles. Around day twelve of your cycle, we'll test your husband's sperm to see if they are compatible with your cervical mucus. If not, we'll have to do a sperm wash and place the cleaned sperm just inside your uterus. Sound okay?"

"Sure." I wonder if my mucus likes Jack's sperm. I never thought to consult my mucus when I decided he was "the one."

"Do you have a drug plan that covers fertility?"

"No, I've checked."

"Okay, that's pretty standard. This country is conflicted about the importance of helping couples create pregnancies. It's something I lobby for – well, don't get me started. Anyway, the good news is some of the drugs we use are actually used for other reasons, like diabetes or breast cancer, so your drug plan will cover some of them. The rest, I'm afraid, is your cost. You can write it off on your taxes, but that's about it." While Dr. Greenberg is talking, he is madly writing in my chart. "Just take this and wait outside for the nurse to get you and explain everything. See you on day eight." And with that, I am dismissed.

I have now waited two and a half hours for a three-minute meeting. If one of my clients pulled a stunt like that, I would have told them off and walked out. I marvel at the lengths to which I am now willing to go to become a mom – although compared to the stories I heard this morning, wasting almost three hours seems hardly a hardship.

Interrupting my contemplation is Smiley Nurse, who invites me to her office. How is it that the name of every person in this clinic, except for Dr. Greenberg himself, has escaped me? They introduce themselves, and their names vanish immediately from my head. She has three bottles of pills I'm to start taking right away, to help thicken the lining of my uterus and stimulate follicle growth. I am to report back to the clinic in six days and have my blood tested and another violating ultrasound performed. Maybe it is from being in the presence of the fertility promoters, but out on the street, I feel stronger, taller – dare I say optimistic – for the first time in months. I grab a latte and apple fritter to go, and race to the office.

∽

"Morning everyone, I'm sorry to be a little late–" I freeze in mid-sentence as I catch sight of Linda at the head of the boardroom table. All eyes swivel in my direction, as Marco taps his watch. Linda's eyes have a nasty gleam. I catch sight of Andrew, our high-maintenance client, and note confusion on his face.

"Oh good, you're finally here." I hear the scorn in Linda's voice. "I just thought I'd fill in for you since you were so late." Marco nods, and all other eyes drop down to the table.

"Didn't Scott give you the message?" I look to Marco, but he looks blankly back at me. "I told him I was running a few minutes behind."

"Scott is tied up this morning. No worries, Abby. I assured Andrew that we all pitch in together around here." Linda sounds sweet, but I feel the evil lurking. "Andrew, such a pleasure to meet you. I'll leave you now in Abby's *reliable* hands." She sweeps from the room, stopping by me at the door. "So glad you finally made it. I'll check with Scott on that message."

An uncomfortable silence fills the room. Smiling with what hopefully shows a confidence I seem to be lacking, I walk to the front of the room to finish my meeting.

∽

Six mornings later, I find myself in the cattle line at the clinic door. I've arrived five minutes earlier than the last time, but somehow still find myself in tenth position. I have religiously taken my three bottles of pills and am, surprisingly, looking forward to the violating ultrasound that will show if in fact these pills are working their magic. I pat my purse, checking for the umpteenth time that I remembered my book.

Silently, I chant my mantra: "I will get pregnant, I will have a baby, I will be a mom."

Cheery Nurse appears and unlocks the door, and we all file politely onto the elevator and flow in order into the waiting room, like a very organized ocean wave. I smile at the Fertility Goddess and scan the room, looking for a safe place to sit. It's amazing how, if you look closely, you can spot the "desperates" in the crowd. They are scanning the room, trying to make eye contact, looking for a sympathetic ear or someone to complain to. I find a seat near the back of the room, with others reading books, deciding I'm safe. As I pull out the latest Sophie Kinsella novel, I recognize the woman across from me as the one who had warned me to bring a book. We smile shyly and settle into our books.

As with last time, I quickly move through the blood and ultrasound stages. The ultrasound tech tells me my uterus is looking good, with multiple follicles growing. This could be it; this could all be working. I'm about to be a mom. Back in the waiting room, I have trouble concentrating on the page, but I keep my eyes down in case a desperate tries to talk to me. I don't even care that it takes close to three hours for Dr. Greenberg to show up.

"Abigail, things are looking good," he says, staring at my thin chart. The charts piled on his table are easily four times as thick as mine, which must mean the other women have either been trying for a very long time or have some exceptionally serious fertility issues. I feel a little less optimistic as he flips through my measly file. "Keep up the drugs and I'll see you again in two days. Any questions?"

"Yes. What exactly happens next?"

"We'll check you every two or three days until you ovulate. Around day fourteen, you and Jack will come in together. We'll check to see if you guys are compatible and then we'll try insemination. Hopefully that will do the trick." He closes my file and puts it aside, my cue to leave. As I open the door, he heaves a very large file onto his lap and calls the next contestant. I avoid eye contact with her and dart out the door for the office.

The next week passes in a blur. I am at the clinic every other morning and working long hours at the office to balance out my late morning arrivals. Marco has been hovering around me, and my fingers are tightly crossed that I'll get pregnant and back to my normal routine at the office. That's the real challenge: Marco is used to me being available.

I've been so busy I haven't even spoken to Jules, and her messages are taking on a very worried tone.

Day fourteen arrives. As I get out of the shower, I catch the distinctive smell of bacon. Downstairs, Jack is laying out plates loaded with bacon, eggs, and toast, with a huge grin.

"Dig in, baby."

"What's with the huge breakfast?"

"It's the breakfast of champions. We need my 'guys' to perform today, so I figured a high-protein breakfast would get them swimming as fast as their little tails can go."

I laugh. I haven't paid his sperm much attention, but Jack's right. We do need his swimmers in top form. I just hope bacon and eggs are truly fuel for sperm champions. I brief Jack on the clinic etiquette as we leave the house.

"He's always late; just don't make a big deal of it, okay? Oh, and don't look at anyone, I mean it."

"Abbs, relax. I've got my phone and some stuff to read. Plus, I'm sure the wait isn't quite as long as you say. No offense, honey, but you do tend to exaggerate."

I smile sweetly in his direction but laugh inside. *Good luck,* I think.

"Wow, you weren't kidding," Jack whispers to me as he witnesses the fertility seekers calmly crowd into the clinic behind Cheery Nurse.

"I'm telling you, I don't exaggerate. Just be ready to wait," I whisper back.

As I sign in for blood and ultrasound, the Fertility Goddess hands Jack a cup and beckons him toward the "sample room." He smiles sheepishly, trying to look cool while he flushes beet red. He winks at me and swaggers toward a black door. I catch him looking back at the front desk with a lopsided grin – I just hope his sperm are more focused on their goal than he is.

Jack is back in even fewer minutes than the last time. "Abbs, you should see the set-up in there: big-screen TV, quality porn mags, and no stains on the furniture. It's not a broom closet, it's a real jerk-off room." There is awe in his voice.

I notice Jack keeps shooting looks at the Fertility Goddess, but otherwise spends most of the next two hours on his phone.

"You weren't kidding about the wait, Abbs."

I glare at him as we get called into Dr. Greenberg's office.

"Well, Jack, Abigail, it's time to find out if you guys are compatible. So here's what we do. We take a drop of Abigail's cervical fluid and a drop of Jack's sperm from his sample and put them together on a glass slide. We put that under the microscope, and if you look at the TV screen on the wall, we'll get to see what happens." A window in the wall opens, and a lab technician hands Dr. Greenberg a test tube, as if on cue.

"Jack, make sure this is you. It's never very popular if we mix these things up." He chuckles. Jack dutifully reads the name on the label and agrees that it is indeed full of his swimmers. All eyes are on the TV screen as Dr. Greenberg puts the slide under the microscope. "So, what we want to see here is a V-shaped formation of Jack's sperm marching confidently through Abigail's mucus."

Everything starts out on track. A distinctive V-shape forms, and the army of sperm heads toward the wall of mucus. Then it's as if the general is taken out, sending soldiers moving in all directions, some apparently in full retreat. Jack and I stare numbly at the chaos unfolding in front of us.

"Well, that's not quite what we are looking for," says Dr. Greenberg. "Abigail, it seems you have hostile mucus."

"What?"

"Your cervical mucus is basically killing off Jack's sperm." As Dr. Greenberg is explaining, I realize Jack is staring accusingly at me. I can almost hear his thoughts. "Not only do you nag me to put my dishes away, your mucus is killing my guys."

"So, if your mucus wasn't hostile–"

"Dr. Greenberg, do we have to use that word? Can we just say they don't get along?" I plead.

"As I was saying, we would have injected Jack's sperm into the entrance of your cervix and let the little guys swim their way to the egg. But in this case, we'll have to give them a little help."

"Yeah, like body armor and assault rifles," mutters Jack. I shoot him a look. Either Dr. Greenberg hasn't noticed the tension or it's commonplace in his line of work.

"The technicians in the lab will put Jack's sample in a centrifuge and separate out the sperm from the seminal fluid. We will then inject the washed sperm directly into the uterus, bypassing the hostile – I mean, unfriendly – mucus. Then, they have a clear path to the egg, and we hope all works out. Sound good?"

Dr. Greenberg leaves us, promising to return in a few minutes when the sample is ready. Jack and I sit quietly until I break the silence.

"So maybe this will do it. I mean, it sounds like, problem solved."

"I just can't believe you kill off my guys. What did they ever do to you?" He's pathetic, really, but what can I say except sorry?

∞

For ten minutes we make small talk, like strangers sitting together on a train. Actually, neither of us is sitting. I'm lying on the examination table with my eyes closed, mentally singing the fertility chant, while Jack paces. Just when I feel like screaming, the little lab window pops open and Dr. Greenberg rolls through the main door. "Okay, let's make a baby," he says, snapping on latex gloves and gesturing toward the stirrups. I let my knees fall open and grimace when the speculum is inserted. Damn, I hate those things. Jack grips my hand tightly and looks a little pale. A syringe is handed through the lab window into Dr. Greenberg's waiting hand, as if technician and doctor are professional dancers, moving in perfect precision. Whether intended or not, this is calming.

At the end of the syringe, where typically a needle would be, is a long, slender, flexible hose. "So Abigail, I'm going to insert this into your vagina. To get around your mucus, we will inject Jack's sperm straight into your uterus. The little hose here allows us to bypass the cervix safely. Usually, the cervical mucus would filter out the seminal fluid and allow only the sperm to pass into the sterile environment of the uterus. The centrifuge does the cleaning work instead, so when we manually bypass the cervix, we don't introduce any germs into your uterus. There, all done. Just lie here for about twenty minutes before you get up." He hands me some boxes of vaginal suppositories, with instructions to insert one three times a day. "These release progesterone and will help sustain the uterine lining. We'll see you back in two weeks for a pregnancy test." Dr. Greenberg yanks off his gloves and gathers up his equipment, ready to leave.

"What should Abby do, or I guess not do, for the next two weeks, Doc? I mean, aside from those suppositories," Jack asks. He looks a little wary of the boxes of suppositories in front of us. Truth be told, I'm a little wary too.

"Just don't overdo it, is all. Try to avoid carrying anything over ten pounds, minimize your use of stairs, try to stay stress-free, no sex, the usual. Good luck, you two." And with that, Dr. Greenberg is gone. I stare at the ceiling, willing Jack's sperm to find their way without needing directions.

"So," Jack begins and stops. He suddenly smiles, happy with himself. "Was it good for you? Wanna cigarette?"

I burst out laughing. "Yes, sweetie, it's just how I pictured it would happen. A romantic sexual encounter with my spouse, the lab technician, vaginal suppositories, and a roly-poly Jewish Santa. I can't wait to tell the kids how they came to be." I'm thankful the tension is gone, and hopeful that someday I will be able to tell our children they were conceived with lots of love and laughter. Not a bad recipe for life.

10

I DIVE FOR the phone as it rings, not bothering to check call display. I'm so bored and desperate for company, I'll happily talk to a telemarketer at this point.

"Abby, how are you? Are you feeling preggers?" Jules's voice greets me like a savior's.

"Jules, thank god. I can't take this waiting. These two weeks are endless."

"So, aside from anxious, how do you feel?"

"It's hard to say. I feel nauseous and bitchy, and my boobs hurt."

"That's terrific."

"Well, the problem is I've felt like that for the last month, and they warned me that the drugs can mimic the symptoms of pregnancy."

"I don't know, hon. Some people swear they felt different right away, but I never really noticed. How's work?"

"The usual fires to put out, egos to stroke, and of course Ms. F&F to monitor. Stress-free, maybe not, but at least it's no worse than usual."

"Aha, how is our lovely buxom office vixen? Blown any clients yet?"

"Don't even joke about that." I can hear Jules chuckling and the soft gurgle as she fills her wine glass. I'd kill for a glass of wine, but I don't want to risk it. "I can barely concentrate at work. If I don't get fired during all of this, I'll be amazed. I'm usually good at multitasking, but I can't focus on anything other than making a baby." I cut Jules off as I hear her start to speak. "Don't bloody well tell me to *not* think about it. Have you ever tried to *not* think about something you can't stop thinking about? It's impossible."

"I'm sorry you're going through this. I can give you the 'what doesn't kill you makes you stronger' spiel, but I'm worried you'll fly here and kick my ass." Jules knows me well – that's exactly what I'd be tempted to do.

"I don't get it. I come from a line of easily knocked-up women. My parents only had to be in the same room. My sister – no, don't get me started."

"Just think of all the money you could have saved on birth control," chimes Jules. Before I can seriously consider hopping on that plane to beat her up, she continues with her unwavering confidence. "Abbs, you will be a mom. This will all work out." Part of me wants to tell her to fuck off. The other part needs a hug.

∽

Finally, the morning of my pregnancy test arrives. I race into the clinic at the crack of dawn. Today, I am number five – that must be a good sign.

The lab technician hands me a special pregnancy-test clipboard. I sign the list – only two names ahead of mine, and in a matter of minutes it's my turn to have the tech draw a small vial of blood and send me on my way. I stop by the Goddess's desk to ask what happens next.

"Off you go, sweetie. We'll call you this afternoon with the results." I really want to dislike her, but she is just so cute and nice. I guess it doesn't matter what the guys think about in the jerk-off room, as long as they get the job done.

It's only seven o'clock and I have nothing to do but go to work, so I pick up a cinnamon steamer at the local Second Cup and head to the office. I've managed to get through the countless emails that materialized overnight and make a good start on the personnel reviews that I've been putting off before I hear everyone else arriving to begin their day.

The morning passes unbearably slowly. I zone out in at least one of my meetings and actually catch myself rubbing my belly, willing my baby to give me a sign that he or she is in there growing. I picture people commenting on my glow and my cute little baby bump. I am in the midst of making a mental checklist again of the baby things we will need when I realize all eyes are on me.

"Abby, you know my policy on cell phones in the meeting room," says Marco, glaring in my direction.

"Of course," I stammer, confused until I suddenly recognize the "Flight of the Bumble Bee" ringtone emanating from my jacket pocket. Jack programmed my cell phone and I still don't know how to fix it. Damn him.

"For god's sake, answer it," Marco barks.

"Excuse me. I'll be right back. Sorry, forgot it was in my pocket," and I flee the boardroom. "Abby Nichols."

"Hi Abby, its Shelly from Dr. Greenberg's office. I have the results of your pregnancy test." It's Cheery Nurse. I can hear the smile in her voice. *Oh god,* I think, *it worked, it worked, it worked.*

"I'm sorry," she says, still managing to sound bubbly, "it's a no." She ends the last word with her voice lilting upwards, not down.

The rest of the conversation I don't really pay attention to. Something about how I need to stop taking the drugs and suppositories and return to the clinic on day two. I feel as if I've been hit in the stomach. I bury my head in my hands and do everything in my power to not cry. Oh god, oh god, the tears are welling. I bite my knuckle to keep them at bay. Then I get angry. Where does that nurse get off being so cheery? Talk about leading me on. Who the hell left her in charge of calling people? The range of emotions I feel in the space of ten seconds is unbelievable. I look around to see if I can sneak away. I have to get out of here before I totally lose it.

The boardroom door opens, and Marco is shaking his head at me.

"Are you finished, Abigail? The rest of us are waiting on you."

"I, um, it's just—" I can feel my tears building, and I need to leave immediately. Marco jerks his head toward the room and mouths the word "Now." I take a deep breath, realizing my fingernails are digging painfully into my palms. Following Marco silently, I resume my seat at the table, feeling everyone's eyes drilling hot holes through me. I stare mutely at the notes in front of me.

"Right then, where were we?" Marco resumes command, beckoning our production director to continue. I take slow breaths, trying to control myself and focus on our weekly managers meeting.

"This campaign will run for nine months—"

A muffled roar in my ears drowns him out. Nine months — I was supposed to be on maternity leave in nine months. Any movement feels as if it would break me apart and I remain immobile. Seconds, minutes, hours may have passed since the phone call, but I have no concept of time.

The next words I can focus on strike through my heart. "Okay, Abby, you handle that, it's your *baby*," Marco says, and a wave of grief sweeps over me at the word "baby." I clamp my lips, curl my fists tighter, feeling my nails slicing my palms, and nod. "I'm expecting a homerun on this project. Let's get to it, everyone," he says.

The second Marco finishes, I grab my notes, rush for my office, seize my purse, and slip out the back door. Sprinting to the subway, I can hear my cell phone ringing. The subway is pulling away from the station as I take the stairs two at a time. The TV screens advise that the next train isn't due for four minutes — I can't seem to catch a break, even when I feel as if *I* am going to break. Holding my breath, I rock myself back and forth, longing for the solitude of my house.

I have vague recollections of the subway's arrival, slumping into a seat, and then the seemingly endless walk up our street. Jack comes home later to find the entire house dark.

"Abbs? You here? Shit!" He trips over my coat and purse on the hallway floor. "Are you okay?" Jack flicks on the living room light to find me curled on the couch, surrounded by used tissues.

"It's a no," is all I get out before the next wave of tears takes over.

⌒◎

When the next morning dawns, I have to get up and rejoin the world. It takes half an hour and a trowel to apply enough makeup to cover the puffiness and blotches on my face. I know I'll fool some people at work, but Scott will see right through me.

Jack is waiting in the kitchen with a steaming cup of tea and a bowl of cereal.

"Hey there. Did you get any sleep?" He kisses me gently on the head as I shrug in response. In the safe embrace of Jack's arms, I feel tears prick my eyes. Blinking quickly, I bury my face in his chest, inhaling laundry detergent and ocean breeze deodorant, all familiar and homey smells. "Do you want to talk about it?"

"I can't." My voice catches. "Not right now."

Disappointment clouds Jack's face, but the fragile wall I have built up is threatening to come down, and I can't fall apart on my way to work.

"I love you," he whispers, and he kisses me gently before leaving. I nod, and a lump forms in my throat.

I don't remember much of the day, but I get through it, barely. Scott tiptoes around me as I go through the motions at my desk. Mostly, though, I stare out the window, watching mothers pushing strollers, doing my best to come to terms with the fact that this will not be me in nine months. I question every sexual encounter I've ever had, trying to account for my inability to conceive. For instance, when I did it with my college boyfriend on a plane, did the altitude damage my ovaries? I feel as though the core of my emotions is naked on the surface of my skin, vulnerable to the slightest touch. I can't call anyone; I know words of comfort from Jules, my mom, or even Jack will be wasted.

I leave work early, no use to anyone there, and count twenty-five mothers with babies on my way home. Jack arrives moments after I do, with take-out Chinese food in hand. I leave mine uneaten. Later, we sit on the porch swing and gently rock through the night. In our speechless rocking, I feel the emptiness in him as well, as we share our grief for our baby who never was.

11

DAY TWO OF my cycle arrives, and for once I'm actually thankful my period has come. I'm slightly more emotional than normal, but I blame that on the drugs. Granted, the whole "I'm not pregnant" emotion is rather large, but I'm looking to blame something here, and drugs seem like a safe bet. I head into the clinic, early as usual, hoping I don't see Cheery Nurse, as I have a few choice words for her about her phone etiquette.

The stench of desperation in the waiting room is particularly potent today. I am very careful not to make direct eye contact with anyone, but it's simple to read the body language. Some couples look to be in trouble, their arms crossed tightly, bodies leaning away from each other, tension radiating off them in visible waves. My guess is that they've been coming to appointments for longer than they had expected and are turning the blame on each other

Three hours later, I'm sitting with Dr. Greenberg. This man has absolutely no concept of time. I contemplate invoicing him for my time and then remind myself he is meant to be my savior.

"So, Abigail, no luck this time. Well, we can either change up the drug protocol or give IVF a try."

"I think we'll still hold off on IVF for a bit."

"Okay." He flips through my chart, scribbling notes. "Let's stimulate the follicles a little more, and we'll try a few other things that will help with balancing your hormones and getting the uterus ready for implantation. We did IUI with you last time." I must look puzzled. "IUI is interuterine insemination, when we wash the sperm and place it in the uterus."

IUI, IVF – I'm going to have to keep these things straight. Dr. Greenberg sends me out to wait for a nurse who will explain the process. The nurse has a gentle manner and makes me feel safe immediately. Again, I don't catch her name – I wonder if there's a suggestion box in which I could drop a note about the benefit of name tags for the staff. She has two bottles of pills on her desk, an orange, and a needle. My safe feeling disappears in a poof.

"Have you ever done an injection before?"

"Um, no," I say, a minor note of terror creeping into my voice.

"Okay, I'll walk you through the process. You'll need to get your partner to help. Dr. Greenberg wants you to inject yourself thirty-six hours before we do the IUI. I'll show you how to do it, and when the time comes, we'll leave a message with the exact time you need to inject. It helps control the timing of the eggs being released."

Lovely Nurse keeps talking to me as she shows me how to fill the needle – with water in this case – so I can practice injecting the orange. She tells me to be quick and inject with some force, like slapping the leg. The needle needs to go into the fatty tissue of my butt cheek. "Since it's going in behind you, you'll have to get someone to do it for you."

Great, Jack will get a thrill out of shooting me in the ass. No doubt he will think of every bitchy comment I have ever made as he hits his mark.

Over the next twelve days, I freeze outside the clinic every three or four days, waiting to get blood taken, follicles measured, and uterine lining checked, and then have a two-minute status meeting with Dr. Greenberg. When day twelve arrives at last, the nurses tell me to wait for the phone call to inject myself. I then have to show up at the clinic thirty-six hours later, with Jack, for another sperm wash and IUI transfer. The nurse has me drop my pants in her office and draws a circle on my right butt cheek as a landmark for Jack.

In the middle of the next Tuesday, Cheery Nurse calls to tell me to inject myself at exactly eight o'clock at night and show up a day and a half later, with sample or husband in hand.

Jack and I eat dinner much earlier than usual, in anticipation of the main event. I can feel his nervousness, and I sure as hell know I'm petrified. My eyes keep darting to the kitchen clock as I finish doing the dishes – I even run vinegar through the coffee maker in an attempt to occupy my mind, hands, and time.

"Here, drink this." Jack rather unceremoniously hands me a glass of wine. It's to steady our nerves, and I gratefully take a swig as Jack gulps his. "Okay, let's do this."

"Are you sure you understand how to do…" my voice tapers off in shock as Jack opens the sterile casing of the needle. "Holy shit, it's huge." The needle looked so small in the office. That thing is going to go straight through to the front of my thigh. Jack swallows loudly. Lovely Nurse told me the entire needle had to go in deep into the muscle. Without asking, Jack grabs our two wine glasses, fills them with red wine, and places them on the counter, our reward for getting through this.

"Just do it fast. Smoothly, but quickly," I say as I drop my pants and grip the edge of the countertop.

"Okay, here we go."

I clench my teeth, close my eyes, take a deep breath, and wait. *Any minute now,* I think; *okay, any minute.* Sweat beads on my brow. What's up? I open one eye and turn toward Jack, who is holding the needle and apparently determining which angle might be the best.

"Just do it," I scream, making him jump.

And bam, he hits me.

"It's in. Hold on, Abbs, almost there. Done." He quickly withdraws the needle and chugs half his glass of wine. I do the same with mine. Actually, it was not as bad as I'd feared. Hurt a bit, but the anticipation was definitely worse than the reality. Jack pours another round. Even though we are headed to the tipsy-drunk-sex-might-be-fun stage, we are under doctor's orders not to "waste" any of Jack's sperm, so we spend the evening getting happily pissed and stagger to bed early.

Thirty-six hours later, we find ourselves back in Dr. Greenberg's waiting room, waiting for our second IUI attempt. Whistling a happy tune and winking at the Goddess, Jack heads off to the jerk-off room, and I do my best to focus on my book and not on the fact that we are making a baby today. My abdomen feels bloated and uncomfortable, and I keep shifting positions, trying to get comfortable. What did I eat last night? By the time Jack comes back, I've been to the washroom three times, trying to expel whatever is causing me such discomfort.

Before I get a chance to tell Jack that I think I'm coming down with something, Smiley Nurse calls my name. "How are we feeling today?" she asks as she leads us to a treatment room. "Sore and bloated?" How did she know? "It's totally natural. I guess no one told you to drink Gatorade, did they? Well, your ovaries are really swollen and the follicles are ready to burst out. Next time, drink Gatorade. The electrolytes seem to help." I want to shout, "Now you tell me!" but Smiley Nurse has already toddled off to share her wisdom with someone else.

I assume the position in the stirrups and wait for Dr. Greenberg to join us. The door opens and in he comes, with a full entourage behind him.

"Abigail, these are medical students on rounds with me today. My clinic works in conjunction with the hospital, and once a semester I take a group for a week. You don't mind if they observe, do you?"

Medical students? They look as if they've barely reached puberty. Jack looks worriedly at me. I'm a little bit torn. On the modest side, I'm not sure I want my "business" put on display. On the other hand, giving birth isn't exactly a modest endeavor either, so maybe I should get used to the exposure.

As Dr. Greenberg sets up between my legs, two of the male interns lean in, searching my vagina for the meaning of life. Jack clears his throat aggressively. I squeeze his hand and pray for this to all be over quickly, and so it is. Snapping off his gloves, Dr. Greenberg reminds me to stay horizontal for the next twenty minutes, to take it easy for the next week or two, and to not forget the suppositories. I'm to report back for a pregnancy test in two weeks. His band of merry men leaves in his wake.

I can hear the words before Jack utters them.

"So, good for you, Abbs?"

∽

Two weeks creep. Life continues, but I am living for pregnancy test day, and nothing else is of any consequence. Thankfully Scott helps me keep on top of work – it's times like this when I fully appreciate his value and am able to forgive his drama. My pregnancy test is scheduled for Friday. After learning the hard way last time that getting results at the office is a bad idea, I'm planning to skip out of the office mid-afternoon. Jack has cleared his afternoon too and is planning on meeting me at home. I am doing my best to tie up loose ends before leaving.

"Scott? Where is everyone? Alex isn't at her desk and Geoff is nowhere to be found."

"They're all in Linda's brainstorming meeting. I thought you knew that."

"All of them? Are you kidding me? I knew Linda was working with Omar and Christine, but not everyone else. Alex and Geoff are supposed to be on my bank project." I can feel my blood pressure rising as I grip the phone with white knuckles. Scott is silent, which is likely wise. "Fine, that's fine." I hang up and take a deep breath. Surveying the files on my desk and mentally reviewing my unfinished task list with no help in sight brings my blood pressure and anxiety to unhealthy levels. Anger propels me out of my chair.

"Marco, this is bullshit." I stomp into his office and slam the door behind me. Marco jumps and quickly closes his laptop, cheeks flaring red. I'm too angry to care what he was doing online.

"Abigail, really, is that language necessary?"

"How is it that all of my staff members are now working exclusively for Linda? I've got the bank pitch to work on. How am I supposed to wow them with no help? What happened to dividing up the team? Math may not be my strongest suit, but

I'm pretty sure zero is not half." I plant my hands firmly on his desk and lean in as I glare at him.

"Look, Linda came to us with major contacts, and she needs extra resources to close those deals," he starts.

"You keep talking Linda up, but honestly, what are these big deals? Who are these major contacts? There seems to be a lot of unknowns here. Something isn't right."

"Are you questioning my judgment?" Marco rises up from his chair, planting his palms on the table, and leans toward me. I pull back and stand as tall as I can.

"I am questioning the decision to take all of our resources off our tried and true clients. The ones we know, the ones that pay their bills." As the words leave my mouth and I see an angry calm settle over Marco, I know I've stepped over the line. I have no idea what hold Linda has over him, but obviously it's pretty strong. If she were young and sexy, I'd think she was doing him, but in truth, I think he's afraid of her.

"I will handle the running of this agency, *my* agency. You worry about your job and keeping it. I expect you to land the bank account," he almost hisses at me, a deadly tone to his voice. "In fact, I'll even give you another pair of hands to help." He grabs the phone and hammers an internal extension. "Trixie, meet Abby in her office in five minutes. She needs your help." He slams down the phone and meets my stare. "Happy now?"

Attempting to tuck my tail between my legs, with dignity, I turn and walk slowly back to my office. Great, just great. I slump into my chair and rub my throbbing temple. Can this day get any worse?

"You wanted to see me?" A perky voice comes from the doorway. I look up and am greeted by the sight of someone I can only assume is Trixie, a.k.a. our latest Ms. F&F. Big blonde hair, Botoxed lips, seriously enhanced boobs, wildly inappropriate office attire, all teetering on stilettos. Yep, this day can definitely get worse, and it has.

"I'm working on a big pitch for the bank and," I practically choke on my words, "I need a little help. We need to see what other banks are doing in North America and

Europe. Who is promoting to a younger demographic? We need to see logos, colors, sponsorship examples, a complete work-up. Can you look into that for me? Here's what we have gathered so far," I say as I pass over a slim red file folder. Trixie stares at it as if it clashes with her outfit and nods hesitantly. "Trixie, can you do this? I really need this research done by Thursday and I have an appointment right now, so you'll have to do this on your own."

"Sure, I mean, I'll do what I can." She teeters toward the door, clashing red file in hand.

A feeling of dread settles over me. This day still has the potential to get worse.

∽

On the way home, I make two quick stops. The first is at the liquor store for a small bottle of champagne in case we have good news and a large bottle of inexpensive wine to get riotously drunk if our results are negative. I promise myself that if it's the celebratory champagne, I will only have a sip. Also, I pop into the grocery store and buy the fixings for a fabulous meal – steaks, heirloom tomatoes, bocconcini cheese, and large artichokes. I throw two microwaveable meals into the basket, in case we aren't in the mood to cook.

Jack's number flashes on my phone as I walk home. "I'm on my way, but traffic is brutal. When are they calling?"

"I don't know exactly; it was close to three last time." Phone tucked to my shoulder, I change hands with the grocery bags, trying to even out the weight.

"I'm doing my best to get there on time."

"I know. Drive safe and I'll see you soon."

"I love you, Abbs."

"I love you too."

I'm barely home when my cell phone rings. Taking a deep breath, I sink into the couch to answer.

"Abby Nichols."

"Hi Abigail, it's Randi from Dr. Greenberg's office." My eyes turn heavenwards with thanks when I realize it's Smiley Nurse, not Cheery Nurse. Her tone is subdued, and I can feel what is coming. "I'm really sorry, it's negative. You can stop taking your medication and suppositories. We'll see you on day two."

At least she has the proper phone etiquette. I feel deeply saddened, but slightly more in control this time. I busy myself cleaning out cupboards in the kitchen that haven't been touched in a while, and when Jack gets home, he finds me surrounded by the contents of our fridge as I scrub it furiously.

I've been sure I'm fine, but as soon as I see Jack's face, his hope and anticipation, I burst into tears. Jack leads me away from the mess in the kitchen and envelops me in a huge hug on the couch. Hours later, I hear the microwave beeping, and Jack returns with dinner on a tray and two glasses of red wine.

"Can we talk about it?" Jack asks, watching me push my food around, eating nothing. I shake my head sharply. "Abby, please don't shut me out. I'm hurting too." Jack pulls me into his arms. Part of me feels the need to hold back, but the rest of me melts in the safety of his embrace. Through all of the fertility treatments, my focus has been on functioning at work and at Dr. Greenberg's, with little thought of Jack's feelings. My tears flow freely as I realize the depth of our mutual loss.

೨

When the phone rings first thing Saturday morning, I don't bother to reach for it. My eyes are so swollen from last night's tears; they wouldn't open if I tried. Jack mumbles something undecipherable and flops over on his side. I attempt to sink back into my blissful state of sleep, but instead hear myself gasp at the grief of an empty uterus. Wiping away the crusty, dried tears sealing my eyelids shut, I punch in our voice mail code in a blurry haze of numbers.

"Jacky, darling, you'll never guess who's preg–" is all I can bear to listen to before I punch the delete button. I'd rather slam the phone down on Marilyn, but will have to settle for violently deleting her voice mail instead. Jack is breathing heavily beside me. Frustrated, I throw back the covers and head into the bathroom and run the shower as hot as I can stand it, letting the water beat down on me for a long time. When I throw the curtain back, I see a rosy red image reflected in the foggy mirror.

"Holy crap, Abbs, it's like a steam room in here." Jack has opened the door and let in a rush of cold air. Shivering, I quickly dry my body and shrug into Jack's bathrobe, wrapping my hair in a towel. "Did you sleep?" I nod, not ready to speak, and head downstairs to switch on the coffee and the kettle.

I stare absently around our cozy little house, and my eyes are drawn to the flashing red light on the wall phone. Another message? Who else could be calling before ten on a Saturday morning?

"Hi, Abby, it's me, Cassie. I just wanted to check in and see if– I mean, how you're doing?" This day just keeps getting better and better; first Marilyn and now Cassie. I make a mental note to pick up another jumbo bottle of wine. I have a feeling we will need it. I delete Cassie's message, less violently this time.

Jack eats as if he's eating for two, a thought that deepens my funk. I, on the other hand, pick at my breakfast. I feel Jack's eyes following me as I clean up the kitchen and head upstairs to change.

"I've got a great idea." Jack walks around the bed to his side, grabbing the sheet to help me make the bed. "Let's head over to Home Depot and get what we need to tackle that bathroom. I know you hate the tiles in there."

"Wow," I say, raising an eyebrow. "You *are* worried about me."

"Abbs, you need something else to think about. You always do better with a project, and you've been bitching about that bathroom for years. Come on, it'll be fun." Jack looks eager, and the thought of ridding myself of the mocking tiles makes me smile. Before my mood changes, Jack grabs my hand and steers me to the door, pausing only to grab coats, wallets, and keys. I focus my eyes on the road as Jack drives, ignoring the happy parents pushing strollers.

We wander the aisles of Home Depot, driving our oversized orange shopping cart. After finding a plain white tile, we head for the paint section. Jack's phone rings and he checks the call display. "Go ahead, honey, I'll right there."

I love looking at paint colors and marvel at the vividly descriptive names: Baby Dreams Pink, Melted Ice Cream Beige, Stormy Monday Gray, Baby Seal Black, Downpour Blue. I have five completely different color samples in my hands when Jack finds me. He looks annoyed.

"What's up?" I ask him and he shrugs.

"Nothing, just my mom. Abbs, you're right, she can be really insensitive sometimes."

"Don't get me started on your mom today," I warn, holding my color chips at arm's length and squinting to imagine our bathroom. "Let me guess, some country club crony is a grandmother again."

"Something like that," Jack mutters. I hear a slight hesitation in his voice and look at him.

"What? What did your mother say? Who's pregnant?" I ask, fearing the answer.

"Sarah," he says. I inhale heavily. Oh crap, Sarah, the "one that got away," is pregnant and poor Abigail is not.

"Are you okay?" I ask tentatively.

"Fine." Silence descends on the paint section. "I told Mom to back off with the who's who of the baby world." He clears his throat. "So, what color should we get?" It amazes me how guys can do that, just move along to the next thing. I take my cue from him and show him my top three color choices, and we settle on a soft but deep blue shade called Jamestown Blue. We collect our supplies and head to the car. As we unpack the bags, Jack stumbles upon another set of paint chips and looks at me inquiringly. Glancing toward our spare bedroom, I look longingly down at Denim Wash, a lovely soft blue, and Marshmallow Bunny, a gorgeous dusty pink. I put the paint samples in my bedside drawer, straighten my shoulders, and put a smile on my face. He was right: I do better with a project.

"Ready?" Jack asks as he hands me a small sledgehammer.

I channel all of my anger, frustration, and sadness into my first swing. It feels good to hit something.

12

WE ATTEMPT ANOTHER cycle of IUI, and every few days I join the mob at the clinic doors and subject myself to blood tests, ultrasound violations, drugs, and tardy meetings with Dr. Greenberg. December is here and everything, including the street lights, seems jolly and festive. When not completely numb, I'm bitchy. Scott is in a full-blown snit, well aware he's being excluded from something important in my life. For a guy who despises being out of the loop, this is really driving him nuts.

I haven't seen Cassie since her "big news," but she bravely calls me every few weeks to catch up. I find myself exhausted after each call. When it comes to her, my emotions are jumbled and irrational. I know I should be happy and supportive, but I can't seem to get past the anger and bitterness. It doesn't make sense, this feeling of betrayal – it's not as if she did this on purpose, but I still find myself gritting my teeth every time she tells me about her latest pregnancy symptom.

My mother, who would love to be my sounding board, is in the worst spot imaginable, torn between two daughters, so happy for one and devastated for the other. Our long-distance phone bill skyrockets with late-night calls to Jules, but I know Jack will never question it.

Day twelve finally rolls around and my phone rings.

"Hi, Abigail." Drat, it's Cheery Nurse. "Dr. Greenberg needs you to inject yourself at exactly four o'clock this

afternoon. We'll see you the day after tomorrow for your IUI."
Her sing-songy voice irritates me to my core.

"Toodles," I say with fake cheeriness as I hang up. It's
already three thirty. I text Jack.

> To Jack: *Shot in ass @ 4pm today. Where can I meet u?*

> To Abby: *Shit, in mtgs, can't escape. Can u do it?*

Okay, no need to panic. Abby, you can do this. I twist in
my seat and mime the motions of shooting myself in the butt,
but I don't seem to bend that way. Frustrated, in pain, and close
to tears, I put my head on my desk, feeling utterly beaten. What
am I going to do?

"I see you're working hard, as usual." I lift my head slowly
and see Linda posing languidly in my doorway.

"What do you want, Linda?"

"I was just thinking that when I become partner, I might
have Marco take down this wall and make my office larger."
She taps on the wall. "There's no reason an underling like you
needs so much space." She chuckles and drifts out of view.

"Over my dead body," I mutter through clenched teeth.
While it is true that I happen to have one of the larger offices,
it's mine and has been for five years. I have no intention of
letting *that* woman have it.

Okay, focus, don't worry about the office, we have
immediate concerns to deal with – the needle.

My mind flips through our company directory like a
Rolodex and I mine our staff for potential needle-givers. I reject
the production team for two reasons: they are all male, and they
would tell everyone they saw my ass. Even though my account
team is predominantly female, I rule them out as well. I hired
each of them, and it's hardly appropriate for me to drop my
pants in front of them.

I check the clock again: twenty minutes till showtime.
Accounting? I only venture downstairs to the accounting
department when summoned for billing issues or my team's cell
phone bills. Our VP of finance is a man, *but* his bookkeeper is a
woman. If only I could remember her name. I pull out our phone
list and scan it. Alice. She's perfect. I grab for the phone.

"Alice? Hi, it's Abby. Look, I was wondering if I might borrow you for a minute." I hold my breath, fingers crossed.

"Okay?" She sounds hesitant. "What is it regarding?"

"It's, well – actually, I need your help. Can you dash up for a minute – now – please?"

"I'm on my way."

I exhale. See, Abby, no worries.

Five minutes later, a diminutive, gray-haired woman arrives at my door, breathless. I am cutting it close on the timing, but I pause to stare at her for a minute. Does she look like a savior?

"Thank you, Alice, you're a life-saver." I get up from behind my desk, glance into the hallway, and, seeing no one, shut my door. She looks around my office nervously. The clock is ticking, but a little small talk is warranted. I hardly know this woman, and I'm about to let her in on my major secret. "So, Alice, are you married?"

"I was, but my Danny passed on fifteen years ago."

"I'm so sorry. Did you have any kids?"

"No," she murmurs. Her hand is clutching her necklace.

"Did you ever think about having kids?" *Throw me a bone, Alice.*

"It wasn't to be."

"Well, it's amazing, these days there are things you can do to help get pregnant. Actually–"

"It was God's will. You don't question God's will." The light glints off her necklace – a cross. This might not work.

"Well, I guess one could argue that we are on this earth to procreate, so really, how can that be against God's will?"

Alice gives me a withering stare. "He didn't intend for me to have children. It would be wrong to interfere with his wishes." This will definitely *not* work. Panic sets in and I can feel a trickle of sweat at my hairline. *Breathe, Abby, breathe.* Five minutes to go. *Get her out of here and try again, on your own.*

"Well, it's been lovely getting to know you, Alice. I'm making it a priority to bridge the gaps between the account team and the rest of the staff." I head for the door, and Alice, looking startled, follows me. "I'll see you at the company holiday party." I smile and guide her into the hallway.

When she's gone, I sink into my chair and silently chant my mantra. "I will get pregnant, I will have a baby, I will be a mom." I open one eye and catch sight of the clock. Three minutes. There has to be a way to do this myself. I Google "yoga twists" and find three that might do the trick. I sit on the floor to try Bharadvaja's Twist, but can't get the right angle. Ardha Matsyendrasana doesn't work either. As I attempt to balance in Pasasana, imagining a sharp needle in my hand, I tip over with a squeak – at this rate, I'll fall over on the bloody needle and really hurt myself.

And Scott appears like a mirage at my door. I stare at him. Do I dare trust him? How badly do I want a child? Can the office gossip keep silent? Maybe we should skip a month. What would happen if we were a few hours late with the needle? Am I willing to risk it?

"Scott," I begin, very hesitantly. "Scott, I need to tell you something."

"Here it comes. Wait – let me sit down for this. Okay." He grips the armrest and I see his knuckles go white. I would have expected him to be gleeful at finding out what I've been up to, but instead he appears nervous.

"Actually, I need to ask you a favor. How are you with needles?" What if Scott passes out and I have to call the ambulance with my pants down? Try explaining that away.

"Are you doing drugs?" He arches a perfectly tweezed eyebrow.

"Piss off, Scott. No, I'm not doing drugs. I just need help with a hormone injection. I can't quite reach." I gesture toward my derriere.

"Hormone injections are easy. My neighbor down the hall is getting them for gender transformation surgery. Hang on, are you…?" He trails off and looks me up and down.

"I'm not becoming a man. I don't know how you guys walk around with those–" I gesture to the general area of his crotch "–things. No thank you. Look, this is really personal and extremely private. I need to know I can trust you to keep this a secret." Scott is nodding furiously. "Seriously, Scott, you are not exactly known for your discretion."

"It hurts that you think that of me, Abby." He holds his hand up to his forehead and sighs dramatically.

"Give me a break. You happily tweeted the bra size of the last Ms. F&F."

"Okay, I'll give you that one, but come on; she was a double-d–"

"Scott, this is for real. I will kill you if this gets out."

He nods eagerly.

"Fine. The truth is, I'm–"

"Oh my god, you're dying. You have cancer and only a short time to live. Oh, the insanity. It's a cruel, cruel world. So young and no time left." He whips out a pink handkerchief from his breast pocket and fans himself. I fix him with a sober glare, waiting for him to run out of steam.

"Are you finished?" My serious gaze prompts him to pantomime zipping his lips. With a sigh, I continue, "Scott, I'm not dying. I'm trying to get pregnant."

"What? You're not dying?"

"No, I'm fine. I'm – well, not just me – we're, Jack and I, are a tad … reproductively challenged. But it's okay, we've got ourselves a membership at a fertility clinic."

"Fertility clinic? Wait, this means you're going to be a mom. My little Abby is going to be a mom." He claps his hands together loudly.

"Hush," I hiss. "I'm not pregnant yet. Can I trust you to keep this between us?"

"Of course, honey. I'm just so glad you aren't dying. This place would be rather lonely without you." His somber expression gives way to a glimmer of hope. "Can I be Uncle Scott? Please?"

"Well–"

"Please, Abby, please. I'll take your secret to my grave."

I crack a playful grin. "I thought you might actually be Auntie Scott."

"Auntie Scott; I love it. I can't believe I get to help make a baby."

"Whoa, I only need you to give me a needle – not your swimmers."

He mimes slapping on a pair of latex gloves, eyes gleaming with mischief. "Bend over, boss, I'm going to enjoy this."

⌒☉

The next two weeks pass in a blur of last-minute Christmas shopping and clinic visits. I am normally efficient with my shopping, but find myself lingering in baby stores, stroking each plush toy and adorable onesie. Hoping not to jinx anything, I buy a tiny pair of knitted booties.

"Is it a gift?" the clerk asks, red and green tissue paper in hand.

"Yes, thank you," I whisper. At home, I tuck the booties into one of my dresser drawers.

Dr. Greenberg's clinic will be open on December twenty-fifth, and my first Christmas present will be a violation by ultrasound. Next year, if all goes well, we could be opening presents as a family. My uterus twinges at the thought. *Please, please, let this happen for us.*

⌒☉

I'm not sure if its self-preservation or just impatience that drives me to the nearest pharmacy on my way home from work. I am supposed to have my pregnancy test tomorrow morning at the clinic, but I'm not sure I can handle another negative phone call, especially if it's from Cheery-freaking-Nurse. I browse the aisles until I find a pregnancy test that promises the earliest results. At least this way I'll be prepared for the phone call.

When I get home, Jack takes the bag. "What's this?" he asks, holding the pregnancy test.

"I thought I'd find out now, you know, so I don't have to be shocked by that horrible phone call. I can't keep leaving the office for a thirty-second call. People are beginning to wonder. I need to know before Cheery Nurse calls. I can't handle her voice."

"Let's do it. Do you have to pee now?" Jack sounds eager.

"Sure." I head upstairs to our bathroom, stick in hand. I smile at the happy color of our new bathroom. We still have some work to do, but what a difference. I can hear Jack pacing outside the door.

"It's got to be midstream, Abbs." Jack must be reading the package directions. "How's it going?"

"Jack, you're giving me stage fright. Stop hovering." I try to relax and ... eureka.

"Great work, Abbs." He barges into the bathroom as I'm washing my hands. Jack settles himself stiffly on the edge of the tub and I lean against the sink. We both stare at the stick on the back of the toilet.

There's the faint wail of a fire truck rumbling along Broadview Avenue, the distant sound of a commuter train in the Don Valley, the miscellaneous honking of rush hour traffic, and voices from the street. Toronto is a noisy city, but instead of annoying me, the sounds are comforting and distracting at the same time.

Jack straightens. Our minute must be over. He checks the instructions again. "We're looking for a plus sign."

I nod. I look down.

A minus sign.

I purse my lips and shake my head, passing Jack the stick. He inhales sharply. "Crap," is all he says. I head downstairs and immediately into the kitchen. Simultaneously, my hands juggle two wine glasses and dial our favorite take-out Thai restaurant – proving that even when I'm down, I can multitask. Jack reappears a few minutes later, carrying the pregnancy test.

"Abbs, I checked again and it kind of looks like the other line is there. Look." He thrusts the tester in my face. My throat constricts and I feel hope rise. Maybe it takes a while if you are just newly pregnant. Jack looks so earnest – he really does want this as badly as I do. I look back down at the stick and stare, then shake my head sadly. Jack puts the stick down heavily on the counter. I rub his back and lean against him.

"You okay?" His voice is soft.

"I'm fine. I guess it wasn't meant to…" I trail off, unable to say, "It wasn't meant to be," because I can't believe that. Jack and I are meant to be parents, I know that. He grabs me tightly and kisses my head.

"It's okay, Abbs. Next month, sweetie, it will work, I know it."

I'm not so sure. I don't know if I can keep doing this, subjecting myself to this bitter heartbreak, not to mention the drugs, the needles, and slapping my career in the face. I just don't know.

ᦉ

The next evening, Jack and I are sitting on the couch, take-out Chinese food spread out in front of us. Jack is eating, but mine sits untouched. I am still in tears after the phone call. So much for my theory of knowing beforehand. There is no escaping Cheery Nurse, I suppose.

"I want to come with you when you go back to the clinic." Jack says out of the blue. I wonder if he's planning on punching out Cheery Nurse.

"Sure, but why?" I ask, pushing noodles from side to side with my chopsticks.

"I'm feeling positive. I think we should talk to Dr. Greenberg about IVF. I know it's a big jump, but I can't watch you go through this every month. It's too hard on you and on us."

"It is hard, trust me. But we don't have that kind of money lying around." Dr. Greenberg's "rough estimation" of fifteen thousand dollars for each IVF attempt still makes my savings account cringe. "You just expanded the company last year and that ate into our savings, so I'm not sure how we can afford this right now."

"But I also got a ten-grand bonus on our Carter contract. I was putting it aside to maybe surprise you with a trip, but I think we should use it for this."

"Do you think we should look at other options?" I see his brow crease. "You know, like adoption?"

"Abigail Nichols, I want to have a baby with you. I want a little girl with your eyes and a little dimple on her right cheek just like her mother's." He strokes my cheek and kisses my nose. "Maybe if we've exhausted all other options, we can talk about adoption, but not yet."

I have saved up for so long; the thought of emptying my coffers almost makes me balk. I desperately want to have a baby, but if I get offered a partnership, I will need the money to buy my way in. *And yet, what is your priority, Abby?*

"Well, I have a little put away in my partnership fund; I guess I could dip into that."

"Okay. Let's do it."

I smile at him and take a bite. Food suddenly has flavor again. Dinner is delicious. Fifteen thousand dollars for a baby: the more I think about it, the more it sounds perfectly reasonable. I wince as I realize my thoughts are making this sound like purchasing a baby off some black market. Although, I suppose if it ever came to that ... no. *Enough, Abby.*

IVF – could it be the answer?

13

ON DAY TWO, Jack and I bundle up and head to the clinic together. We wait the allotted two and a half hours to see Dr. Greenberg, who is surprised to see Jack.

"We're ready to try IVF," Jack announces, holding my hand.

"Great. Let me walk you through the process." For the next ten minutes, Jack and I are on the receiving end of a mountain of medical jargon. From what I can gather, the goal is to make as many follicles as possible – way more then we have to date – because this procedure is expensive and invasive. He will stimulate the crap out of my follicles with a laundry list of drugs, some of which I swallow, many of which I need to inject into my stomach and ass. Wonderful. I will be a full-fledged pin cushion this time. Then when they feel I'm at my peak, they go in and retrieve the eggs. He doesn't share much detail on how one retrieves the eggs, and before I get a chance to clarify, he's on to the next stage.

Immediately after the eggs are removed from my body, they are mated with Jack's sperm. There are apparently two ways to do this. I suddenly have images of different sexual positions between sperm and egg, like the F&F logo, and snicker. Jack looks at me inquiringly, but Dr. Greenberg plods on; he's obviously seen it all before.

Stop it, Abby, be serious.

They will take half of the eggs and let Jack's sperm inseminate them naturally. If it turns out my eggs are as hostile toward Jack's swimmers as my mucus was, they will perform

ICSI with the rest of the eggs. Damn, another acronym. Just when I'm about to ask, he explains.

"We use a syringe to inject one of Jack's sperm directly into the egg. That way we know it made it inside. We then grow the embryos for between three and five days – they have to have at least ten cells. That's all done in the lab. Finally, we will implant two or three inside your uterus, guided by ultrasound, nice and snug up against your uterine wall. We hope at least one implants and, well, there you go." Jack and I make eye contact and I know we are both thinking, "Sounds simple enough."

"Abby and Jack, you need to understand that in vitro fertilization is all a numbers game. There is only a forty to sixty percent chance of it working for most normal people. The older you are, the lower the percentage. Given your age and good health, Abby, I think you are at the higher end of that range. Any way we can increase the numbers, the better. I'm not a huge fan of herbs and natural remedies, but it's been proven that acupuncture in conjunction with IVF increases your chances. I would highly recommend it."

This might be the ice breaker I need with Cassie.

We leave the office a little lighter in the wallet after paying our IVF deposit, and with a bag of drugs and needles. All that aside, I am feeling more positive than I have in months. This is going to work.

Jack and I don't seem to be in any rush to get to work, so we walk hand in hand to a coffee shop where I indulge in a rich hot chocolate with lots of whipped cream and he orders an espresso. "This is it, Abbs, I can feel it," he says, reaching to wipe a dollop of cream off the end of my nose.

"I could be pregnant in the next two weeks. We could even have twins – how cute would that be?" Images of matching pink dresses and double strollers fill my thoughts.

"Twins would be awesome. Instant family."

∽

"Accidental-Baby on line one," Scott hisses at me from the doorway. Ever since I let Scott in on the baby-making plan, I have slowly filled him in on the whole story. As far as I can tell, he still hasn't said a word to anyone at the office, but I follow his blog regularly, just to be sure. He used to love talking with Cassie when she called, but these days he's rather short with her and keeps referring to her as "Accidental-Baby." As weird as it sounds, it's nice to know Scott has my back and, well, my butt when I need a shot during the day. I straighten my shoulders and close my eyes for a moment, then reach for the phone.

"Hi, Cass."

"Oh, hi, Abby. Is Scott okay? He seems, um, different when I talk to him."

"It's nothing; he's probably menstruating. There's nothing worse than a man with PMS."

"Interesting, I just saw something online that there is some evidence that men appear to have a hormonal cycle similar to ours–"

"Cass, I'm really busy here. What's up?"

"Oh, right, sorry. Um, I just wanted to see how you were doing. We haven't talked in a while." A teeny tiny whine creeps into her voice. I pause before speaking, ready for the bitterness to overtake me, but this time it doesn't. I actually feel a little sorry for Cassie. I mean, she didn't set out to get pregnant before me. I know that wasn't her plan or intention. She sounds lonely.

"I know, and I'm sorry about that. You kind of threw me for a loop with your news. It took me a while to process it. Actually, we have some news of our own. Jack and I have decided to go ahead with IVF."

"Wow, Abby, that's great news. I'll do some research for you, but I know acupuncture is going to really help," she says, enthusiastically.

"Actually, our doctor is a big proponent of acupuncture." I know what the next words out of her mouth will be. Surprisingly, they don't scare me.

"You should give Mom's naturopath a call. She can also give Jack some great ideas on how to boost his sperm output." She sounds hesitant, probably unsure of my reaction.

"I know, I was planning to call her, and Mom too."

After I hang up with Cassie, and before I lose my nerve or my mind any further, I call Serenity. She sounds thrilled to hear from me again, and when I explain my needs, we both clear some time later in the day, after my production meeting. Hanging up, I feel a hint of confidence.

⁓

"I'm not sure this will sell them," I say, surveying the boardroom. Empty coffee cups and the remains of a bakery tray sit in the center of the table. Four potential logos for the bank are projected on the whiteboard. "They want to move away from the stodgy-bank feel, and this still feels too old. Trixie is supposedly doing competitive research, but I don't know where she is with that. In fact, where the hell is she?" Both men snicker, and I roll my eyes and check my watch. I have to meet Serenity in thirty minutes.

"They are an institution. They are old. I know there's younger blood over there, but do you really think the upper management guys will go for edgy? What if we go too far down that road and they reject everything we have? Where are we then?" Kevin, head of our design team, has his sleeves rolled up and looks tired.

"Abby, you've met these guys, do you think we can introduce a new color? Their logo guidelines are pretty strict." Russell, head of Production, flips through a large binder supplied by the bank.

"Look, you are probably right, they may steer back to tried-and-true, but all we can do is try. That's what they hired us to do. We have to nail the logo before we can work on a rebranding campaign. Can you work up something that will fit the edgy feel? I can present it and we can have one of these," I gesture at the board, "ready to go if we scare them off."

Kevin nods and starts sketching on his pad. I stand up and stretch my back. We've been working on this for the last two hours. Russell picks at what's left of the doughnuts as the door opens.

"How's it going?" Marco asks, and Trixie slips into the room behind him. At least she has the grace to look slightly guilty.

I curse inwardly and turn to meet Marco's questioning face. "We're getting there. We need a little more work, but I think we're heading in the right direction."

"We see the bankers next week. I'd like to review the presentation by Friday."

Kevin, Russell, and I nod in unison.

"Well then, I'll let you get back to it." After Marco leaves, we all watch as Trixie rejoins us at the table and tries to look busy. She must sense all eyes on her as she straightens her papers and meets my look.

"So, what did I miss?"

"Trixie, you've been gone for over an hour. No, don't tell me," I raise a hand as she tries to speak. "I don't want to know. We have a ton of work to do. I expect full participation. Either you are on this team or I can have you transferred to Linda's group." She looks scared by my Linda suggestion, but nods.

Kevin and Russell keep their heads together discussing a new logo idea, but I can see a hint of a smile on their faces. I can only imagine what crazy F&F ideas are swirling through their heads at the thought of Trixie's missing hour and her return with Marco.

"Okay, why don't we break for now. Trixie, I need that research by tomorrow. Kevin, Russell, you guys okay with the direction? Let's regroup at the end of the day and see where we net out. Thanks, everyone."

～

I sneak out for my acupuncture appointment, nodding at Scott, who crosses his fingers and tugs on his ears, his wordless sign that he's keeping my secret. I'm expecting a secret handshake and a team shirt any day. I hold my breath as I take Serenity's stairs two at a time, expecting the fog of incense to beat me down, and don't exhale until I shut her door behind me.

"Abigail, are you okay?" Serenity is sitting cross-legged on the floor.

"I'm fine." I shrug out of my coat and drop my briefcase and purse next to the beanbag chair with a thud. Serenity unwinds from her pretzel and leads the way to the treatment table.

"So, we have some work to do."

"Serenity, have you ever done this before? Not acupuncture, but actually helped someone with IVF?"

"Oh yes. I'd say the majority of patients I see are women just like you. My success rate with patients undergoing IVF is about eighty percent."

"Wow, that's terrific." Maybe I haven't given her enough credit.

On the table, I close my eyes. I can feel Serenity moving around, but still marvel at how I can't feel the needles being inserted, a welcome relief from my injection-riddled life. She rolls up my shirt to place needles above the ovaries and uterus. That's to focus positive energy and help with stimulation, she says.

"Just lie still now," she tells me. I open my eyes a crack and survey my body. I look like a bloody porcupine.

"So, my sister thought you might have some ideas for boosting Jack's sperm?" I'm not sure how much I'll be able to convince Jack of, especially if it's weird.

"Oh, sure, that stuff is easy. I'll write you a list of the foods he should avoid and some herbs that will help with semen production." She reaches for a pad of paper and a pen. "No red meat and no alcohol," she starts. Well, I guess we can kiss that idea good-bye. There is no way my husband, Mr. Meat and Potatoes, is going to give up steak and wine. It's amazing the man doesn't have gout. The only thing worse would be if he had to eat tofu. "Tofu is great for the sperm," she continues. And there it is. I'm just going to have to hope his swimmers are good enough the way they are. Serenity is still talking, but I tune her out, imagining the conversation with Jack, which I know will end in a big, fat "no way."

"Here's what I'd like to do, Abby." I refocus on Serenity. She's off sperm production and onto our IVF attempt. "You are on day two, right? I want to see you every third day until the retrieval. We will work on helping with the stimulation and preparing the uterus for implantation at the same time. It is really important that I see you just before the transfer and ideally after it as well."

"Okay," I say, mentally picturing my work calendar for the next fifteen days. "But right now I'm on track for the transfer to be on a Sunday. I didn't think your office was open on Sundays."

"It isn't, but what works best with the transfers is if I come with you." What? She sees the obvious concern on my face. "Relax, it's okay; I do it all the time. Just tell them you need a bed while you are waiting for your transfer. Trust me, this is best." I nod, not quite trusting myself to speak. Jack gave me such a ribbing my last time with Serenity, I was kind of hoping to keep these appointments to myself. Well, between me and Scott.

∽

"Scott, can I borrow you for a minute please?" I yell from my desk.

"Yes, fearless leader?" Scott pops through the doorway, dressed from head to toe in bright green. Not hunter green – more like neon celery.

"Wow, quite the monochromatic outfit today."

"I read that green is a calming color. I am doing my part to keep your stress levels down, given, you know." He winks conspiratorially at me.

"Green can be a calming color, but I'm not sure that particular shade qualifies. Did you put this on my desk?" I point to a thick binder in the center of my desk and avert my eyes from Scott's headache-inducing outfit.

"Nope, wasn't me."

"Okay, thanks," I say, waving him out of my office. I sit back and wait for the spots in my vision to clear. Once I can see straight again, I open the binder and am blown away. There are two main headings: North America and Europe. Following each heading are tabs for different banks. I shake my head in disbelief as I leaf through the pages. Trixie, if this is indeed Trixie's work, has included each bank logo, their logo color rules, screen shots of advertising campaigns, copies of press releases, and sponsorship examples. This is remarkable work. Maybe I've misjudged her. I grab the binder and head for her desk.

"Trixie, did you pull all of this together?" She hurriedly shoves something into her desk drawer as I approach. "Really, Trixie, this is terrific work. In all honesty, I wasn't expecting anything quite so thorough. You're putting some of our more senior staffers to shame."

She beams with my praise. "I did have a little help. I'm not the best with computers, so the guys in Production helped me with the screen shots and stuff."

"Well, thank you. This is exactly what we need. Well done."

14

THE NEXT FOURTEEN days are tough. I see Serenity every third day, and I'm at the clinic every other day for the first eight days and then every morning for the next six days. I have blood drawn at each visit. Can you actually run out of the stuff? I get violated by the ultrasound tech every morning, and Jack wonders why I don't feel like having sex. I take a handful of pills every morning, more at lunch, and again at dinner. One is making me incredibly nauseous, which is to be expected, so I barely manage to choke down dry toast or a muffin for breakfast. Every morning before we leave the house, Jack has to inject me in the butt cheek. We alternate sides every day, as Lovely Nurse suggested. I spend an entire day leaning to one side at my desk because I'm so sore.

"Abby, you're listing to starboard," Scott notes as he walks by my office. Starboard? After four "ahoy mateys," I realize he must be dating a sailor. I lean a little to port the following day.

Just before Jack injects me each morning, I also have to inject myself in the abdomen with another drug, which is basically a blood thinner. Giving yourself a needle is far more difficult than I'd expected, as if the body has some sort of protective mechanism against self-inflicted pain. The needle for my stomach looks like a large ballpoint pen, and it comes fully loaded with a mini canister attached that contains the drugs. I just turn the top to load the dosage, fire it quickly into my gut, and then depress the end. Sounds perfectly simple, but as I go to do it on the first morning, my hands are shaking and a bead of sweat trickles from my underarms.

Jack looks up from the newspaper. Maybe my hyperventilating has distracted him.

"You okay?"

"Yep," I mumble. *Get a grip, Abigail; you have fourteen days of this.* One for the money, two for the show – I take a deep breath and bam, I inject quickly. Jack raises an eyebrow. "*Man* that burns. It's like a bee sting," I say, but I'm proud of myself.

By day twelve, this morning ritual has become totally routine. Jack barely glances up from his paper as I drop my pants and he shoots me. My hands stop shaking and I can breathe evenly as I inject my stomach. My abdomen and my butt are black and blue and very sore. I can barely stand the waistband of my pants on my bruised tummy and forgo belts most mornings. I'm nauseated and the hormones are making me nutty. Basically, I am a walking weapon of mass destruction.

∽

"Abby, my office, *now*," Marco barks into the phone. We sit four offices away, so I hear him yelling down the hall in stereo. Fabulous, just what I need. I hustle to Marco's office and knock.

"You called?" I ask with sugar-coated sarcasm.

"What the hell is this?" Marco is pointing to his desk. From my vantage point all I can see are framed pictures.

"What the hell is what?" I ask, coming around the desk. "Oh," I say in surprise. In the center of his desk is a voodoo doll that bears a striking resemblance to Marco, a long needle sticking out of his groin.

"I want that psycho fired, immediately. I knew it would be a mistake to have her work here." Marco is almost hyperventilating. As I pick up the offending doll, which I am desperately trying not to laugh at, I want to smack him. He knew it would be a mistake to have his latest conquest work in our office? *Really?* On what planet would hiring her have been a good idea?

"Marco, do you have proof that Trixie did this?" Seriously, who else would?

"Abigail." Damn – my full name. "Whatever you have to do, you do it today."

So much for staying stress-free. At my office, Scott raises an eyebrow and snickers when I show him the doll. Then he checks the clock like a surgeon pronouncing death and records the date and time in his notebook. No doubt he's marking the official F&F record as he hums "Another One Bites the Dust" under his breath. I have the bloody standard termination letter memorized, and as I sign it tiredly, Scott skips out of my office to ask Trixie to join me.

"You wanted to see me?"

"Hi, Trixie. I was wondering if you could tell me where this came from." I gesture toward the Marco voodoo doll and see a half-smirk appear.

"I don't know what you're talking about."

"Oh, that's too bad. I actually wanted one of an ex-boyfriend and I have no idea where to get it," I say sweetly.

"Well actually," she pauses. *Busted.* "That one came from a guy in Chinatown. I know, weird, voodoo doll from Chinatown, but seriously, I'll give you his stall number."

"Trixie." I have to stop her before she buries herself any deeper. I can hear the muffled laughter of Scott, who must have his ear pressed to the door. "Trixie, I'm not sure what your last, um, position was," louder laughter from the hallway now, "but this kind of behavior is not appropriate in our office." Any office, to be true, but I'm trying to wrap this up. "I'm afraid that threatening a member of our staff is grounds for immediate dismissal. Scott will help you gather your things, and he has some paperwork for you." I watch her for the usual signs of impending tears. Surprisingly, she smiles.

"It's been fun working here, but I don't really think I'm cut out for this industry. I was about to quit anyway. I found another job."

"That's terrific. Congratulations, and I'm glad there are no hard feelings. Well, none with me." I incline my head in Marco's general direction.

"It's okay, Abby, really. Can I give you a piece of advice?"

"Sure," I say, uncertainly.

"You always look so stressed. You wouldn't want to get wrinkles prematurely. You should call my dermatologist – he works wonders." She hands me a card and is gone, leaving me to pull out my compact to study my face. When I frown at my reflection, two baby wrinkles appear.

15

DR. GREENBERG'S OFFICE calls me the afternoon of day fifteen. Apparently my ovaries are ready for the retrieval, and we are to report to his office at ten o'clock the next morning with an empty stomach, as they will be sedating me. I dash off a quick note to Marco, Charlie, and Scott to excuse myself for the day, due to a medical issue. I cringe as I write that, figuring it will add fuel to any rumors, then text Jack to let him know to clear his schedule for the next day. As I set about cleaning up my desk and inbox so at least I'm up to date, Linda appears at my door. Squaring my shoulders, I meet her gaze.

"I know what you're up to."

"You know what, Linda, I've just about had it with the veiled threats. If you've got something to say, just say it." I shove my chair back and stand, a little stunned by my anger and confidence. Linda looks pretty surprised as well, and she straightens her blazer uncomfortably, her usual haughty air disappearing. I gather my things and brush past her, leaving her staring.

Jack and I spend a low-key evening at home. We order in sushi, hoping it will be the last time for nine months that I can eat raw fish and have a glass of wine. We watch all the baby shows we can find on TV – even the childbirth ones, which are beautiful to me. I surprise myself by falling asleep quickly, in a haze of baby dreams.

We are at Dr. Greenberg's office at exactly ten o'clock. Ordinarily I'd be early to such an important appointment, but history has taught me that punctuality is not worth it with this man. I quickly change into my hospital gown, and Jack is handed full hospital gear to wear as well, including booties and hair net. He heads to the jerk-off room for what we hope will be his last deposit. Lovely Nurse happens to be on duty in the IVF suite. She walks us through the procedure and sets me up with an IV for the sedation.

"You won't be completely out, but you won't feel much. Put it this way, it's like having twelve margaritas: you'll know you're in pain, but you won't care." She pulls Jack off to the side to have a discussion.

"What was that about?" I ask as he returns to my side with a smile.

"They just wanted to know if I was squeamish. I guess a couple of guys hit the floor each month and they want to be prepared. I told her I'm fine." We are not the only ones who have a retrieval today; there are two other couples ahead of us. We pull out our books but find we can't concentrate.

Suddenly the music in the suite changes from the local Top 40 radio station to a classical channel, as Lovely Nurse injects what she calls the "first batch" of sedation drugs into all the women's IVs. The retrieval process must be relatively quick, since the first woman is soon helped out of the procedure room by her husband and Lovely Nurse. She looks woozy but wears a hint of a smile, either drug-induced or because she knows she may be one step closer to becoming a mom. The procedure room gets cleaned up quickly and the second couple heads in, a petite woman and a very tall linebacker type. Okay, we're next. Jack squeezes my hand and I close my eyes, feeling suddenly quite relaxed. I'm liking these margaritas.

A few minutes later the door to the procedure room flies open, and out comes the football player with Lovely Nurse leading the way. The color has drained from his face and he looks ready to vomit or pass out. She dumps him in a change room, barks at him to keep his head between his knees, yanks the curtains closed around him, and rolls her eyes in exasperation. I'm pretty sure I hear her mutter "pathetic" as she passes. I have to agree with her. I mean, come on buddy, all you have to do is sit there and hold your wife's hand. She has had weeks of needles and drugs and is now having her eggs surgically removed. I open my mouth to say something, then realize that Jack has gone a few shades paler. I squeeze his hand and he takes a deep breath as he meets my eyes. I'm sure he will be fine. He'd better be fine.

When it is our turn, Lovely Nurse checks that Jack is all suited up and leads us into the procedure room. My first impression is that we've walked into an operating room. On one wall is a small door that opens into the lab. As Dr. Greenberg empties each swollen follicle, he will pass the vial to the lab technician behind the door. She will isolate each egg under a microscope – some follicles might contain nothing but fluid – and do a final tally. This is the same room we will return to in three to five days for the embryo transfer. Jack helps me climb up onto the table, and Lovely Nurse covers me with a warm blanket. She administers the second dose of the sedative and tells me that might be all I need, but reassures me that if I feel any pain during the procedure, she will top me up. Jack is told to sit down on the stool beside the bed, near my head. He cradles my hand that has the IV.

"Abby, how are you feeling?" asks a gowned and masked Dr. Greenberg.

As I open my mouth to respond, I realize that I am feeling pretty good, actually; pretty darn good. Lovely Nurse was right. I could be sitting on a beach sipping margaritas. I'm not at all concerned about the procedure room or the scary-looking instruments Dr. Greenberg is picking up. The lights are dimmed and the room suddenly feels a little cozier.

"It looks like we're ready," he says.

I am aware of what is going on. Dr. Greenberg directs our attention to two small TV screens above our heads, one focused on the lab so we can watch the technician isolate the eggs, and one on the ultrasound of my uterus, so we can watch the actual extraction. Dr. Greenberg shows me the ultrasound wand he'll use. Picture an elephant's penis. As wonderful as *that* sounds, this special wand is outfitted with a needle that pops out and punctures each follicle. Jack blanches again, and I can see the nurses exchange a roll of eyes. I can't say I remember too much more. I know I saw a few extractions and a few follicles being isolated, but mostly I remember the cream-colored ceiling tiles.

After a few minutes, I suddenly gasp aloud as I feel a very sharp stabbing pain down in my "secret garden." I don't know why that term pops into my head, but I suddenly remember my grade seven sex education teacher calling it that. I'm tipsy enough that I want to giggle, but the pain is too intense. Lovely Nurse doesn't hesitate. She immediately empties a syringe into my IV and tells me to hang on a second. My body is suddenly very warm and the pain is gone. I also realize how tired I am and close my eyes just for one brief moment.

The next thing I know, the lights are up a bit and I can hear Jack calling my name.

"Abbs ... Abby, wake up."

Dr. Greenberg is gone. Lovely Nurse smiles her happy smile and asks how I am. I feel groggy and fuzzy, but surprisingly pretty good. My eyes close again.

"Up you get," says Lovely Nurse. "Let's get you into the other room. You can rest there."

She wasn't kidding about the sedation. All I want to do is go back to sleep. Somehow, Lovely Nurse and Jack manage to get me into a lounge chair, back where the day began. I have very little memory of the next few hours. Eventually he wakes me again and convinces me to get changed so we can leave the clinic. I pass out in the car again, and he has to carry me into the house and up the stairs to the bedroom.

I sleep away the next few hours and wake late in the afternoon. Jack is working from our spare room-slash-office and comes running in to check on me.

"Hey, Sleeping Beauty. How are you feeling?"

"Hi. What time is it? I'm–" I pause and take a mental check of my body, "–sore, down low."

"They said that was to be expected. You can take some Tylenol for the next few days. Abbs, it was incredible. They got ten eggs. Five follicles were empty, but they seemed excited about the ten. They're calling us later today to tell us how many eggs fertilized." Jack's enthusiasm is infectious. He brings me a bagel with cream cheese while I watch season two of *Ally McBeal* on DVD.

The phone rings around dinner time. For all of the waiting at the clinic, they get credit for the hours they work. It is practically a round-the-clock operation. Dr. Greenberg himself is on the line with mixed news. Five eggs were allowed to fertilize naturally and nothing happened. My stomach drops.

"Abby, you need to understand, this is good news." Good news? "Look at it this way: we may have isolated the issue you and Jack have in conceiving. His sperm can't get into your eggs. We haven't solved the problem, but at least we know what we're dealing with. The great news is that we successfully fertilized the other five eggs with the ICSI procedure. We'll let these grow for the next two days, and then we should be ready to implant. I'll have Sandy call you in two days. This is positive news, Abby. We're on our way." He rings off.

"So? What did he say?" Jack is staring at me expectantly. I relay my conversation with Dr. Greenberg. "That's terrific. Five, wow. We only need one."

I "work from home" on Thursday and Friday and then spend much of Saturday lounging around the house. I am tender and raw inside and find myself moving slowly, which, given I have been punctured fifteen times, I guess is to be expected.

We get a call from the clinic on Saturday afternoon that our embryos are ready for transfer. We are to report to the IVF suite at one o'clock on Sunday with a full bladder – mine, not Jack's. I am allowed to bring my acupuncturist with me and she can do a treatment on-site. I'm not sure which I'm more nervous about, the transfer or Jack meeting Serenity.

～

Sunday. Pregnancy day. P-Day. It's weird to wake up in the morning and know – really, truly know – that life may be changing forever. Most people don't know the moment they get pregnant. They certainly don't know in advance that today is the day. I'm not quite sure how I feel – excited, anxious, worried, and giddy all at the same time. I stop before getting into the car and stare at our house. It is just the two of us leaving our wonderful home. Coming home, there will be, in a way, more of us.

I am fidgeting in the car, shifting positions every few seconds and flicking the door locks with fingers that can't be stilled. Jack takes it for nerves, but it's my full bladder making me move. Apparently it pushes the uterus up, giving the doctor easy access for implantation. I pray silently that Dr. Greenberg shows up on time for once. If I have to wait too long, I'm sure I'll burst.

"Wow, check her out." Jack cocks his head at a stocky woman with tangerine hair headed for the clinic entrance. "Who wears spandex outside of the gym – especially if you have that figure?" he mutters.

I follow his gaze and make eye contact with Serenity.

"Oh, I forgot to mention Serenity is joining us. She's going to do acupuncture just before the transfer." As I step forward to greet Serenity, she gives me a huge hug and then moves onto Jack. He stares at me over Serenity's shoulder and I shrug. We head up to the IVF suite, and Lovely Nurse greets us with a wonderful grin. That woman never leaves this place. Dr. Greenberg really did hire his staff well, I think. Not only does he have the Goddess to exude fertility in the main office, but Lovely Nurse exudes happiness in the procedure rooms. I find myself relaxing in her presence.

"Instead of changing into your gown right away, Abby, why don't you work with your acupuncturist and then we can check you." Lovely Nurse smiles and I wonder what she thinks of Serenity. I lie down on the gurney as Serenity slips into the bathroom to wash up.

Jack leans over and whispers, "Abby, are you kidding? She's ... she's–" A pause. "Hell, I don't know what she is, but I thought you were kidding, about the spandex and hair and all."

"Jack, I couldn't make that up if I tried. Just don't laugh if she chants."

He moves to my side as Serenity reappears. Within minutes she has me set up like a porcupine again. Jack stares disbelievingly at all the needles. I get the impression he has only recently clued in to what lengths I have gone to in my effort to get pregnant. One of the women ahead of me in the transfer line passes our alcove, catches a glimpse of me, and looks confused. After she returns to her alcove, I hear her whispering questions to the nursing staff. A nurse leans around our alcove and asks if Serenity can answer some questions. She agrees, but warns the nurse that under her oath, she can't treat as a patient anyone she doesn't know. Jack snickers at the oath remark.

Serenity returns after handing out her card to a few couples.

"So, Serenity, what made you want to go into naturopathy?" Jack asks, trying to get a conversation going.

"Shh, I need total concentration to work with Abby's chakras."

"I'm guessing you didn't see *House of Cards* last night?" Jack winks at me as Serenity looks up from her meditation and glares at him. "Okay, I'll be quiet." He throws his hands up in surrender.

After what feels like an eternity – twenty minutes with a bladder seriously going to explode – Serenity removes the needles and tells me that in an ideal world I should be treated again following the procedure, but as it is a Sunday, she has to get back to her family. *Family*? I can see my astonishment mirrored in Jack's face.

"Treatment prior to the transfer is the best option, since we can only do one today," she says as she packs up her supplies.

"Well, thank you, Serenity. I really appreciate you coming to do this." I head to the bathroom to gingerly get changed into my gown. Jack is waiting for me with an ultrasound tech when I return, and we all walk to the ultrasound room together to see how full my bladder is.

"I owe you an apology, Abby," Jack starts. I don't bother looking in his direction; I'm too busy trying not to pee myself as I climb on the ultrasound table. I'm so single-mindedly focused on the intense pain in my bladder that he could confess to being the second shooter of JFK and I wouldn't care.

"Wow, that is really full. You must be uncomfortable," the tech says. Understatement of the year, lady. I feel like a cartoon character that has a hose in its mouth and is so rapidly filling with water that fish swim past its eyeballs.

"Do you think you can pee out one cup and then stop?" Whether I can or not, I assure her I can. She gives me a Dixie cup the size of a thimble and I waddle into the bathroom where, shockingly, I manage to stop after one cup. I diligently pour it into the toilet and am about to flush when I realize I don't feel much relief. I debate for a second or two and then think, "Oh to hell with it" and pee out another two cups. I'm feeling much better and decide what they don't know won't hurt them.

Jack is waiting for me back in our alcove.

"Feeling better?" he asks. I give him a winning smile.

"Much. You were saying?"

"Right, it's just I thought you were totally exaggerating about Serenity, but she's ... something." I just smile and close my eyes, sending positive energy to my uterus. I guess Serenity's rubbed off on me. I tune Jack out and chant to myself, "I will get pregnant, I will have a baby, I will be a mom."

With closed eyes, my hearing is heightened. The music changes abruptly to the classical SiriusXM channel and I sense an electric energy. As I open my eyes, I see Dr. Greenberg slip into the procedure room. The two other couples pass through quickly, while I make one more quick trip to the bathroom. This time I'm a good girl and only pee out one thimbleful. Lovely Nurse materializes at our alcove, and without a word we follow.

"Good morning, Abigail, Jack." Dr. Greenberg nods as we enter the room. I quickly but gingerly climb up onto the procedure table and slot my feet into the stirrups. "So, everything is looking pretty good. We have three embryos at ten cells and they look terrific. Here, take a look." He nods at the lab TV screen, and sure enough, we can actually count the cells. It's truly amazing, knowing how small those things are. "I would suggest we insert either two or three today. What do you guys want to do?"

"What happened with the other two?" I struggle to raise myself on my elbows. "I thought we had five fertilized eggs?"

"We did, but only two of them are at ten cells. We'll let the other two grow for another day to see if they will make it. If they do, we can freeze them for future use."

"Well, I guess we'll go with three." I speak for both of us, and Jack holds my hand, nodding.

"You do understand that there is a chance, albeit a small one, that you could get multiples. I always suggest that if three or more take, you seriously consider a reduction. Twins are considered high-risk, but the major complications tend to occur with more than two."

"Supposing all three take, what exactly is a reduction?" Jack asks.

"Well, we go in around week thirteen and reduce the number. There are risks involved, but I'm getting ahead of myself. If that does occur, we can talk when we are further along." Jack looks at me to see if I'm fine with Dr. Greenberg's latest pronouncement. I shrug it off and concentrate on settling myself as comfortably as possible in the stirrups with a nearly full bladder. Jack and I exchange glances. The talk of reduction and potential risks is making me a little nervous, but I can't tell what Jack is thinking. He squeezes my hand tightly and smiles at me.

"Hey, Dr. Greenberg," Jack says, "I hope these are the three best-looking ones. Oh, and make sure they're smart. I don't want to insert the kid who's going to steal my car."

"Okay, Abigail, just lie still." He inserts the dreaded speculum. An ultrasound tech materializes at his side and puts cold gel on my belly.

I grit my teeth as she sweeps the wand over my belly, applying quite a bit of pressure to my full bladder.

"Here we go. Just watch the screen."

I realize I can actually follow the grainy black and white-ish blobs on the screen, but Jack looks completely confused.

"I'm just putting all three against your uterine wall. We want these little guys to stick. There, done. Theresa, freeze that, please." Dr. Greenberg snaps off his gloves and hands me a grainy printout with a tiny speck of white at the edge of a black blob. "Here's the first picture of your babies."

Jack and I just stare. I don't really notice the ultrasound tech cleaning off my stomach or Lovely Nurse taking my feet out of the stirrups and covering me with a warm blanket. I know she told me to lie still for a while, and instead of feeling antsy to get to the bathroom or get home, I'm totally content. Jack keeps one hand on my shoulder, and we both hold a corner of our first family picture. We've never come this far down the baby-making path before. It's exhilarating.

After waiting nearly thirty minutes, we slowly make our way from the procedure room. I relieve myself, and does it ever feel good. Jack helps me into my clothes and we are ready to go.

"Abigail, remember to take it very easy. No heavy lifting, don't take the stairs, do your best to reduce any vigorous activities. Dr. Greenberg has given you a note to stay home from work for this week."

"It's okay, I've already booked off for a holiday this week. I haven't exactly had full disclosure with my office. This is a really busy time for me, but I promise to take it easy."

"That's great. Remember, we need you off your feet for a week, Abby. Dr. Greenberg insists." She watches me nod. "We also recommend you don't have sex until after your results. You need to continue your stomach injections and the blue and white pills, and don't forget to begin the progesterone suppositories. Minor spotting is perfectly normal – many women spot at implantation. We'll see you back in two weeks for your pregnancy test. Good luck." Lovely Nurse escorts us to the door and hands us papers that describe all of the things she has just said. I want to take her home with us. She's just so, well, lovely.

Jack bundles me into the car like a breakable package, his smile contagious. It's still Sunday, although it feels like days since we met Serenity at the clinic. At home, Jack and I curl up on the couch and spend the rest of the day napping, watching TV, snacking, and doing crosswords. Jack fetches my slippers, a quilt, and any food or drink combination I require. I could get used to this. It's too bad he can't take the week off as well.

I send an email to Charlie, Marco, and Scott, reminding them I'm away on holidays but checking email. I debate using

Dr. Greenberg's note, but then decide that will just throw fuel on the gossip fire about me dying. Scott immediately calls me and I fill him in on the real story, sparing most of the gory details.

"Abby, don't you worry. Auntie Scott is in charge." Somehow I'm not entirely relieved, but it is what it is, and my orders are to stay put and stress-free.

16

"I'M BORED," I whine into the phone.

"Abby, darling, you are growing a family. It's hard work." Just hearing Jules's voice makes me feel better.

"Hard work, ha. I feel like a lump. I've caught up on my reading, and daytime TV really sucks."

"Look at it this way: when you're up to your ears in screaming babies and poopy diapers, you are going to look back and wish you could have a week to yourself to do nothing. Trust me. Enjoy it. Watch a movie. Surf the net. Hire a manicurist to come to the house; whatever. Just remember *why* you are flat on your back. You'd never forgive yourself if you overdid it and something bad happened."

She's right. Abigail Nichols, get a grip.

◈

Monday morning rolls around, *finally*. I've taken Jules's words to heart and managed to keep myself occupied – somewhat – but I'm itching to get back to the office, back to work, and away from my dreaded couch. Six days to go until the pregnancy test.

I arrive early, expecting to be the only person around, until I notice my office lights are on.

"What do you think you're doing?" I enter my office and come to a full stop when I catch sight of Linda rummaging through files on my desk. She has the decency to look sheepish, but her piercing stare and prickly demeanor drop quickly back in place. She straightens up slowly, like she has every right to pilfer my desk.

"I was just looking for something Scott thought he might have left it in your office by accident. I wouldn't want sensitive materials to get out." She walks around my desk and looks me up and down, a truly annoying habit of hers. You can almost hear her mind at work, cataloging my outfit and mentally comparing it to hers. I know you can afford more expensive clothes, lady. I'm practically broke, what with Jack's company's expansion and our fertility treatments.

"I would appreciate it if you left my office. Next time, why don't you get Scott to find it for you? We both have confidential files to maintain." I brush past her, and without trying to look paranoid, I scan the files left on my desk. I'm relieved to see nothing too sensitive, but my unease doesn't abate completely. There is just something about this woman that I don't trust.

Watching Linda leave, I exhale and kick off my shoes. I pull the files together and start to put them away in my drawer. I always keep my current projects in my bottom right drawer, which I tend to lock at night. As I slip each one into its respective hanging folder, I catch movement at my door.

"Seriously, get out of my office," I bark toward the door before catching a glimpse of Charlie, thick glasses, rapidly receding hairline, golf shirt, and all. I plaster on my corporate smile.

"Is this a bad time, Abby?"

"Good morning, Norman. Sorry about that; please come in." I do my best to sound like Cheery Nurse.

Charlie takes a seat across from me, with an amused look on his face. He brushes the crisply ironed crease of his khaki pants, and I catch a glimpse of white athletic socks that disappear into what my grandmother would call "comfortable walking shoes." He can't hold a candle to Marco's sense of style, but there is something comfortable and safe about Charlie's appearance – I'm sure his ability to bring in the big clients has something to do with it.

"Sure. What's up?" I can't get a read on him: is this good or bad?

"Did you have a good holiday?"

"Yes, thanks. It was nice to get away."

"You know, when Shelia and I were first married," he starts. *What?* Charlie is married? You'd think after seven years of working for the man, I might've acquired a few details about his personal life. He glances around my office, taking in the framed photos and artwork from some of our more successful campaigns, and continues. "We struggled for a long time to have children." *Kids?* The man has kids? Are you kidding me? I am having trouble reconciling a family man with the mysterious Charlie.

"We ended up having to do fertility treatments. It was a really tough road – toughest on Shelia, of course, but pretty hard on me too." *Why is he telling me this?* "She was so crazy on all of the drugs they put her on. She used to call herself a whack-job." He chuckles and nods at me knowingly.

Oh my god. The light goes on in my head. *He knows. He* freaking *knows.*

"Anyway, I just wanted to stop by and see how you were," he finishes.

"I don't really know what to say Char– Norman. How did you, I mean…?"

"A little birdy confirmed my suspicions. Don't worry; your secret is safe with me. I hope this works for you, Abby, I really do."

"Thanks, Norman, that means a lot." I squeeze my knees together to keep them from bouncing and smile at Charlie as he leaves. A little birdy, my ass. I'm thinking a big gay jaybird. I leave a nasty note on Scott's desk telling him to see me immediately and grab the phone to call Jack.

"What do you think he means?"

"Relax, Abbs. He's got your back." I can hear Jack mumbling something to someone in his office. He sounds busy.

"Can I trust him? I mean, I know he's my boss, but I'm hardly the model employee these days. What if this is a setup? How can I ever make partner?" What is with me? I have my boss in my corner; I should be feeling relief. These hormones are making my head spin.

"It's fine. He's looking out for you – just don't screw up."
Jack's parting remarks do little to settle my nerves.

∽

"You wanted to see me?" Scott is peeking through my door,
afraid to enter. I point at a chair in my office and fold my arms
across my chest. Scott flutters in and perches nervously on the
edge of the chair.

"Is there something you need to tell me?"

"I like your sweater, Abby, very 'saucy school-marm'–"

"Scott," I hiss. "Would you care to explain how Charlie
knows I'm trying to get pregnant? And at a fertility clinic to
boot?" He flinches and looks away. "I'm waiting."

"I didn't mean for it to happen, Abby, I swear. You know
how nervous I get around Charlie. He kept asking me 'Where's
Abby? Why is she away? Is everything okay?' I just cracked
under the pressure." Scott slumps down in his chair, sweat
beading on his forehead.

"You didn't tell me Charlie was around last week. I asked
you to keep me informed. Why was Charlie in the office?" I
hold Scott's eyes with mine.

"It was nothing. You're supposed to stay stress-free,
remember? I didn't want to worry you."

"Okay, now I'm worried. Scott, what the hell happened last
week?" I can feel a lump forming in my stomach, and it's not a
hopeful pregnancy lump.

"Well…" He looks toward the door, either thinking of
making a break for it or seeing if anyone is listening, I can't
tell. "Marco was trying to sack you."

"What? And you think that is *nothing*? Oh my god. What
happened?" I stare numbly at him, feeling as if I might
hyperventilate.

"He and Charlie got into a big fight. The door was closed,
but I could hear parts of it. Marco said he was tired of you
always being out of the office and that you'd screwed up a
few times. Charlie was defending you." Scott pauses and
watches me clutching my stomach and rocking in my chair. "I
couldn't let them sack you. I grabbed Charlie while he was

leaving Marco's office and filled him in on your whole situation. I know you didn't want me to say anything, but Abby, I had to tell him."

I sit silently, continuing to rock.

"Are you okay?"

"I'm fine. Thank you, Scott. I mean it. You are a good friend." My breathing sounds ragged, but the lump lessens.

"Here's your mail and messages from last week." He passes me a bundle and picks through my out tray before leaving. I continue sorting the files on my desk, slotting them into my bottom right drawer.

"Hey," I say as he reaches the door. "Linda thought you had misfiled something in my office. What was it?"

The confusion on Scott's face is clear. As my hand touches the last file on my desk, I see the bank's logo on the label. Opening it, I see the pages are out of order. I knew I couldn't trust her.

"Never mind, Scott."

⟳

Sunday morning finally rolls around. Pregnancy Test Day. Knowing I have fewer hoops to jump through at the clinic – Pregnancy Test Day people are on a special sign-up list, like a FastPass at Disney – I don't bother arriving at the crack of dawn. Instead, I follow what has become my morning ritual: shower, dress, eat dry toast since the drugs are still making me feel nauseous, and inject myself in the stomach. The sight of my abdomen with its black and blue band running just below my belly button is shocking. It is swollen and so tender. I can barely do up my pants. This morning I choose a loose-fitting pair of yoga pants, and I wonder if I can wear them to work. Jack joins me in the kitchen as I finish stabbing myself.

"You okay?" he asks.

"Yep. *Man*, does that hurt." I pack up my needle set, swab myself with an alcohol wipe, and rearrange my clothes carefully over my throbbing tummy.

"Why don't I drive you down and we can grab breakfast when you're finished?"

☙

Jack is checking his phone when I emerge from the clinic building. "That was fast." He watches me settle gently into the car. I'm careful of my seat belt placement.

"There was only one woman ahead of me. It's quick if you don't have to wait around for Dr. Greenberg."

"Abbs, are you going to be up for Mom's party this afternoon?"

Oh no, I'd forgotten all about that. Every year, Marilyn throws a party to kick off the golf season, and it's a command performance for us and a huge bore. With snow still on the ground and at least two months until the golf courses open up, I never understood the need for – or timing of – this party.

"They'll call at three o'clock with our results. Your mom would kill me if I skipped out early, but I can't take that call at her party, I just can't."

"Okay, don't worry. You stay home. I'll tell her you're sick. I'll go for a bit and then slip out in time for our call."

"Please don't miss the call. I want you with me."

"I won't, Abbs, I promise. Let's go eat."

☙

After a hearty breakfast of eggs and bacon for Jack and French toast for me, I spend the rest of the morning working on my laptop from the couch. With Marco's bull's-eye on my back, I'm determined to make up for missed time.

By mid-afternoon I'm pacing between our front window, to look for Jack's car, and the kitchen, where my phone sits silently on the counter. Five minutes to three; where the hell is he? I'm grateful we don't have a grandfather clock or some other ticking timepiece that would announce every second that passes. Jack's cell phone sits on the front hall table. I have no way of reaching him.

It's three o'clock now.

I will it to not be Cheery Nurse who calls. If the answer is no, please don't give me Cheery Nurse. No sign of Jack and it's five after three. I'm sure Marilyn has distracted him or barred him from leaving – I realize he is a grown man, capable of making his own choices, but I *need* to make this all Marilyn's fault. My fragmented thoughts are pierced by the ringing phone. I reach for it with a shaky hand and brace myself against the kitchen counter.

"Hello?"

"Hi, Abby." Smiley Nurse – I silently send a thank-you to the heavens. "I'm really sorry, but it's a no." She continues, telling me to stop all of my meds and come back on day two. I thank her and hang up. My legs feel numb – all of me feels numb. I slide to the floor of the kitchen in silence and desolation, and that's where Jack finds me. I hear him yelling my name as he comes through the door, but I don't have the energy to answer.

"I'm so sorry. I forgot my cell and couldn't call you from the car." He falls to his knees and touches my shoulder.

"I needed you. I needed you to be here." The dam breaks and I sob.

"I know, I know. I'm sorry, Abbs, really. Mom asked me to drive…" I shove his hand away.

"I don't give a shit about your mom. You need to decide where your priorities lie. Don't give me your 'I'm all she's got' line, because you know what? You're all I've got. *We* are in this together. *We* want to have a baby. That means you and me – not your mom. Don't you think getting our pregnancy results is just slightly higher on the importance scale than your mother's stupid golf party?"

Jack sits back against the counter across from me and stares, shocked. I'm sure I am a sight to behold. When I wind down, he scoots over and takes me in his arms.

"You're right, I'm so sorry. This *is* important; this is the most important thing for me – for us. I totally blew it and let you down. I'm so sorry you were alone for the call. I will never do that again. Can you forgive me?" His voice is heavy with regret. He doesn't ask for the results; I guess they're pretty obvious.

"I can't do this alone, Jack. I need to know we're on the same team here." I'm sobbing hard.

"We are, baby, I promise."

Jack helps me to the couch, covers me with Nana's quilt, which is quickly becoming my security blanket, and makes me tea. Over the course of the evening, he screens and fields calls from Cassie, my mom, and Marilyn. I hear him whispering in the kitchen, obviously filling everyone in on our bad news. Jules is the only call he allows through to me.

"Oh, honey." I can hear the emotion in Jules's voice, and a fresh waterfall of tears hits me. "I'm so sorry, Abby. This sucks. Jack told me what happened, with the call. Boys are idiots, they just are." I nod into the phone, unable to get words together. Jules lets me cry on her long-distance dime. She is my rock. She doesn't offer any platitudes of "This wasn't meant to be" or "Next time will work." She pretty much sums it all up with "This sucks." And it really does.

17

DAY TWO FINDS us back at the clinic. There has been frostiness between Jack and me since the missed phone call, but I feel myself thawing as Jack strokes my hand. For some reason, I think back to when we were planning our wedding, before any of this baby-craziness started. All I wanted was a small wedding with family and close friends. Of course Marilyn had other thoughts. She had thoughts about every aspect of my wedding – the bridesmaid dresses, the groomsmen's ties, the venue, the menu, the wine ... the list goes on. After one particularly nasty exchange, Jack found me on the couch in tears, the seating chart in tatters on the floor. I was ready to call the whole thing off. Jack stroked my hand, kissed away the tears, and whispered, "Fuck it, let's run away."

"We can't. We've sent out the invitations, booked the restaurant ... you mother would kill us. You can't be serious."

"Abby, I am serious. I want to marry you, not fulfill my mother's weird dream of being a wedding planner. Let's run away. We can pack a bag and head to the airport. Where do you want to go – Paris, Vegas, London? You pick."

Of course we didn't end up eloping, but I loved him more in that moment than I thought possible. We stayed to face the music with Marilyn, but Jack took a more active role running interference. We bowed to most of her demands, but we did it knowing we could run away together if we really wanted. For the first time, I really felt we were a team. I remind myself of that feeling as we sit together in Dr. Greenberg's office, waiting for his prognosis.

"Good morning Abigail, Jack." Dr. Greenberg seems to have taken a page from Cheery Nurse's playbook.

"Good morning," I answer. Jack is quiet. Dr. Greenberg flips through my file, which has doubled in size.

"I have some good news and some bad news. We look at the quality of embryos on a scale of one to five – one being the best, five being not really viable. Your embryos are a two, which is not bad, but there is definite room for improvement – which is good news. Now, unfortunately the last two embryos didn't grow enough, so we weren't able to freeze any."

Oh no; what are we going to do now?

"But you think you can do something about the quality? How can we get number one embryos?" Jack asks, squeezing my hand.

"Looking at Abby's chart here and reviewing the drug protocols we used, yes, I believe I can improve the quality. But of course, that does mean another full retrieval." I feel my stomach drop. No frozen embryos and a depleted bank account do not add up to another full retrieval.

"I just know that I can't watch Abby ride this roller coaster much longer."

I look at Jack in shock. "Jack," I say. "We can't afford it."

"It's okay, Abbs, don't worry," Jack says, turning back to Dr. Greenberg. His bonus must have been larger than he told me. Where else could the money be coming from? I am returned from my money thoughts as Dr. Greenberg speaks.

"Abby, are you okay to do this again? We can start right now, seeing as it's day two."

Am I okay with this? More injections, more drugs, more time with Serenity, more time off work – well at least on that front I know Scott has my back, and hopefully Charlie as well – but am I willing? Damn right. At least this time I know the deal, how everything works and how much it hurts.

"Yes."

As we leave the clinic, fully stocked up with drugs and needles, I ask Jack about the money. "Seriously, Jack, how are we going to pay for this?"

"Abbs, don't worry. I've been saving up, so we're fine."
He holds my door open for me. It's not that I don't believe him
about the money, but there is a nagging thought eluding me. I
push it away when it doesn't come easily and close my eyes as
Jack navigates through the traffic to my office.

∽

"Are you sure you're up for this?" Jack asks as I pull the
makings of our dinner from the fridge. I can tell he's worried
about me. I nod and watch as he reaches for two wine glasses
and the corkscrew. I'm glad Jack is beside me in all of this.

"I'm fine. Only, I think we need more ground rules this time."

"Sure, like what?" he asks as the satisfying pop from the
cork being released echoes in the kitchen.

"Well, I'm doing everything I can, with acupuncture, the
drugs, and needles, but there are a few things you could be
doing to increase our chances. I didn't want to say anything
earlier, because I knew you won't be thrilled, but they could
really help." *Great sales pitch, Abby.* I don't sound convincing
to myself, never mind to Jack.

"Okay," he says hesitantly. "What things?" As he lifts his
wine glass to his lips, I reach over and hold his arm.

"For starters, no alcohol," I say, watching him grimace.
"And no red meat," I add, and see him cringe. I rush on, before
I lose him completely. "And Serenity has some herbs you
should take every day."

"You've got to be kidding me," he says, but I notice he
carefully puts down his glass.

"Jack, this is costing us a fortune. I think we need to take
our best shot. Surely you can live without red meat and wine
for the next two weeks. We need the best, soberest, most
vegetarian swimmers you've got. Just think, if I get pregnant,
I'm giving up a lot of things for nine whole months." He
doesn't answer. "Hey, if I can handle the needles and drugs,
I'm sure you can handle this. It *has* to work this time, Jack."

Jack puts his nose into his wine glass, like a wine snob, and
inhales deeply. He holds the glass up to the light and stares
longingly at the burgundy liquid.

"One sip can't hurt," he says in a small voice, but I stare him down. He sighs and then carefully pours the wine back into the bottle. "You're right. I will survive. And Abbs, it will work this time."

∽

The next two weeks pass in another painful and hormone-induced haze. Jack is grouchy every morning taking his Serenity-prescribed herbs, but he seems to be following her regime. Marilyn keeps a low profile, but I wouldn't be surprised if she is sneaking burgers to Jack's office at lunch time. I run constantly between the clinic, the office, and Serenity's purple room. I have blood drawn, ultrasounds, acupuncture, drugs, and injections. Between the needle marks on my arms, my stomach, and my butt, I look like a serious but confused drug user.

I snap at everyone who pisses me off, and even at those I imagine are *thinking* about pissing me off. Scott runs around the office behind me doing damage control, cleaning up the swaths of destruction I leave in my midst. In my sane moments, I remember to thank him, and he insists I'm "not that bad," but apparently I've left a few people crying near the copier, our receptionist is terrified to put another wrong call through to my office, Linda is even hiding from me, and Production has come up with a logo for "Hurricane Abby."

Marco appears at my door. "Abigail, I have a bright young star I'd like you to personally train." I guffaw, remembering how I fell for that line the first time he dumped an ex on me. "She's very talented and–" I hold up a hand to stop him.

"We're fully staffed right now, Marco," I say through gritted teeth.

"Now, Abby, you're always saying we could use more people."

"We could use more *qualified* people." I hope he hears my emphasis.

"She's highly qualified. I'd like you to meet with her tomorrow."

"No way," is all I can manage in a colossal internal struggle to stay polite, when I want to tear his head off.

"Excuse me?" His eyes shoot a questioning glare in my direction.

"You heard me, Marco. No way. Give this one to Linda or dump her yourself. I'm sick and tired of cleaning up your messes. This isn't kindergarten, this is real life. Grow a pair and dump her," I snarl. Shocked, he leaves my office without another word.

Oh god, I sounded awful. I heard myself being a bitch; I just couldn't control myself. Marco might fire me – actually, he probably should – but I don't really care. I am surprised that he gave up so easily. I wonder if there really is an office rumor that I'm dying of some horrible disease and that's why everyone is putting up with my behavior. I'll have to check with Scott.

∽

As I get ready for the clinic on the morning of our retrieval, I rummage through my top drawer, searching for socks, making a mental note to throw in a load of laundry as we leave. At the back, in the void between my bras and underwear, my fingers brush a small package, which I pull out with surprise. I sit on the bed, cradling the tiny red-and-green-wrapped package in my hands. It's the booties I bought with such joy. As we leave, I tuck the booties in my purse, and on the way to the clinic I ask Jack to stop the car. I slip them through the donation slot of a local women's shelter. It feels like the right thing to do.

∽

I walk confidently into the retrieval room, the original fear of the unknown gone, and smile at each staff member, then get myself changed and seated in a comfy recliner. Jack whistles as he leaves for the jerk-off room, cup in hand. He comes back a minute later.

"No way, there is no way you did the deed in under a minute," I say.

"There's a huge lineup. Some poor schmuck is obviously having stage fright. His wife is at the door trying to whisper sexy encouragement, but it doesn't seem to be working. There are at least six guys waiting. She even told him people were waiting, like that's going to speed things up."

"Jack, we're first today, you've got to get your sample." I am acutely aware of the music being played in the suite. Any minute now the switch to the classical channel will signal Dr. Greenberg's arrival.

"Okay, don't worry. I'll be right back." He disappears as Smiley Nurse arrives to insert my IV. Five minutes later he struts back into our alcove. "Done," is all he says.

"Really? The shy guy came through and the other six are finished too?" Seems to me like Olympic and world records are being broken for the speed of ejaculation around here.

"No, the poor bastard's still in there. The natives are getting restless, and they might lynch the guy when he comes out."

"What? So, how did you?" I'm confused.

"I just went to the bathroom and took care of things. So, is he here yet?" I shake my head to indicate no, but also in disbelief. My husband just ejaculated in a cup in the stall of the men's room? Talk about potential stage fright – I'm impressed.

Suddenly the music changes. I don't remember much else. Knowing that last time I needed three doses of the famous margarita drugs, Smiley Nurse starts me off with that amount. I wake up in my own bed and remember absolutely nothing. Jack tells me that they retrieved twelve eggs this time. I was out for so long that I even missed Dr. Greenberg's phone call, telling us that of the twelve, ten had inseminated this time.

☙

Three days later, Serenity joins us at the clinic for our transfer. Maybe it's all the time I've spent with her lately, but I'm happy to see her waiting for us, spandex and all. In fact, my stomach is so tender that the thought of the continued injections every day makes me re-evaluate spandex as an option for work attire. It's a fleeting thought, quickly dismissed. If I show up in spandex, I'm sure Scott will take that as carte blanche to wear it all the time.

I lie on a table in our alcove, and Serenity has me looking like a porcupine in no time. I close my eyes and relax. Knowing how long the wait was and how bloody uncomfortable I was with a full bladder last time, I haven't had nearly as much water today. Instead of downing two full glasses at home and three bottles in the car like last time, I've limited myself to one bottle. I figure that by the time Dr. Greenberg arrives, I should be relatively full, just not bursting.

I hear the music switch over, and Jack and I settle in to wait. Three couples are ahead of us today, and again it amazes me that it takes only a few minutes for each transfer. Of course, sex is sometimes over in mere minutes as well. I see fear and hope mixed on the faces of all three women as they emerge with their partners. The butterflies in my stomach cause me more discomfort than my full bladder. Smiley Nurse beckons us.

"Good morning, Abigail, Jack." Dr. Greenberg seems to be in a great mood. There have been times throughout the last year that his bedside manner has needed some serious work, but there have been other times, like today, when hugging seems appropriate. I smile nervously and climb up on the table. "So, great news. Out of the ten embryos we inseminated, six have grown to ten cells. Two others are at six cells, so we'll try to grow them for another day before freezing them. This is great; you should be really proud. The quality looks good, but I won't have that report for a day or two. Now, we did three last time, I presume we are doing that again?" He looks expectantly at us and we both nod. "Okay, let's get you pregnant, Abigail." I smile nervously and settle into the stirrups. It's hard to believe that doesn't faze me anymore – some man, not my hubby, saying "Let's get pregnant." Look how far we've come.

"We are in the midst of a test study," he says as he snaps on his latex gloves, "using a laser to crack the outside shell of an egg in which an embryo is already growing. We are hoping that it might assist in implantation, especially for those that have hard shells. Last time we confirmed that Jack's sperm couldn't inseminate naturally, so one theory might be the hardness of your egg. I think you're an ideal case, and our initial results have been quite positive." Guided by the ultrasound wand on my belly, Dr. Greenberg carefully inserts three of our precious embryos deep into my uterus and parks them gently against the back wall. The ultrasound tech takes a grainy photo and we are finished.

"We'll see you in two weeks, Abigail. Good luck," and he's gone. For such a large man, he is surprisingly nimble in his arrivals and departures. Smiley Nurse bustles around the room cleaning up. She covers me with a warm blanket, dims the lights a little, and squeezes my hand.

"Take your time." She smiles her winning smile and vanishes as well. Jack and I sit in companionable silence until he suddenly leans over and kisses my temple.

"I'm so proud of you, Abbs. You've been through so much for this." He waves his hand around the room. "I have a really good feeling. I think we're going to have a baby, and you're going to be a great mom." I inhale quickly. I feel tears prick my eyes and blink rapidly to clear them. I squeeze his hand tightly three times in quick succession, silently saying, "I love you."

Again Jack helps me home as if I'm an invalid and organizes me on the couch, Nana's quilt over my legs, slippers within reach. When he heads off to the kitchen, I close my eyes and listen to him whistle as he prepares a plate of cheese, crackers, and grapes, a tall bottle of water and a glass, my iPhone, the portable phone, the latest *Oprah* and *People* magazines, and two books he grabbed from my bedside table.

"Thanks, Jack. I could get used to this."

"Doctor's orders, Abbs; you're to take it easy." The phone rings and Jack dives for it. "I'll get it."

He backs away toward the kitchen. I hear him answer the phone and then his voice drops lower, so I can't quite overhear. But I know who he is talking to, and it's not a secret lover, although his guilt-ridden handling of the phone might drive suspicions that way. No, I believe he's filling Marilyn in on the day's activities. Part of me feels as if an affair would be easier to deal with in the short run than his mother. It's amazing how anxious I get at the thought of her.

Abby, stop this, he's talking to his mother. Relax, breathe; who cares about Marilyn?

"Who was that?" I ask when Jack reappears. I'm stirring the pot, but I can't help it.

"My mom. She's just checking in to see what's new. She wanted to come over for dinner..." *Oh god, no.* "But I told her we were busy." He collapses onto the couch with me and reaches under the quilt to find my foot and massage it.

"Oh god, yes," I moan aloud, and we spend the evening happily cocooned on the couch.

∽

I spend another week prone while Scott plays defense for me at the office and I try to remain a vision of part-serenity and part–baby oven.

"Keep me up to date on what's happening at the office, okay? Let me know if Marco is out to get me. I kind of lost it on him the other day."

"We know *all* about it. Marco's been trying to drum up sympathy. The problem is he's not sure what's wrong with you, so he won't come out and say he's pissed, but he's been pretty whiny." Scott turns on his best Marco impression. "'I don't know what's up with Abby; I mean, I just thought she'd like to meet a really talented young woman. She always says we don't have enough staff.'" Scott breaks off to laugh as I shake my head at how thick my boss is. "Gotta run, Abby, I've got a big date tonight. He's a dancer, can you believe it? Keep your feet up." He is laughing as he hangs up.

I read two newspapers a day, I catch the daily guests on *Ellen*, I attempt a crossword, but mostly cheat to fill it – thank goodness for Google – and I finish six books. I get daily phone calls from Jules, my mother, and Cassie.

For a while I call Scott every hour until he starts screening my calls. I try emailing him, but only receive jokes and chain emails in return – infuriating, but some of them are pretty funny. By the middle of the third day, I resort to checking in at the office only twice a day, and Scott finally takes my calls and keeps me up to date.

I spend the second week being chauffeured by Jack to and from work, where I seem to have a lighter load than usual. Is Charlie doing his best to help?

The weekend arrives again, and I am sequestered back on the couch. I long to be active and outside, watching the warm March sun start to turn everything green in anticipation of spring. Jack, or my manservant, as I've come to call him, has piled me with supplies, those that are edible and others for entertainment, before he leaves to join Marilyn for an early round of golf on Sunday morning. Spring has barely begun, but the die-hard golfers are warming up for the season. This was a Sunday morning tradition for Jack and Marilyn before I arrived on the scene. In the early days, I attempted to join them, but was probably better suited for church, as I shouted the Lord's name with each swing. I've never understood the game nor liked it. Marilyn and Jack can have it.

"You'll be home, right? You'll be here on time?" I feel as if I'm begging, but I can't take the phone call alone, not again.

"Abbs, I promise. I will be here on time."

"I mean it, Jack, you *have* to be here. No excuses." I love my husband, but he does not have a great concept of time. Jack puts his hand on his heart.

"I solemnly swear that I, Jack Williams, will be here on time for the phone call. Okay?" He leans down and kisses the top of my head. "Just relax today. I love you." He heads to the door.

"I love you too." I can't help myself; to his retreating back, I yell, "Don't be late." The door has closed, so I'm not sure if he didn't hear me, or if he ignored me.

18

IF HE MISSES this call again, I will kill him. It's five minutes to three and they always call at three. I try his cell for the fourth time, but it goes right to voice mail. Shit, Jack, where the hell are you? I grip the couch to steady myself. I can't take this call alone again. Tears are welling and I hyperventilate a little. Two minutes to go. *Breathe, Abby, breathe.* Even if I am pregnant, I think I'll divorce him anyway. The sound of the phone breaks my internal ranting. No, no, not again. I take a deep breath and three steps to the kitchen where my cell phone sits on the table. One more ring of the phone and one more giant deep breath for me.

"Hello?" Even I can hear the fear and tears in my voice.

"Hi Abby, its Sharon at Dr. Greenberg's office calling." Lovely Nurse; okay, I can handle Lovely Nurse.

"Hi," is all I can muster. I am clutching the phone so tightly, it might crack.

"I have great news. Congratulations, you're pregnant."

The front door bursts open and Jack races in yelling, "I'm here, I'm here. Did I miss it? I'm so sorry, Abbs, my phone died. Did they call already?" He stops short when he sees me on the phone and looks crushed. I realize that the tears streaming down my face are probably sending the wrong message, so I smile through them and gesture at the phone.

"I'm pregnant?" I say into the phone. I'm trying to listen to Lovely Nurse talk about my blood levels and also mime to Jack that I'm fine, but I can't think straight.

"Woo-hoo!" Jack screams and picks me up and twirls me around. We are both laughing and crying at the same time. Lovely Nurse giggles into the phone. I'm sure this is the part of her job she loves.

"Congratulations again, Abby. We'll need you to come back every three days for more blood work, and then if all goes well, you'll have your first ultrasound in four weeks. Keep taking all of your medications, needles, and suppositories until we tell you to stop. You still need to take it easy, too – these are early days."

"Thank you, thank you so much." I hang up and look at Jack.

"We're having a baby. I knew you could do it, Abbs. I love you. I'm so sorry I was late," he starts. I kiss him. Truth is, I don't care anymore that he was late. It doesn't matter. We have a family on the way.

"I'm pregnant. I just can't believe it." I rub my hands over my belly. "Jack, we're going to be parents."

Jack takes me in his arms and rests his chin on my head. "Believe it. This is going to be awesome."

I listen to Jack's heartbeat and feel the weight of all of our failed attempts lift. We are having a baby.

"This calls for a celebration." As Jack reaches for our champagne flutes, I glance at the phone. "Go ahead, you know she's waiting." I quickly dial.

"Yes!" I scream into the phone as Jules answers on the first ring. She must have been sitting beside it, waiting for me to call.

"Oh, Abby." Jules is crying and I'm crying too. "I'm so happy for you. I knew this would happen."

Jack passes me a box of tissues and wraps his arms around me. Jules and I hang up, with promises to talk again in the morning, and Jack leads me to the couch. We curl up together, and Jack places his hand on my belly. "Abbs, you've got a little one in there. This is so amazing." He sounds in awe of our news still. So am I. "Do you think it's a girl or a boy? Whatever it is, I hope it has your smile."

"Your blue eyes will work for a girl or a boy. I can't quite believe this is happening."

"Do you feel any different?" Jack searches my face.

"I just feel so happy and relieved and a little scared. Look, I know we need to tell our families, but let's keep it pretty quiet until I'm further along. I don't want to jinx anything." Jack nods and kisses the top of my head.

∾

Over the next four weeks, I stop by the clinic every three days for blood tests. Cheery Nurse phones every afternoon to tell me my hormone levels are increasing – when she has good news to impart, she's not so bad on the phone. I pop by Lovely Nurse's office on my way out one day.

"Abigail, good morning. How are you feeling today?"

"I'm fine, thank you. I need to pick up a few more supplies; I'm running low on the injections and suppositories." I settle into the chair across from her desk. It's way too early in my pregnancy to be showing, but my abdomen is swollen and tender from the endless needles.

"Let me just look at your file." She opens my file, which has tripled in size since we started this process. "Wow," is all she says.

"What? Wow what?" I ask, leaning forward over my sore stomach to catch an upside-down view of my file. I can see a column of numbers, starting around two thousand and steadily doubling and tripling down the column.

"Well, I'm not really supposed to say." She stops and looks around.

"Are my numbers okay? Is everything fine?" I ask, getting more nervous by the second. I wring my hands in my lap. She closes my file and seems to notice my hands.

"It's fine, Abigail. Let's just say that if I were a betting woman, I'd say you have more than one in there," and she points toward my belly.

"Really? More than one? You're sure?" *Twins?* I suddenly picture myself walking along Danforth Avenue, pushing a beautiful double stroller, everyone stopping to comment on how gorgeous my babies are.

"No, I'm not sure. The ultrasound next time will confirm it, and it's very early days still, so anything can happen. But in my experience, and I've worked here a long time, your hormone levels indicate more than one."

I leave the office in a daze. More than one baby – I can't seem to wrap my head around that. Scott greets me at the door as I slip in to work. I've managed to arrive on time every day, even with the morning blood tests, but somehow I've wound up late.

"Abby," Scott hisses, breaking me from my romantic notions of twins. "Marco's in the boardroom waiting for you. The bank people are here. You're late. I tried calling you." He is speaking quickly and in hushed tones as he strips me out of my jacket and shoves my presentation papers into my arms. He steers me toward the boardroom and gives me a shove in the back, propelling me forward.

"Gentlemen," I say as I enter the room, a smile plastered to my face. "I'm terribly sorry I'm late. Let's get started." Marco is frowning at me from the head of the boardroom table and he not-too-subtly taps his watch, but my clients smile back. I manage to push away the baby thoughts, and my work alter ego takes over.

⟋⟍

"Abby." Marco appears at my office door after seeing the bankers out.

"I know what you're going to say, Marco. Look, I'm sorry I was late, but I think the meeting went really well. They like the direction we're headed in."

He stops me before I can continue. "It did go well. You really have a way with them, I'll give you that. But you don't seem as dedicated to your job and this place as you used to be."

"Look, I know I've been a little detached and maybe even hard to deal with lately, but I promise, things are changing. I've just had some really tough personal stuff to deal with, but it's all working out. The old Abby is back." I flash him a brilliant smile and hold my hand across my heart as he turns to leave.

৩

Jack comes with me for our ultrasound appointment. He's like a kid, practically skipping down the pavement to the front doors. We join the herd of cattle at the entrance and make it into the first group of ten. I can still smell the stench of desperation in the waiting room, but Jack and I feel safe and warm in our cocoon of pregnancy. The desperates seem to gravitate in our direction, like moths to a flame, but we have our shields up and keep our noses buried in our phones.

When Dr. Greenberg finally arrives, although the time hasn't mattered much to us, he surprises me by calling us first. I was number ten on the sign-up list; I've never skipped forward before. Holding hands, Jack and I walk into the ultrasound room.

"Abigail, Jack, congratulations. Your levels are looking very impressive. Let's take a look." He puts on his gloves and I bare my soul on the table. Being violated by the ultrasound probe doesn't even faze me. I'm staring intently at the screen, looking for my baby – or babies, if Lovely Nurse is right.

"Here we go. Look at that." He cranks the volume knob on the machine and the room fills with the most beautiful sound, our baby's heartbeat. I blink back tears, and Jack's hand practically crushes mine. Dr. Greenberg takes a few measurements and jots them down in my chart.

"Size is good, everything is looking good." He pauses, refers to his notes, and looks up again. "Let's see what else we can find, shall we?" He moves the probe a little to the right, and suddenly another grainy but moving blob appears. "There's another one." I know I was prepared, but I'm still surprised. "Great, this is really great, Abby, another strong heartbeat and a healthy size. Let me see what else we can find."

He says it so matter-of-factly. *More? There are more?* I suddenly have the image of a dozen clowns piled in a teeny clown car. *Oh my god, I'm the clown car.* I feel the room spinning a little and look up to see the color draining from Jack's face. I clutch his hand tightly, hoping he won't hit the floor. Dr. Greenberg continues to move the probe around, like an explorer looking for life on a strange planet. I am holding my breath.

"Well," he says at last. "We have two very healthy embryos growing here. Congratulations, Abby and Jack. I think you'll be pretty busy around early December," he says. I exhale quietly and see Jack's color return as Dr. Greenberg removes the probe and takes off his gloves. "We'll see you next week," Dr. Greenberg says, and Jack and I leave the room in stunned silence.

We ride the elevator down to the lobby without speaking. A woman riding with us is weeping silently, her back to us. My heart breaks for her; I can feel her pain, but remain quietly holding Jack's hand. When we get into our car, he makes no move to turn the key. "Twins. Abbs, we are having twins." He sounds amazed.

∽

"Accidental-Baby on line two," Scott's voice floats through my phone. "She sounds weird; you know, weirder than normal." My pregnancy has done little to thaw relations between Scott and Cassie.

"Cassie?" I say, picking up the flashing red light. She doesn't respond right away, and I hear grunting and deep breathing. "Cass? You okay?"

"Abby, Mom told me your news." She breaks off to suck noisily on more air. "That's great. Congratulations. You guys must be thrilled." Her voice sounds strained.

I feel awful. Jack and I have been keeping our news under wraps for weeks. I told Scott, who has sworn on his latest boyfriend that he won't say a word, and I obviously told Jules, who phones every day to see if morning sickness is taking its toll. I quietly told my mother, but I half-forgot and half-decided not to say anything to Cassie. I knew her due date was looming and I didn't want to spoil her big day. I hear my sister pant, as if she's hyperventilating, and then it hits me.

"Cass, are you in labor?"

"Yes, it started in the night. My midwife says I'm dilating nicely. I just finished a bath and now I am walking around the living room. Whoa, ouch; that was a big one."

"Shouldn't you be on your way to the hospital? Does Mom know?"

"Mom's on her way. Roger and I have decided to have the baby right here at home. I've been following this fantastic blogger who just had a baby at home and she's all about the baby's first memory. I want this one to always remember the first glimpse of our home." She breathes deeply, and in the background I can hear Roger coaching her.

"Seriously, Cass? I'm not so sure the baby will remember anything right off the bat."

I can't imagine giving birth at home. Not only do I want to make sure the best of western medicine is at my disposal, including a massive dose of drugs for the pain, but imagine the mess – I'll think twice about sitting on her couch the next time I visit. I'm amazed my mother hasn't mentioned Cassie's home birth plan.

"Ouch. Okay, wow. Abby, I'd better go. I think things are moving along here." She is breathing very heavily now.

"Good luck, Cassie. I love you." She's gone. I sit back, a little stunned, and realize that unconsciously I am rubbing my belly, for comfort and also a bit like a genie in a bottle. I send my sister positive thoughts. There will be a baby today. I will be an aunt. I'm an aunt and a mother-to-be. It's amazing how much the world has changed in the last year. There might be economic turmoil in the world, unrest in the Middle East, and new babies in the royal line, but in my little slice of the world, there is bliss. I take a deep breath and turn back to the realities of my job.

~☙~

My cell phone rings as I'm on my way home from work. "Abby, it's Mom. It's a girl, a beautiful baby girl." Mom is crying happily. I catch sight of my reflection in the rearview mirror and realize I'm crying and grinning too. "Your sister was terrific. It was so incredible and so personal having the baby at home. You should really consider it. They didn't allow it in my day."

"Sorry to disappoint you, Mom, but I will be happily tucked away in a delivery room with the very best of drugs in my system." I can't help but laugh and shake my head at how different I am from my family. "I'm so glad everyone is okay. What's her name?"

"Moonjava."

"Hello, Mom? Are you there? I don't think I heard you correctly." I wonder if my cell provider has dropped yet another call.

"Moonjava. Isn't it beautiful?"

"Seriously? Moonjava? What kind of a name is that?" Our call must be overlapping another cell signal. I definitely can't be hearing that correctly.

"Moonjava Betty Ashfield. It's perfect. Did I ever tell you that was the name I had picked out for you? Your father took one look at you and decided you were more Abigail than Moonjava." My mother sighs wistfully.

"Um, no. I'm sure I would have remembered that." I make a mental note to hug my father next time I see him.

19

THE BATHROOM SCALE says I've gained two pounds in the last two weeks. According to the pregnancy books, most women can lose some weight in the first trimester, but to keep the nausea at bay, I am eating constantly. At this rate, I'll be plain fat before I even begin to look pregnant. I glare at the naked reflection in the mirror.

At nine weeks, my belly is still flat; no sign of any cute little baby bump. Pilates and work stress have helped keep me in shape all these years. My boobs, on the other hand, have definitely changed. I cup each one with my hands to feel their new heaviness and wince at their tenderness. The women in my family are not overly well-endowed, but overnight, it seems as if the Breast Fairy has paid me a visit. Oh sure, where was she in high school when I needed her?

"Do I get to play with them?" I jump and see Jack checking me out from the doorway.

"No way. They may be turning you on, but they hurt. You can look, but no touching." Jack looks gloomy. "The damn things are going to give me away," I groan, turning back to the mirror.

"What do you mean?" Jack is still eyeing me hungrily.

"Well, I don't look pregnant, but my boobs are suddenly bigger. How do I explain that?" I turn sideways to stare at my stomach again, willing a little bump to show to offset my expanding chest.

"Tell them you had a boob job," Jack shrugs.

"Thanks, that's very helpful." I sigh and hope I can stuff my new friends into one of my sports bras so that maybe no one will notice.

⟡

Scott knocks on my office door as I am finalizing the budget for the bankers. I wave him in and continue to jump between multiple spreadsheets on my screen, inputting final numbers. I have spent a lot of time on this, not just in an effort to make amends for missing the initial pitch, but to help cement my dedication to my job and my future here. I am about to attach the final file to an email when Scott drapes something over my shirt.

"Scott, what are you doing?" I look up from my computer screen and push his hands away.

"Put this on," Scott says, still trying to wrap me in a long scarf.

"Quit messing around. I'm not wearing your scarf. I have to get this budget out in the next few minutes. They're expecting it by close of business." I glare at him, ball up the scarf, and throw it at him. "Plus, it's a million degrees in here. I've already taken off my jacket. What's your problem?" I blow my hair off my face and turn back to my computer, attach the open spreadsheet, and start typing to my clients.

"I'll get you a fan if you're hot, but Abby, you have to put something on. Your girls are getting noticed."

I look down and realize that without my blazer, my "girls" look as if they are trying to burst from my lightweight sports bra. So much for trying to hide my new friends.

"Oh crap," I mutter, shrugging back into my jacket. I finish typing, hit send, sit back, and look down at my chest. Even in my blazer, they are still noticeable. Maybe Scott's scarf idea isn't such a bad one. "Has anyone noticed?"

"A few people might have casually mentioned something..." Scott looks away. "Marco might have made a comment; I don't really remember."

"Figures he'd be looking at my boobs. I'll try and keep them under wraps. Thanks for the heads up." Scott winks and heads for the door.

I am about to close up my email and shut down for the night when my eyes flicker to my sent emails. The title of the most recent attachment says "c monitoring," not the bank budget I have so diligently worked on.

No, no, this cannot be happening...

I open the attachment and my stomach drops. Instead of our budget spreadsheet, I have attached my old cycle monitoring file. Oh god, this is so bad – so very, very bad. I just sent the senior vice president of a major bank a file filled with my daily temperature readings and cervical mucus discharge description.

The room starts to spin. I shove my chair back violently and throw my head between my knees. Marco is going to lose it for sure. Good-bye partnership, good-bye job. I draw in a ragged breath and tears prick my eyes. Maybe he's right. Maybe I'm not cut out for management. I can't concentrate on anything anymore, and now I'm making junior mistakes. How can I explain that I was distracted by the size of my boobs? *Oh Abby,* I wail.

"Abby? Are you all right?" Scott is suddenly at my desk. Maybe I wailed out loud?

"I screwed up, Scott, big time." I sit up, hoping my office will have stopped spinning, and gesture at the open attachment on my screen. I grab a tissue and stifle a sob as I watch his eyes widen. He looks confused.

"What is that? I don't understand what these numbers mean – and why do you mention egg whites? Is this a menu?"

"Scott, this is horrible. I am in so much trouble. I hit send when we were discussing my–" I gesture toward my breasts.

"Oh," is all he says. My shoulders droop, and I'm sure defeat shows on my face.

"Marco is going to kill me. This will make us look like hacks. We'll lose the account for sure. How can they have any faith in our company – me in particular? I missed the pitch, and now this?" I hold my breath, waiting for the bellow from Marco's office. Scott looks at me and takes off at a run. Great, just great; I'm a sinking ship and the rats are leaving. I rest my forehead on my desk and await my fate.

Scott races back into my office and shuts the door behind him. I don't bother to lift my head. "Abby, can you smooth this over with the bankers?" he whispers. I turn my head to the side, resting my right ear on the desk, and look up at him. "Well? Can you?"

My head feels heavy, but I make my neck muscles work to support the weight and pull it off the desk. "I probably can, but it won't matter, Scott. Marco will still fire my ass. He's going to be livid. It's no use." The weight gets the better of me and I rest my face back on my desk.

"Abigail Nichols, I'm ashamed of you." Scott's sharp tone slaps me. My head rises slightly to hover over the desk. "I don't really understand what you've sent out, but when life hands you lemons, you don't suck on them and cry, you squeeze them in a glass, add sugar and vodka, and voilà – a Lemon Drop."

"Scott, I don't think that's quite the expression," I say, straightening and attempting a small smile. "What's your point?"

"Just smooth it over with the bankers and I'll handle Marco." He leans over and pulls a paper clip off my cheek. "Pull yourself together. You can fix this." He pats me on the head and saunters to the door, opens it, and darts a glance in both directions before sneaking out. The heaviness of failure pulls my head to the desk again. I appreciate Scott wanting to help, but I'm sure he is destined to fail.

My phone rings and, without looking, I grope for the receiver and rest it against my ear. "Abby Nichols." I sound deflated.

"Abby, hi, it's David at the bank. Do you have a minute?" David, Mr. Orange Tie. I close my eyes and sit up, feeling slightly lighter, thankful it's not Marco on the other end.

"David, hi. Yes, sure I've got time." What should I say? *Think, Abby, think.*

"I just got your email. I'm not really sure what to say." He chuckles and I sit up much straighter. I was expecting bankers to be conservative and stuffy. Mr. Orange Tie doesn't sound fussed.

"Mister – I mean, David – yes, I'm so sorry. That file, it's, um, I don't actually know what to say. I was a little distracted and I'm sorry. This is entirely my fault and I hope my mistake won't reflect on the entire firm." What else can I say? I cradle the phone between my shoulder and ear and reach for my keyboard and mouse, trying to attach the correct file.

"Look, don't worry about it. You're not the only one whose personal life seeps into their work life. Please don't worry; I won't hold it against you or your agency. I like working with you, I think you are great at your job. And to be honest, if this file is what I think it is, I admire you more and I wish you the best."

"Really?" My voice is almost a whisper, and I choke back the tears.

"Really. Just send over the budget now and I'll sign it back." He rings off, and I sit back and exhale.

Very carefully, I attach the correct spreadsheet to a new email, triple-check it, and send the correct file to David, cc'ing Marco and Charlie. I can only hope that Marco will overlook my latest gaffe.

I turn off the computer and half-heartedly organize my desk before heading out. As I step into the hallway, I see Scott sneaking out of Marco's office.

"Scott?" I hiss.

"We're all good. Go home and relax." He steers me toward the front door.

"What did you do?" I turn to face him in the glow of the streetlights through the frosted doors.

"Relax, Abby; what Marco doesn't know won't hurt him. I deleted the email."

"How did you get into his computer?" Marco brags about how unbreakable his password is. I'm sure he keeps the computer protected to hide his porn.

Scott kisses me on the forehead. "Go home, Abby."

20

"NO," I SCREAM, and sit bolt upright in bed. My heart is pounding, my brow is beaded with sweat, and I'm all tangled up in the bed sheets. I clutch at my stomach and cry out.

"What's wrong? Is something happening?" Jack is awake beside me, eyes wide in terror at my obvious distress. I shake my head, brush away the tears, and take a ragged breath.

"I just had a horrible dream. Jack, one of the babies died," I wail.

"Shh, relax. It was only a dream. You're okay, the babies are okay, and it was just a dream." He rubs my back and strokes my hair, trying to calm me down. He reaches across to the bedside table and hands me a box of tissues. I blow my nose and mop up the tears.

"It was so real; you don't understand, it felt so real." I snuggle into his warm embrace as Jack continues to stroke my hair, making shushing noises.

"It's okay, Abbs, everything is fine," he croons. I can hear the sleepiness in his voice and know he's about to drift off. I lie quietly in his embrace, listening to his breathing. I can't shake the unease, but realize it's probably left over from my last work screw-up. I seem to be in the clear with Marco, but I keeping waiting for something else to go wrong. I take a deep breath and close my eyes. Jack's right; it was only a dream. *Happy thoughts, Abby; think happy thoughts.*

In the morning Jack joins me in the bathroom as I am putting on my makeup. He places a steaming cup of tea on the counter, closes the toilet lid, and sits down to watch me apply mascara. Crying in the night has made my eyes puffy.

"You want to tell me about the dream?" he asks.

"It was so weird." Putting down the mascara tube, I lean against the countertop to face him. "Part of me knew it was a dream, like the colors were too bright or something. But it felt so real." I shudder and wrap my arms around my body.

"So what happened?" Jack is looking at me as if I might be a bit crazy. Even when I was hopped up on serious hormones for our IVF procedure and probably *was* certifiable, he never looked at me quite like this.

"It's not like anything happened. It was more like a feeling. I could see myself and I knew a baby had died." I realize I do sound a little crazy. "Okay, I sound nutty, I know. I can't explain it, but it sure felt real." I throw up my hands in surrender.

Jules emails me back later in the day after I've recounted my dream to her, sending me links to articles about vivid dreams women experience while pregnant. "Honey, just you wait till the horny dreams start," is her parting line.

∽

Each week I head back into Dr. Greenberg's clinic to have another ultrasound. The embryos are growing according to plan; the heart rates are strong, the length is good. They still look like little beans, but they are beautiful.

Secure in knowing I'm pregnant, I feel as if I have a force field around me that fends off the depressing atmosphere of the clinic. Jack comes with me each week, wanting to catch a glimpse of our growing family in the grainy black and white blobs on the ultrasound screen. We do our best not to sit in the waiting room grinning like idiots. Not that long ago, I was like the others.

"How are we feeling today, Abby?" asks Dr. Greenberg.

"Great." I have to endure vaginal ultrasounds until I'm twelve weeks along. I am only at eleven weeks, so there's one more to go. I should plan a small celebration.

"Terrific. So, no morning sickness?" he asks as he gloves up.

"Actually, I still feel pretty awful. If I let my stomach get empty, I tend to get really nauseous. I haven't thrown up yet today, but we did have to pull the car to the side of the road on the way over here."

"Sounds pretty normal. You might want to stash some granola bars in strategic places in case you get hungry. With most women, morning sickness tends to end around the beginning of the second trimester, and you're only a week or two away. I think you'll feel better soon. Okay, let's take a look." Baby A comes into view on the screen. Dr. Greenberg has the monitor turned up, so the room is filled with the sound of the heart beating. It is still the most amazing sound I've ever heard. We can actually see the heart beating on the screen. Dr. Greenberg takes his time making measurements and jotting notes in my file.

"Okay, Baby A looks good. Let's go see what contestant number two is up to." He moves the ultrasound around, trying to get a fix on Baby B, who is usually behind or beneath Baby A. As soon as Baby B comes into view, I inhale sharply. I'm no doctor, but over the last two years of clinic visits, I've learned a little about how to read an ultrasound – at least, I know what some of the blobs are supposed to be, and that the heart should be visibly pumping in an eleven-week fetus. Silence fills the room. Baby B is smaller than Baby A, and very still. Dr. Greenberg doesn't say anything right away; he only takes a close look and makes a few measurements.

Jack looks bewildered. "What's going on, Doc?" he asks.

"It looks as though the heart has stopped."

"What do you mean? Baby B has been the same as Baby A every week, and Abby hasn't had any pain or cramps or bleeding. How does it just … stop?" Jack wrings his hands and paces two steps in each direction in the tiny ultrasound room. The joy and bliss of listening to Baby A's heartbeat has quickly turned to confusion, panic, and fear.

"I realize this is very difficult, but unfortunately it's rather common. Over the last two weeks, some pretty major organs have been forming. In fact, in the tenth week, the embryos become fetuses. In this case, I'd say that something probably didn't form correctly. Nature has a remarkable way of taking care of itself. I know this is hard, but if something major, like brain, kidney, or liver, doesn't form correctly, the odds of a baby surviving are pretty slim." Dr. Greenberg speaks calmly, talking us off the ledge. I'm numb as I listen to the men talk over me.

"Then how do we get it out? I mean, we can't leave a dead– I mean, you get it out somehow, right?" Jack asks, running his hands through his hair.

"Well, no; we call it a vanishing twin. It will either come out on its own and Abby will have some spotting, or it will be reabsorbed back into the uterus."

"Reabsorbed?" I finally pull myself to the surface of my shock.

"That's why it's a vanishing twin. In a few weeks, we won't be able to find it on the ultrasound. This situation happens outside of the fertility world as well. Lots of women can get pregnant with twins and have a vanishing twin and never know it. The average pregnant woman not using a fertility clinic doesn't have her first ultrasound until twelve or thirteen weeks. By then, the twin is gone. We only know about it because we have ultrasounds done early and every week." Dr. Greenberg turns off the monitor and gathers up my file.

"I don't get it," Jack says. "Everything was fine last week. When could this have happened?"

"Given the look of the fetus, I'd say it was within the last couple of days." Dr. Greenberg catches the look that shoots between us.

"Abby had a dream two nights ago that one of the babies died." Jack grips my hands and turns to me. "I'm so sorry, Abbs. I thought it was just a dream."

"That's not totally surprising. I've had a few other patients tell me similar stories. On some level you might have had an awareness of what was happening. Scientifically, I can't say for sure."

"But is Baby A okay? I mean, can this happen again, out of the blue?" I ask, terrified of the answer.

"Baby A is growing strong. Just continue to take it easy, try to keep your stress levels down, and I'll see you next week."

Jack and I walk stiffly and silently toward the elevator. Again, a woman is quietly weeping on the ride down, and this time I feel like joining her. I know I should be overjoyed that I am still pregnant, but I feel empty from losing Baby B and terrified of losing Baby A. If it happened once, Jack's right – what's to say it won't happen again? The thought of another dream is terrifying. I'm not sure I'll sleep at all for a little while.

"Do you want me to drop you off at work?" Jack asks as we get to the car.

I shake my head. I don't think I can face the office. "I think I'll go visit Cassie," I say, surprising even myself.

∽

"I'll be fine," I tell Jack when he drops me off at Cassie's house. "Don't worry. I'll take a cab home. Jack, it's fine, go to work." Giving him a final wave, I turn toward Cassie's front door, which is badly in need of a new coat of paint. I fish through my purse and pull out my phone to call Marco, clearing my throat as I wait for him to pick up.

"I won't be in today." I swallow hard, trying to push down the lump in my throat.

"Are you kidding me? We're presenting the final design to the bank. You know you have to be here." I can hear Marco's fury. "Attendance is not optional."

"Look, I can't. I'm sorry. I can try to reschedule–"

"Abigail, this is unbelievable. What could possibly be more important?"

"Marco, I'm sorry, it's just that ... something personal has come up." I stifle a sob and think, *I've just lost a baby; surely that is excuse enough*, but the words won't come.

"Well, if you can't be bothered to join us, I'll have Linda do the presentation." His threat hangs heavy in the air. I close my eyes and cup my forehead. I'm most likely serving Linda the partnership on a silver platter, but even with that threat to my career, I can't possibly face everyone. Maybe I'm not meant to be a mom *and* a partner. I exhale slowly.

"Fine. Tell Linda to take the meeting. I'm sure she's up to speed anyway." Once the words are out, I feel lighter. She's been sniffing around the production studio; I'm sure she's sussed out the new campaign for the bank.

"Fine, then." We both hang up without good-byes. Fresh tears spring forth and I make no effort to wipe them away, feeling them forming little rivers through my moisturizer. I drop the phone into my purse and reach out and pick at the peeling paint before I knock on Cassie's door.

"Aren't you supposed to be at work?" Cassie asks as she ushers me inside. A curry is cooking on the stove and nature sounds are playing on the stereo. I spot a well-swaddled bundle rocking in a baby swing that looks homemade. My sister looks great. I think I was expecting her to look sleep-deprived, harried, and unwashed, but she's the opposite. The house even looks surprisingly clean. My eyes dart to the couch, but it too looks spotless. I walk over to the swaddled bundle and gaze down at my new niece.

"Are you okay?" Cassie asks, and I realize I haven't said a word. I've arrived on her doorstep out of the blue and haven't bothered to explain myself. I nod, but that quickly turns into a shake and my eyes well with tears as I meet Cassie's worried gaze. As she guides me to the couch, I hesitate.

"Did you have her here?"

"Goodness, no, we would have ruined the couch. My midwife brought a birthing stool. Sit, Abby, and tell me what's going on." I wonder what on earth a birthing stool looks like, but I don't want to ask.

I tell Cassie about the dream first and then that one of the babies has died. After she hugs me tightly, she gets up to make tea – herbal, of course. I move over on the couch while she is in the kitchen and focus clearly on my niece. She is gorgeous.

"Abby, I'm so sorry. You guys have been through so much. Let's all be thankful that you have a healthy baby in there. Your doctor is right; the other one most likely wouldn't have made it in the long run. There could have been more serious complications down the road if this had happened later. I realize that doesn't soothe the loss now, but…" She trails off as Moonjava lets out a wail.

She reaches down and, in what seems like one fluid motion, unbundles the baby, sits on the couch, and lifts her shirt, and suddenly her daughter is latched on. She gazes down adoringly. It amazes me how easily my sister has taken to motherhood. Most of my friends have looked so frazzled in the early days, and here is my sister with everything well in hand. I only hope I take to motherhood as easily. Maybe that, at least, is genetic.

"Cassie, I've been a crappy sister. I should have come to visit sooner. It's just been such a roller coaster for us. It's no excuse, I know."

Before I can go on, Cassie interrupts me. "It's fine, Abby, really. I know our baby news was hard to handle – we had trouble too, trust me. The past few weeks have been a total blur. Our midwife suggested no visitors for the first two weeks, mostly to help keep Roger's family in line, but also for us to try and bond as a family. You're here now; that's all that counts. Thank you for the flowers you sent; they were beautiful."

"Well, I have a few cute outfits at home for her. I wasn't planning to bail on work today, so I'll bring them next week. Once I find the perfect 'My aunt rocks when she's not so self-absorbed' onesie, I'll let you know."

When she finishes breast-feeding, Cassie changes her daughter's diaper – cloth – and hands her over to me. I sit back on the couch, careful to cradle the tiny head and neck, and just stare. It's amazing how contented babies are once they have clean bums and full tummies. As Moonjava drifts into a milk-drunk doze, I finally work up the nerve to ask the question I've been dying to ask.

"Why Moonjava?"

"I don't know. Mom told me once she almost named you Moonjava. It's always stuck with me. The way we grew up was so different from Roger's childhood. We just wanted to bring those two worlds together. Do you like it?"

"It's a little different. It'll just take some getting used to. More importantly, how are Roger's parents adjusting to it? Moonjava Ashfield is hardly a family name."

"I won't lie, it hasn't been an easy sell. They sent out a birth announcement and called her MJ. You know, initially I wasn't impressed, but they are so happy to have a grandchild, and MJ is kind of growing on us."

I spend a little more time with mommy and baby and then decide it's time to head home. I kiss MJ gently on the head and hug my sister.

"Cass, you look great. I'm really happy for you," I say, and Cassie hugs me tighter.

"I am happy, and you're next. Abby, this is you next. Everything is going to be great."

∾

I unlock the front door and am about to drop my keys on the hall table when I spot a Gucci purse sitting on it. Marilyn. Great, just what I need. I notice Jack's briefcase on the dining room table. Maybe they haven't heard me come in; maybe I can slip out without them knowing? The thought of fleeing the house and wandering aimlessly in the May heat wave until the coast is clear is just too tiring. I want to curl up on the couch and tune out the world. As I kick off my strappy sandals, I catch snippets of their discussion. Actually, it sounds more like an argument. I tiptoe barefoot to the kitchen door to eavesdrop a little more.

"Seriously, Mom, this is not cool."

"I'm sorry, Jacky. The girls thought it would be nice."

"Mom, you are unbelievable. I told you not to say anything, and now this, today of all days. Abby's going to freak." Oh dear lord, what has this woman done to me now? Part of me wants to barge in and catch them in the act – of what, I have no idea. The other part wants to slink off, hoping that whatever it is will just go away.

"I'm sorry, Jacky. I was just so excited. The girls are so thrilled for me."

"Dammit, this isn't about you, don't you get that? This is about me and Abby. This is private information that you shared without my permission. I don't care about your golf-club biddies." *Yes, way to go Jack, you tell her,* I cheer silently. I have never known him to stand up to his mother like this. "You're going to have to tell them what's happened. Don't you

dare let another one of these enter our house. Honestly, sometimes I understand why Abby finds you so difficult."
Ouch, okay, not ending on a high note for Abby.

I push the door open and survey the scene. Jack and Marilyn are surrounded by enormous bouquets of flowers and balloons. They are hastily trying to deflate each balloon and remove the little signs from each bouquet. Our kitchen is not huge, but from the door I can see what has Jack so flustered. Every bouquet and balloon screams, "Twins, congratulations!"

"Oh my," Marilyn starts, and I turn to walk out. "Abigail, I'm so sorry," she yells to my back.

"See, Mom, nicely done. Abby, wait," Jack calls and I hear him following me upstairs. I go to the bedroom, strip off my sweaty blouse, and let my skirt fall in a heap to the floor. I climb under the duvet, suddenly chilly and utterly exhausted.

"Abbs, honey, I'm so sorry. When I told Mom what happened this morning with Dr. Greenberg, she told me about the flowers. I was hoping to beat you home and get rid of everything." Jack picks up my skirt and lays it carefully and crease-free on the chair in the corner. He sits beside me, and the bed dips a little. I can see real worry in his face as he tries to read mine.

"It's fine, Jack; I'm fine."

"Can you believe she announced it to all her friends at the club?"

Actually yes, I totally believe it, but instead of fanning the flames of discontent, I find myself soothing them.

"She's just excited. Those gossipy golfers have formed a clique, and this was her chance to get accepted. And twins? Christ, they might have erected a statue in her honor. I'm not saying we should let her off the hook, I'm just really tired and I don't think I have the energy for her. Do you mind if I stay up here?"

"You're taking this surprisingly well." Jack looks confused.

"Let's just say nothing your mother does surprises me anymore."

"Okay. You relax, I'll get rid of the flowers *and* my mother, and then bring us something to eat up here. Deal?"

"Sounds great. Oh, but don't throw out the flowers; they really are beautiful. Maybe just the cards and balloons." I turn on the TV as Jack heads back downstairs. I can only hear murmurs from the kitchen, but Jack's tone still sounds clipped. I flip through the channels and settle on a home decorating show featuring a nursery makeover. Scott has been begging me to let him design the nursery. I'm not sure I want to let him loose until I have a firm grasp of what we really want. Lord knows what we'd end up with if we gave Scott a long leash. I'm thinking Martha Stewart, Liza Minnelli, and Cher all channeled into baby accessories.

As the show is ending, I hear tentative steps on the stairs, which can only mean one thing: Marilyn. I sit up, smooth the covers around me, and take a deep, calming breath, bracing myself. Marilyn clears her throat and taps lightly on the bedroom door.

"Abigail?" She pushes the door open so just her head peeks in. Her usual haughtiness is gone. She looks apprehensive, even scared. She clears her throat again. "Abigail, I just wanted to sincerely apologize to you. Jack told me what happened this morning and I'm so sorry. Once I told the girls, they were very upset, but there was no way to stop the deliveries." She hovers in the doorway, unsure.

"It's fine, Marilyn."

"Jacky's right, I shouldn't have said anything. I am sorry." Wow, coming from her, this is big. Jack really must have told her off.

"Thank you, Marilyn. If you don't mind, I'm rather tired right now."

"Oh, right, of course dear. You rest up. Jacky's making you a lovely dinner. I'll just show myself out, don't you worry."

Despite what she says, worry is something I can't help but do around Marilyn.

21

SOMEHOW I MAKE it through the next week, despite getting little sleep at night. Scared of images that might haunt my dreams, I toss restlessly. During the day, doing my best to keep my nose clean at work, I hole up in my office, leaving it only for meetings or increasingly frequent bathroom visits.

Scott has been trying to show me his nursery designs, but I've managed to put him off. I need to get to my twelve-week ultrasound and then I know I will feel better. Meanwhile, the heat and soggy humidity of Toronto's early summer do little to lift my spirits.

Jack holds my hand as we ride up the elevator together to the clinic, where the Goddess greets us in all of her fertility-ness, pointedly looking at my belly. Jack and I nod nervously back and take seats in the waiting room, still holding hands, clammy with anticipation. Knowing neither one of us will be able to concentrate, we've come empty handed. We hardly speak, just making eye contact every so often.

When my name is called, Dr. Greenberg greets us in the ultrasound room. I climb up on the table and assume my regular stirruped position, while Jack stands by my head, in his usual spot.

"How are you feeling today?" Dr. Greenberg pulls on his gloves as he checks my chart.

"Not bad," I say, although in fact my nerves are churning up waves of nausea.

"Let's take a look." I hold my breath as the probe is inserted and exhale when I instantly hear a heart beating. *Thank you.* Jack sags a bit with relief and grins at me. Dr. Greenberg takes his measurements, nodding and mumbling to himself. As he puts the ultrasound equipment away, he prints out a picture and hands it to Jack.

"Everything looks great. The heart is strong and the size is good. Your baby is doing really well."

"Oh, thank you, Dr. Greenberg. We were so worried after losing the other one." I feel so elated.

"This is it, you guys. You've graduated. Congratulations." He passes Jack a slim file folder.

"Graduated? What do you mean?" Jack looks at me, but I'm just as confused.

"My work here is done. It's time for me to pass you on to either your family doctor or an obstetrician. I used to deliver the babies, but it messed up my schedule and made me horribly late at the clinic," he says chuckling. *Used* to make him late? I can't help wondering how much later he used to be.

"Wow, Doc, thank you. I'm not sure what to say. 'Thanks for getting my wife pregnant' sounds a little weird." Jack smiles.

"Best of luck to you both. Don't forget, you have some frozen embryos for the future." I hug Dr. Greenberg, and he and Jack exchange handshakes. It feels odd, knowing we won't be back here any time soon, after the place monopolized my life for over a year.

At the front desk, Lovely Nurse and Smiley Nurse are standing with the Goddess. "Abby, congratulations, we're so happy for you." They take turns hugging both Jack and me. Jack is grinning like an idiot as he pulls away from the Goddess.

"Thank you so much for all of your help." I'm sniffling, trying to keep myself from crying. At the elevator, I wave. They must love this part of their job. For once, there is no weeping woman in the elevator. Jack grabs me and twirls me around.

"You did it, baby, you did it, we're having a baby! I can't wait. Abbs, this is so awesome, I want to yell from the rooftops."

"Well, we've graduated, so I guess it's okay to tell people now – not that there are many people left who don't already know." I mentally draw up the list of who's in the know: my family, Jules, Scott, Marilyn, the entire golf club. Who's left? As far as I know, Marco and most of my staff are in the dark, and my clients. I have no idea how many others Jack has let the news slip to, but if he's as discreet as his mother, his list is probably pretty long.

"My wife is pregnant!" he screams as we step out on the sidewalk.

"Shush, stop it." I laugh as my husband spins, his hands upraised, looking like Julie freaking Andrews in chinos and a button-down.

"Congratulations!" I flush as strangers yell from across the street and a cab driver honks his horn and waves.

"Now who's crazy?" I say, pushing Jack toward the parking lot before he makes any more of a spectacle of himself, or of me.

∾

"Okay, Mommy, design time." Scott enters my office unannounced and heaves a huge binder onto my desk. Since my pregnancy news has made it mainstream, he's taken to calling me Mommy. Marco tried it once, but it sounded creepy, so I told him off. We seem to have settled into an uneasy truce.

I knew this time was coming. I sigh, close the file I've been working on, and give Scott my undivided attention. The faster we do this, the faster I can get back to reviewing our second-quarter sales numbers.

"Wow me," I say, as Liza Minnelli as I can manage.

"Okay, I have three different visions here. Be honest, be brutal, but remember, this is for baby."

"Right. Let's move this along, Scott. I have a conference call in an hour." I tap my watch.

"Vision one: close your eyes and think about Le Moulin Rouge," he says in a flourish.

"What? The Moulin Rouge is a whorehouse. Next."

"Okay, I did say be brutal, and I know the hormones in pregnant women are off the charts." Scott sounds wounded but continues. "Close your eyes." I sigh loudly. "Just do it. Okay, vision two, think the ocean, and think boats." I nod. This could work. "Think white uniforms, think navy officers, think hunky sailors..." He drifts off into his own fantasy.

"Oh for god's sake, Scott, this is a baby's room, not *your* dream room." I open the file on my desk and shoo him toward the door.

"Wait, one more, give me one more chance," he pleads.

"Fine, but enough screwing around. Last chance." I sit back, arms firmly crossed across my chest.

"Okay, close your—" he starts.

"No way, enough drama."

"Fine, Little Miss Hormones," he says in a prissy voice. I raise an eyebrow and he flips to the back of his binder in a hurry. "Vision three. Think warmth, think safe, think chocolate. Chocolate brown is the main color. All of the furniture should be the shade of espresso. Now, if it's a girl, we introduce pink into the mix, or more of a dusty rose, actually. If it's a boy, we can use either a light blue or a green apple color, and the accent colors will be highlighted in the bedding, drapes, and area rug. So, what do you think?" He looks anxious.

"I love it. It sounds perfect." I beam at Scott, who squirms in his chair in a happy dance.

"I can source everything we need," he continues eagerly.

"Great, just give me a list and the prices. But don't go overboard on the cost," I warn. This baby has already cost us a small fortune. He scampers out of my office, and I lean back in my chair with a hand on my belly. My pants are feeling a bit tight today.

My email chimes. One message is from a client with a last-minute design change, the other a one-liner from Charlie: "Abby, congratulations on your big news. Norman." I smile, send him back a quick thank-you, and head to Production to work through the emergency changes. Everyone in the office smiles as I pass, glad my reign of hormonal terror seems to be over, or at least dulled.

I wake up on my own, no alarm in my ear and no clinic to rush off to. I cherish the mornings now. I touch my belly.

Hello baby, can you feel me? It's so amazing to know you're in there. It's too early to feel you, but I want to believe you can sense me and feel me. I'm going to take very good care of you, I promise. Your daddy and I have worked very hard to bring you to us. All you have to do is be healthy, keep growing, and be safe.

"Hey, you gorgeous pregnant lady." Jack rolls over and smiles at me lazily, his hair dishevelled and his eyes a shimmering blue.

"Hey yourself," I say, and I snuggle into his embrace. Jules has been regaling me with stories of the crazy sex drive in the second trimester, but that hasn't hit me yet. Part of my problem might stem from all the internal ultrasounds, but they are becoming a distant memory.

"What should we do today?" Jack asks.

What bliss. It's Saturday morning and the day stretches, free of plans, in front of us. My stomach growls loudly, making us both laugh. "If I wasn't starving to death, I'd suggest staying right here." The empty beast roars again, making its point.

"Right then, up we get." Jack kisses my forehead and rolls off the bed. He grabs a pair of boxers on his way to the bathroom, and I hear the water turn on and the sounds of him brushing his teeth and spitting in the sink. His toothbrush clinks back into the holder, and he appears in the doorway, drying his face and hands in a towel. I smile at the penguins on his boxers, picturing him proudly wearing goofy Father's Day gifts from our children.

"The short order cook is on duty. What can I create for the hungry woman with child?"

"Pancakes would be divine, but if that's too much trouble, a bagel and cream cheese would do the trick." My stomach voices its emptiness again.

"Pancakes it is, my lady." He bows and goes downstairs as I throw back the covers and head for the bathroom. My morning sickness has abated, but I take a nibble of a granola bar I keep in the top drawer in the bathroom, trying to ward off the growling.

I stare at my reflection in the mirror. It's almost as if there is a slightly different person staring back at me. She's happy; maybe that's what it is. This woman in the mirror feels joy and seems at peace. Glorious smells waft up from the kitchen and my stomach complains loudly, breaking the magic mirror spell. I cinch my robe around my waist and head downstairs. As Jack places a steaming mug of decaffeinated chai tea and a stack of pancakes in front of me, I think to myself that life is pretty darn good.

∽

"MIL on line one," Scott announces, popping his head in my door early Monday morning.

"Ugh, what does she want?" I'm surrounded by project updates that are due to Marco by Friday, but I'm doing my best to have them completed early. Dealing with Marilyn is the last thing I have time for right now. We haven't spoken since the flower-and-balloon incident, but Jack has been giving her daily updates on the pregnancy.

"Probably your firstborn son."

"Don't even go there."

"Relax, I've already worked the Scott charm. She'll be purring like a kitten."

"Hardly," I snort. "A saber-toothed tiger, maybe." I blow my hair from my face and straighten my posture before I pick up the phone. "Hello, Marilyn," I say in a fake cheery voice.

"Abigail, darling, how is my grandchild doing today?"

"I'm feeling quite fine, Marilyn, thank you for asking." I realize I'm just the vessel bringing forth her grandchild. Seriously, who talks like that?

"Oh, right, that's lovely dear." Total disinterest fills her tone, and I grit my teeth.

"Can I help you with something?" I look up when I notice Scott hovering in the doorway with a weird grin on his face, looking as if he's waiting for something.

"Yes, Abigail, you can. I've decided to host your baby shower." I am silent. Scott points an imaginary finger gun at me and shoots. Bugger, he knew this was coming. He darts away as I hurl my stapler at him.

"No need to thank me, dear." She pauses, waiting for my thanks.

"Sorry, Marilyn. You just caught me off guard, that's all. I know my mother and sister are planning something."

"Well, I was just having the loveliest chat with the girls here, and we would all like to celebrate my grandchild. I was telling your wonderful assistant about it, and he's offered to help out. Imagine that." Yes, I can imagine that. I pick up my tape dispenser and hold it ready to throw when Scott reappears to gloat. "We'll host it at the golf club, just some nibbles and a few light cocktails. I won't step on your mother's toes. She can host all your friends and family. This is really just for the girls."

Taking a deep breath, I roll my eyes heavenward. Marilyn has been dying to have grandchildren. Here is her chance to be initiated into the Grandparent Clique at her club. As crazy as she can drive me, she will love this little one so much – too much, likely. But I could never deny her this momentous event. I exhale slowly.

"That sounds lovely, Marilyn. Just let me know when it is. I can't wait." My cheeriness is a bit forced, but she seems to miss it and rings off. I picture my wardrobe and realize I haven't anything suitable for Marilyn's stuffy club that still fits, which means I'll have to go shopping soon. Hearing footsteps at my door, I let the tape dispenser fly without even looking.

"Hi, Abbs, whoa, hey, careful there, someone could get hurt." Jack ducks as the tape dispenser thuds into the wall, where seconds earlier his head was. Scott's reflexes aren't as quick as Jack's. Scott's darn lucky – I would have nailed him.

"Oops, sorry, I thought you were Scott. What are you doing here?"

He bends to pick up my stapler and tape dispenser and returns them to my desk. "What on earth has he done to warrant death by office supplies?" Jack leans over the desk to give me a kiss and then sits down.

"Apparently, he's teamed up with your mother to throw a baby shower at the club for the girls. I will play the role of incubator, and I'm sure Scott will spice it up singing 'Circle of

Life' or some such nonsense. Actually, it could be a hoot. Wanna come?"

"Not on your life. Sorry, you're on your own." Jack smiles but looks distracted.

"Hey, everything okay?"

"Do I need a reason to come see my lovely wife? I thought I'd take my favorite incubator out for a meal. Do you have time for lunch?"

"I'd love to, but I'm seeing a new client for lunch. Can I get a rain check?" I look at Jack and wonder what's going through his mind. He seems unsettled.

"No worries; thought it was worth a try. I'll see you at home tonight." He jumps out of his seat abruptly.

"Jack? What's up? I have a few minutes before I have to go."

"I'm good, don't worry. Knock 'em dead at lunch." He blows me a kiss and leaves. I pack up my stuff and check my makeup. I can't help but feel there was something more to Jack's visit, but before I can analyze it any further, Marco is in my doorway.

"Let's go, Abby, show time." I nod at Marco and head out the door, thoughts of Jack giving way to my sales pitch.

∞

The day of our eighteen-week ultrasound is finally here. Holding hands, Jack and I walk into the waiting room. I adjust my pants, trying to stretch the waistband a little, and sit down beside Jack, who is engrossed in his phone. I really need to think about maternity clothes.

The room feels different from the clinic – no stench of desperation. The woman across from me is beaming, and I recognize a fellow first-time mom in her. She and her husband are leafing through a baby-name book and pointing at various entries, quietly giggling. That reminds me, we should probably think of names.

The other woman in the room looks much more seasoned; actually, she looks totally exhausted. I'm betting she has other children, maybe quite a few. Her husband is dozing off in the corner, perhaps the only sleep he's had in a while.

"Hey," I whisper. "Honey, isn't this exciting?" Jack nods in my direction, but doesn't break contact with his phone. "Jack," I say, slightly louder. He looks up, appearing guilty. "We might find out if it's a boy or a girl today. Isn't that exciting?"

Just then my name is called out by a lab-coated woman, and we gather our things and follow the white coat into the ultrasound room. Without needing any prompting, I climb up on the table and expose my belly. The technician punches information into the computer and readies the gel. As I wince at the gel temperature, she moves the probe across the surface of my abdomen. A grainy picture appears.

"We have some measurements to do first, and you want to know the sex, yes?" She doesn't introduce herself and speaks with a strong accent, Russian or something Eastern European – I'm never very good at placing accents.

"Yes, please," I say and Jack catches my eye. *Chatty sort,* I know he's thinking. She slides the ultrasound around my belly, pausing to enhance images, take measurements, and punch indecipherable things into her keyboard.

"Here is your baby." She points to a full image of our little one, the entire shape. She pauses to take a picture and then takes us on a guided tour, this time talking and pointing out landmarks. We marvel at all ten fingers and toes, watching one hand curl tightly into a fist. We pause at a close-up of the face in profile. Jack grips my hand and I hear him exhale a "wow." Here is our baby. I know we saw it every week in the clinic, but it looked like a peanut most of the time.

White Coat lowers the probe for a close-up view of the nether regions. Just as we are about to zero in on any tell-tale sign, Baby clamps a hand over its "bits." "Must be a boy," I say, laughing. "He's already playing with himself, for goodness' sake. You boys and those things," and I gesture toward Jack's pants. He laughs, but looks sheepish at the same time.

The tech pokes me in the side a few times, and I look at her enquiringly. Just as I'm about to ask her to stop bloody poking me, the baby moves, and without a moment's hesitation, the tech zooms in. "There you go," she says triumphantly.

"What?" Jack says. "I don't see anything."

"There isn't anything. It's a girl, right?" I look to the tech for confirmation and she nods. Tears well up in my eyes and I look back to Jack.

"A girl? I'm having a daughter?" he asks.

"We're having a girl." I'm having a daughter.

We find our way, a little stunned, out to the street moments later. "You okay?" I ask gently.

"I would have been fine either way, but truthfully, I've always wanted a daughter." He smiles at me, his eyes a swimming-pool blue. My breath catches. I know this little girl will have him firmly wrapped around her finger in no time, just as I did with my dad.

We walk slowly to the busy downtown corner. Jack looks east, in the direction of the subway, and I look west, toward my office. We are reluctant to leave each other. He pulls me to him and kisses me gently, but with such passion. I am aware of the blur of people and taxis and streetcars around us, but it feels as if we are inside the calm eye of a tornado. When Jack releases me, we've suddenly caught up with the world around us. Without a word, Jack flags down a cab and opens the door for me. "We're having a girl," he says with a grin. I smile back, and he shuts the door with a thud.

"We're having a girl," I repeat as the driver pulls away from the curb. I watch Jack walk with a spring in his step toward the subway entrance.

"A girl."

22

I'M STILL LYING cocooned in bed when Jack comes home from his Saturday morning run. I put down my copy of *What to Expect When You're Expecting*, which is frankly scaring the pants off me, and pick up *The Girlfriends' Guide to Pregnancy*, which Jules swears by. This one at least makes me laugh, while terrifying me about bowel movements in the delivery room.

"Hey, sleepyhead, are you ever getting up?" Jack asks as he pushes the door open with his foot, while balancing a tray of food, drinks, and the paper. My stomach growls at the sight of food. This kid is hungry.

"Why get up when I get waited on right here?" I offer my lips to be kissed. Jack smells like outdoors, sweat, and a hint of his deodorant when he leans in to kiss me, still balancing our breakfast. He places the tray in the middle of the bed, and we prop ourselves up on the pillows and dig in.

"So," he says through a mouthful of bagel, the cream cheese on his upper lip. "What do you want to do today?"

"Well," I say, pausing to take a sip of tea. "I have a list of things we need to get done."

"Of course you have a list. That's why I love you," he says. I dunk my finger in the cream cheese and poke him in the nose. "But seriously, what's on it?"

"We have to tackle the baby's room. Scott came up with a brilliant color scheme, and now that we know it's a girl, we can get going. Maybe we shouldn't gender-stereotype, but my room was yellow as a kid and I hated it. Plus, I don't want to be like Jules."

"What happened with Jules? I thought I knew all of the famous Jules stories."

"Liam put off painting the nursery till the last minute. When Jules went into labor in the middle of the night, she woke him up and got their things ready. Liam disappeared and Jules assumed he was warming up the car. After ten minutes of waiting in the front hall with her contractions getting stronger, she went looking for him. He was in the baby's room painting as fast as he could. I'm surprised you've never heard that story. He still hasn't lived it down."

"I promise the room will get done in time. What else?" Jack is idly flipping through the paper.

"I have to find maternity clothes. I don't have anything to wear to your mother's shower tomorrow." I want to say "dreaded shower," but I know he'll get defensive. "And, we could maybe make a list of baby names." From the pile of books on the bedside table, I pull out one promising a thousand names for girls and boys. Jack puts down the newspaper and tidies up our leftovers.

"I've actually been giving it some thought already," he says.

"Really?"

"What do you think of Emmaline?" he asks.

"Um, wow, I don't really know what to say," I flail around for words that aren't, "Are we living in Victorian England?"

"You don't like it?" He sounds hurt.

"It's not that I don't like it. It's just, well, a bit too formal for a kid. Plus, there was a girl in my school named Emma and I never liked her. It doesn't really work for me."

"Okay, what about Sandra?" he tries again. Dear lord, it's getting worse.

"Didn't you date a girl named Sandy?" When he doesn't meet my gaze, I continue. "I think we should rule out ex-girlfriends, ex-fiancées, and any other people we didn't like growing up." I desperately want to add "and your mother," but I think he knows not to go there.

"Fine, let's hear your ideas," he pouts.

"What about Alexis?" I watch his reaction. He shrugs non-committedly. Okay, so not a total yes, but it's not a no either. "Or maybe Anna?"

"Those aren't bad," he says, so grudgingly that I can tell we aren't getting very far. I pass him the book.

"You should check out the crazy names in here." I get up to brush my teeth and take a shower while he thumbs through the book.

"Abbs," he yells as I strip off my pajamas and turn sideways to look at my blossoming belly and backside in the mirror. Even at twenty-five weeks, I'm still in the "gee, she's put on some weight" stage, not the obvious-pregnancy stage. I realize I'm probably going to be one of those women who expand everywhere, not the ones with a beach ball out front who don't even look pregnant from the back. Sigh.

"What?" I yell back, still analyzing the changes to my body. Jack appears in the doorway and whistles at my nakedness.

"Moonjava's in here. It's a real name."

෴

A few hours later, I'm in the change room of a maternity store with my third round of wardrobe basics – jeans, dress pants, one skirt, three blouses, three casual tops, and a wrap dress – to try on. The patient sales assistant must be well-versed in the hormones of pregnant women. I've attempted multiple pairs of pants, but just can't seem to find a comfortable waistband. All of the pants seem to cut in at the bladder and make me want to pee. I'm hot and sweaty from struggling into and out of clothes, and close to tears. Two other women have come and gone with new purchases in the time it's taken me to secure even one pair of pants. One of them looked like a size zero. I hate her.

"Okay, how about we try the larger belly band?" my assistant asks in a voice that I'm sure could be used to relax a charging rhino. I nod, blinking rapidly. *Get a grip, Abby.*

Twenty minutes later, I carry my meagre pile of clothes to the cash, cringing at the total price. I could probably do with more pieces for work, but at this rate I'll be well-dressed in the poor house. Oh well, Scott is just going to have to get over my repetitive wardrobe, unless he wants to start a collection for me.

My phone rings as I leave the store, and I see Scott's number on my display. His spidey senses must be in overdrive. "Abby, I'm just calling to remind you about the shower tomorrow."

"I remember. You don't have to worry."

"You're not going to skip it, are you?" He sounds worried. I wonder if Marilyn has asked him to check on me.

"Relax, I'll be there." There are a thousand things I'd rather do, but I know where I'll be tomorrow at two o'clock.

"Don't forget, you need to wear–" he starts, but I cut him off.

"Geez, Scott, I'm not a child. I just finished shopping and I have plenty to wear. I'll see you tomorrow," I say firmly, and hang up the phone.

I pick up lunch and add an apple fritter to my order on my way home. I might as well test out my new elastic-waistband pants. "Jack, are you here? I brought food," I call as I dump my clothing bags and purse on the floor and head for the kitchen.

"I'll be right down," he yells from upstairs. I busy myself with organizing our sandwiches on plates and pour a glass of milk for me and water for Jack. "It looks like shopping was a success. Are we broke?" he asks, sauntering into the kitchen.

"Almost. I didn't go crazy, just a few basics. What have you been up to?" I spear a piece of pickle while Jack tucks in to his pastrami on rye with extra mustard.

"I looked over Scott's designs and thought I'd get started on the baby's room. I don't want to be accused of being Liam," he says between mouthfuls.

"Really? Can I see?" I ask excitedly.

"Actually, I wanted to surprise you. Do you think you can wait a few weeks?" I want to shout no, but I can see the eagerness in his eyes.

"I'm sure it will be wonderful. I won't peek."

"Promise?"

"I promise." I cross my heart. "I love you, Jack. You're going to be an awesome dad."

23

I PULL INTO the visitor parking lot of Marilyn's stuffy golf club, turn off the engine, and rest my forehead on the steering wheel with my eyes closed. I was half praying for a minor traffic violation to delay me on the drive over, but no such luck. I guess I should be thankful to be safe, but that also means I'm here. A knock on my window startles me, and I look out to see Scott. Even before I open the door, I can see him pointing at his watch and tsk-tsking my tardiness. It's true I took the longest route possible from our house to the club, figuring that if an accident didn't help me out, maybe arriving a few minutes late would cut down the pain of the party. Now I resign myself to my fate and get out of the car.

"You're late."

"I know, traffic was awful," I say, practicing my excuse.

"Mm-hmm." Scott looks me up and down with his critical eye. "That's what you're wearing?" From his tone, you would think I'd showed up in a bikini or ripped jeans.

"What? There's nothing wrong with what I'm wearing." I sound defensive as I push past him. I look fine in a flowered maternity skirt and a soft blue blouse. The blue brings out my eyes, and I'm having a decent hair day.

"Abby, you're having a girl. The whole theme is pink. You were supposed to wear pink today." I realize Scott is dressed in pink from head to toe.

"How was I supposed to know?"

"It was on the invitation, you ninny. Didn't you read it?"

Crap, I definitely hadn't read the invitation. It's posted on the fridge, and I marked August thirtieth in my calendar, but I did not read it. I can feel a trickle of sweat at my hairline. The party hasn't even begun and already I've messed up.

"Scott, she's going to kill me. What am I going to do?" I can feel panic rising.

"Relax, Abby. I always have your back, even your ever expanding backside." Right when I want to love him, he gets snarky, but I decide to accept his help. Scott rummages through his messenger bag and in a flourish pulls out something very pink. "Here, put this on." I drape what looks like a pashmina over my shoulders and wait for his approval. "You look like a beggar woman. Turn around." He speaks to me as if I'm a slow child. I turn around, and Scott crisscrosses the pink shroud around my body and ties it neatly at the back. He stands back and tilts his head to the side to review his work. "It will have to do. Let's go."

He strides toward the front door of the club and snaps his fingers for me to follow. I'm not sure when the balance of power shifted, but I'm not liking this new arrangement. Still, I find myself hurrying to catch up. As we reach the massive carved front door, I catch my reflection in the glass panels that flank it. I look great. The new makeshift pink top works with the skirt, and the soft blue blouse blends into the background. I mouth a thank-you to Scott, and he nods as the doors open. I am anxious, but at least this minor disaster is averted.

Scott offers me his arm, and we walk through the grand foyer into the Ladies' Tea Room. This club is so old that for years women weren't allowed until, in a bow to the changing status of women, the club converted the servants' break room into the Ladies' Tea Room a few decades ago. Today, women are allowed in all areas of the club, but the two main rooms are still called the Men's Lounge and the Ladies' Tea Room.

As we enter, I pause, stunned by what I see. The room, normally decorated in pale yellow and green, is stunningly pink. There are pink balloons and streamers, pink pillows have been added to the couches and chairs, and each guest is dressed in pink, including pink feather boas. Most of the women have a pink cocktail in one hand and a pink napkin in the other. I spot pink hors d'oeuvres – I'm guessing salmon mousse and smoked salmon.

"Holy gender-stereotyping–" I start, squeezing Scott's arm.

"Abigail, darling, you're here." Marilyn breaks through the crowd to my side, and grips me in a tight embrace, which is totally out of character for her, but probably true to the doting grandmother-to-be persona she projects to her friends. *Shame on you, Abby,* I think. Marilyn has obviously gone to a lot of trouble and expense to make this party special. Granted, it's more about her, but outwardly it is for me. I am still chastising myself as Marilyn pulls me around the room introducing me to her golf cronies.

I am feeling much more warmly toward my mother-in-law when a stunning young woman approaches. She has a baby strapped to her in one of those complicated-looking carriers and she offers her hand to me. I feel Scott stiffen slightly beside me.

"Abigail, I don't think you've ever met Sarah before. Sarah, this is Abigail."

Sarah? She invited *Sarah* to my baby shower? The room spins a little and Scott grips my elbow.

"Abby, it's so lovely to meet you. I've heard so much about you." Her voice is sickly sweet and I feel nauseous, as if I've gorged on too many candies. I stare at her dumbly until Scott nudges me from behind.

"Um, Sarah," my voice comes back to me. "Wow, I didn't expect to see you here." I can't come up with anything else to say. I keep thinking, *You've heard so much about me? Like what?*

"Sarah had a baby six months ago, Abigail. You could learn a lot from her." Marilyn's voice sounds genuine, but I'm sure she's relishing this moment.

"Oh, right, baby, um, congratulations." I was pretty sure this party was going to be painful; I just had no idea it would be excruciating. Conversation around us picks up, and Scott steers me to the drinks table and away from Marilyn and Sarah.

"Did you know she was here?" I hiss at Scott as he hands me a crystal champagne flute of pink punch. What I wouldn't give for something alcoholic right now – damn medical community and its studies.

"I'm sorry, Abby, I could tell Marilyn had something up her sleeve, but I didn't get to see the guest list." Scott looks upset. He can be a real drama queen sometimes, but I know he's got my back.

"Jack said she was pretty..." I can't help but speak out loud. He did not do her justice. She has raven-black hair, swept tidily up on top of her head, tendrils framing her almond-shaped face. Her eyes are dark and her lips perfectly plump. Having recently had a baby, I'm sure she has extra weight on her, but she looks like a size two. Instead of feeling lovely and pregnant, I find myself feeling large and ungainly compared to her.

I watch as Marilyn holds court in the middle of the room, Sarah at her side. Sarah laughs dutifully at Marilyn's jokes, and on every third sentence, Marilyn reaches out and touches Sarah's arm or strokes her hair. Sarah regales the women with stories of her pregnancy and the birth and how she wore her pre-pregnancy skinny jeans home from the hospital – what a bitch. As I watch, the baby is passed around and everyone takes a turn holding the child. I spend the next hour sitting on the sidelines of my own party. Thankfully Scott stays faithfully beside me. Neither one of us speaks as we watch the daughter-in-law Marilyn always wanted.

"Oh, Sarah, you are lucky. It is wonderful to have a son," Marilyn crows. "Your parents must be thrilled. I've always hoped for a grandson."

I can't seem to win today. Now I'm a disappointment because I'm having a girl. I get up from the couch and walk to the bathroom without looking back. I can't bear to see Marilyn and Sarah together any longer and I know I will cry if I look at Scott.

I lock myself in a stall, put the lid down, sit heavily, and sigh. *You are not allowed to cry, Abby. Do not give them the satisfaction.* I close my eyes and think happy thoughts of Jack and me walking along the Danforth, pushing our beautiful baby girl in a Bugaboo stroller. I jump forward and see Jack pushing her on a swing and imagine the cries of "Higher Daddy, push me higher." But my happy place is interrupted when I hear someone enter the bathroom. Taking one more deep breath, I stand, flush the toilet – even though I didn't use it – and open the door. With the way my luck has been going all day, I know without a doubt that Sarah will be standing there.

And she is.

"Hi, Abby. Is everything okay?" Her voice drips with honey. I never have liked honey.

"I'm fine, Sarah, thank you for asking." I move to the sink and wash my hands. She makes to enter the stall, but pauses and looks back at me.

"You know, if you ever need anything, or want to talk…" she stops.

"Sure, great, thanks." *Fat chance, lady*, I think, and I clamp my hand over my mouth to make sure I don't say it out loud. I pinch my cheeks to get some color back and straighten my shoulders. *You can do this, Abby.*

Sixty very long minutes later, I am allowed to leave. Scott packs the presents into my car, and I go through the motions of thanking everyone and saying good-bye. I will say this about Marilyn and her golf gals: they are very generous. I have more knitted blankets and booties than I know what to do with, and no fewer than three shirts that say "I love Grandma," which I will have to ensure the baby pukes on.

I park in front of our house. Jack will want to hear all about the party, and I'm not sure what to tell him. I pull out my phone and compose an email to Jules, giving her the true version of the party and how awful it was. I put all of my negative thoughts and feelings in the email, hoping to purge them from my mind before I face Jack, and hit send. Finally, I grip the steering wheel tightly and give myself the pep talk I know Jules will send me later.

Okay, Abby, that totally sucked. Marilyn broadsided you and left you for roadkill. You met the famous Sarah. You're not entirely sure why Jack is with you and not her, but the fact of the matter is that he *is* with you. None of this other crap matters. You are having a baby. You and Jack are having a baby. Deep breath. Put a smile on your face, and when Jack asks, focus on the positives. You can do this.

"I'm home," I announce gaily as I unlock the front door. Jack comes down the stairs looking worried. "Your mom sure knows how to throw a party," I add, knowing my voice sounds a little high, reminiscent of Cheery Nurse.

"Are you okay, Abbs? Mom called after you left and said you weren't quite yourself."

"Really, your mom said that? Did she maybe mention that she invited Sarah?" Jack's shocked expression gives me my answer.

"No, she must have forgotten. Are you okay? Did she say anything to you?" He shoves his hands in his pockets and looks at the floor.

"I'm fine, Jack. I wasn't quite myself because your mother shanghaied me with Sarah and her baby. The party was a huge success from your mother's perspective and about as much fun as a root canal from mine."

"I'm sorry, Abbs. I'll talk to her, okay? Do you want me to unload the car? Did we get some good stuff for the baby?" I swear I am watching a cartoon character pick up the corner of a rug and sweep everything underneath. He rubs his hands together and bounds outside to get the gifts.

The tears I have managed to hold back all afternoon spring forth. I drop my coat and purse at the foot of the stairs and head upstairs, kick off my shoes, crawl into bed, and pull the duvet over my head.

24

"HAVE YOU HEARD?" Scott hisses late on Monday, and shuts my office door behind him with a thump, oblivious to the fact that I'm on the phone. Raising a hand, I narrow my eyes at him and continue my gory description of the baby shower to Jules. Scott rushes over to my desk and grabs the phone from my hand.

"Hey–"

"Jules, honey, hi. Look, Abby can't talk right now, but she'll call you back with huge news soon. Kisses." He hangs up and turns my chair toward him, gripping the armrests.

"What the hell was that? You can't interrupt my calls. What if that wasn't Jules?"

"Pu-lease, Abby, I checked before I came in. But pay attention, this is big."

"I don't care what's big. Wait, you checked? Are you listening to my phone calls?"

"What? Um, of course not." He waves off my inquiry and moves on, but I will definitely circle back later. "Anyway, apparently our little friend Linda has been a very naughty girl." Scott's eyes gleam with mischief. My interest piques.

"What sort of naughty are we talking about?"

"Well, as I understand it, she was asked to leave her last job. Apparently she was dipping into the company's coffers."

"No, that's how she affords her clothes? She didn't jump ship for us?" I grip his arms tightly and feel the baby kick, sharing my excitement.

"Hardly," he snorts. "More like she had to walk the plank. They wanted to keep it quiet."

"Of course, they wouldn't want their clients to find out and panic. Where did you hear this?" Scott looks guilty. "Scott?"

"My source is highly confidential."

"Give me a break. Have you been eavesdropping on Marco's calls too?" Before I can administer any form of torture to break him, my phone rings. We both check call display and see Marco's extension.

"Shh, you didn't hear it from me," Scott whispers at me, and darts from my clutches. I rub my belly for luck and pick up the phone.

"Hi, Marco."

"My office, now. Um, please."

∽

"You wanted to see me?" I ask with a hint of a smile.

Marco is pacing, his hair in disarray from running his hands through it. He's probably been trying to pull it out. He waves me in and I close the door behind me. I've never seen Marco this unnerved. His usual suave swagger has been replaced by muttering under his breath and jerky movements. He drops into his chair, grips the desk, and pulls himself toward me as I move back involuntarily. "We've got big problems, Abby, really huge problems. How were we to know?"

He's babbling, but doesn't seem to notice. Thank goodness Scott tipped me off. "She came so highly recommended. Well, of course they recommended her, just to get her out the door. This could ruin us," he wails.

"Marco," I say sharply. He ceases his blathering, and I watch him attempt to focus on me. "I'm sure it, whatever it is, can be solved."

"You don't understand. We hired her and touted her as the next partner here." I wince at the confirmation that I was officially out of the running. Marco is oblivious to my discomfort. "She embezzled from her last company, and who knows how much damage she's done here?" He collapses on the desk, his head in his arms.

What's that expression? When a door closes, a window opens? I straighten, knowing my window is creaking open, and arrange my features to show surprise. "She embezzled? Are you sure?"

"I was trying to land a new client, who turns out to be a former client of the Cooper Group. Once they heard Linda was on our team, they didn't want to hire us. When pushed for a reason, they opened up and told me the whole story. She fudged budget numbers, submitted bogus expenses, and double-billed the clients. Her old company wanted her gone with little attention, so they made her seem like a hot commodity." Marco sighs deeply, head still on his desk.

"Okay, here's what we need to do." No use all of us falling to pieces – I have a baby to support, and this company going under will not help. "Marco!" I shout to get his attention. "First, we need to fire Linda – *immediately*. Second, Accounting needs to comb our books and all of her expenses. Ditto with any budgets and invoices she's submitted to her clients. She wasn't here very long; let's hope she was waiting until she'd been here longer, or–" I pause, swallowing before I say it aloud, "until you made her partner."

Marco's head snaps up and he looks away quickly. Good.

"If she has cooked the books, you have to call the police," I continue. Panic crosses Marco's face. "You and Char– I mean, Norman need to meet with each of her clients and talk this out. We should offer to keep their accounts, but maybe give them a discount to overcome any discomfort. I won't lie; we might lose a couple, but maybe we can stop a major hemorrhage. I can talk to our PR people and come up with some solid talking points if the media get involved."

Marco goes green at my mention of media. I push out of my seat and kick his garbage can around the desk to him, just in case.

"I'll pull the account team and Production together first thing tomorrow, and we'll see if we can figure out the status of her projects," I continue, ticking off the actions needed. Marco's color is slowly improving, and he nods.

"Thank you, Abby. You're right. I knew we could count on you."

"You're damn right you can count on me, Marco. But I'll be blunt. This time it comes at a price. I will clean up this mess as best I can, and when I do…" I pause, glaring at him, daring him to deny me.

Marco nods once, but I know we understand each other. I leave him, head on his desk, and go in search of Scott, who materializes in my office as I heft myself into my chair.

"What's the plan, boss?"

"We are in damage-control mode. I'm going to need everything Linda was working on, now. I want to familiarize myself with her projects. Can you set up a meeting first thing tomorrow with Accounting, the account team on her projects, and then our PR company? Let's just cross our fingers she hadn't started to supplement her income here yet. We might just survive this." I lean back and rub my temple, which is starting to throb.

"You okay?" Scott asks as he moves to rub my shoulders.

"Thanks, Scott. I was hoping to get out of here in good time, but that won't happen." I straighten up, stretching my neck. "Okay, let's get started on the files. The sooner we get through them, the sooner we know what we're dealing with. Let me send a quick note to Jack and tell him I'll be late, if you can round up what we need." Scott kisses my head and leaves as I reach for the phone.

"Jack, I'll be late tonight. Something major has come up. Call me when you get a chance," I tell his voice mail.

Clearing my desk to make room for Linda's files, I pause. Here I am, helping the very people who were planning to pass me over for promotion. Truth is, I've put so much time into this company and have such great clients, I would hate for anything bad to happen. I pull out a take-out menu as Scott reappears with a stack of files.

"Chinese or Thai? We're going to be here for a while."

25

"JULES, YOU WOULDN'T believe the people in our group."
Easing onto a plastic folding chair I hope will hold up under
my weight, I glance around to make sure the weirdos are not
within earshot. Jack has disappeared with the promise of fresh
pastries. We are on a break from our intensive prenatal-class
weekend. The hospital gave us a choice to come once a week
for five weeks or to an intensive weekend-long class. Five
weeks seemed like an eternity, and so here I sit, kicking myself
for losing a weekend to a bunch of pregnant strangers,
especially in the wake of my baby shower disaster. Two
weekends down the drain.

"I remember our class being rather odd, too," says Jules
sympathetically in my ear.

"Yeah, but you're normal and we're normal – so where are
the other normal people who are having kids?" I'm exhausted
from the long days at the office dealing with "Linda-gate," as
Scott has coined it, and uncomfortable as hell in my seventh
month, knowing I have another eight weeks to go.

"It can't be that bad."

"Oh yeah? One guy has the worst comb-over in the world.
Seriously, who at the age of thirty-five has a comb-over? And
his wife doesn't speak a word of English. Jack is sure she's a
mail-order bride. It's a bit freaky, I have to say. Two of the
couples have rhyming names; that's almost as bad as
matching tracksuits."

"Really? What are their names?" I can hear Jules's interest now.

"Carrie and Jerry are one, and Simone and Jerome are the other." I giggle just saying them out loud.

"Not much rhymes with Jules, so I never had that problem."

"Jack is the oldest and I think I'm next, after Mr. Comb-Over. Everyone else looks about twenty. I thought the average age of mothers was on the rise? I know I sound totally judgmental and catty, but we have nothing in common with anyone."

"Ha, Liam and I felt ancient compared to our group too. Did you watch the movie of the birth yet? As I recall, we lost a few with that one."

"Yep, Carrie left the room in tears and three of the guys looked pretty green. I don't get it; how did they think the baby was coming out? Jack looked a little stunned, but at least he didn't throw up or anything." Wincing, I move to find a slightly more comfortable position, which is proving difficult these days. "Ouch." I draw in a quick breath as the baby nails me in the ribs.

"You okay?"

"Yep. This little girl is going to kick her way out, I'm sure of it."

"Did you do the breathing exercises yet?"

"No, that's after the break," I say, checking my watch and wondering where Jack has gotten to.

"Every time we did the relaxation breathing, Liam fell asleep. I could have killed him. Thankfully he stayed awake for the actual birth. But just to change the subject, how much damage did Linda do?"

"We got really lucky. I've spent hours with her project files, and Accounting has gone over her invoicing and expenses with a fine-tooth comb. She was probably waiting for a little more time to pass. Whatever the reason, we seem to be okay. Marco confronted her, and she quit before he could fire her. All I care about is that she's gone. The atmosphere at work feels better; lighter somehow."

Jules and I chat for a few more minutes, and then I hang up as I see Jack reappear with two cups and a bag of what I hope is something yummy. Propelling myself off the chair, I shuffle down the hall toward him.

"Nice waddle," he says with a smile.

"Shut up. You walk around with a watermelon about to drop from between your legs and see how graceful you are. What heavenly delight did you bring me?"

"Was that Jules?" Jack gestures toward my phone as he hands over his greasy paper bag of goodies. I peer inside and smile – apple fritter, my favorite. I love my husband. I nod and take a bite. It's almost orgasmic – and it's been a long time since I've had one of those too. This apple fritter might actually be better.

"Did you give her the lowdown?" he asks. I nod again, too busy letting the cinnamon glaze melt on my tongue. "You told her about the Rhymers? The Mail-Order Couple?" I keep nodding as our instructor waves us back into class. "Two more hours, Abbs; we're almost done," Jack whispers, and he hands me another greasy bag from under his coat. Another apple fritter – he walks me through the door, with his hand resting on the small of my back. This is true love.

☙

Jack drives us home from the marathon prenatal class with me lying back in the passenger seat.

"What about Marigold?" I ask, breaking the silence.

"You want to name our kid after a flower?" Jack sounds happy to veto one of my ideas.

"So, I guess that means Lily is out too?"

Jack doesn't answer, but gives me a sideways glance.

"Okay, do you like Archer?"

"Seriously? Do we call her Bow or Arrow as a nickname? You've been spending too much time with your mom and sister. I think the hippie gene is rubbing off."

"Okay, okay, I'm just brainstorming here. Do you have any other ideas?"

"I kind of like Sally," he says quietly.

"That's not bad."

"You like it?" He sounds surprised and takes his eyes off the road to read my expression.

"It's cute. I'm not saying it's the *one*, but it's definitely an option." I smile warmly, but thankful we are having a girl. I can only imagine the pressure Jack would feel from his mother to name a boy Jacky Junior.

26

OKAY, ABIGAIL, I think, *almost quitting time.* Just finish this last briefing and you can go home. I take my hands off the keyboard to rub the small of my back and tilt my head slowly from side to side, stretching and willing the muscle strains to melt away.

"Am I interrupting?" asks Charlie, entering my office regardless of my answer.

"Hi, Norman; no, come in. I'm just finishing up a brief."

"You look great, Abby. You really glow. How much longer now?"

"I'm eight months. You know, the light at the end of the tunnel and all that." I know I'm not glowing – hot-flashing and sweating, yes; glowing, no.

"Look, I just want to say thank you. Marco and I didn't entirely see eye to eye on the choice of Linda or her future here. But, you jumped in to help, and frankly, we wouldn't have bounced back so quickly without you. I know I'm pretty hands-off with the daily running of this agency, and that probably contributed to this last problem, but I've been that way partly because of you."

"Me?"

"You keep this place running. I know I'm telling you this just before you go on maternity leave, but I want you to understand your value. Over the next year or so, I'm planning on making some changes, which involves a more active role for me and branching out in a new direction for the company. There's not much I can do about Marco; he is effective in his own way." I chortle, and Charlie smiles knowingly. "And you have proven yourself more than capable of handling him and keeping him in line." A thank-you, I think; an award or danger pay would be more appropriate, but I'll take the praise. "Anyway, this is the long way of getting to my point. It's something I should have done a while ago, but I want to make sure it gets done now, before, you know." He points at my belly.

"Make sure what gets done?" I ask.

"I want to make you a partner," he says. My hand flies up to my mouth.

"Charlie– I mean, Norman, really? You mean it?" I feel giddy. *Abigail Nichols, Partner.* I like the sound of that.

"Yes, of course I mean it. I also meant what I just said, that this place wouldn't run without you. You've worked really hard, and you deserve it. And given that situation with Linda, you have more than proven your loyalty. I have the papers drawn up for you to look over. We need to find a replacement for you while you're away, so it would also be a good time to audition someone for your spot permanently. What do you think? Are you interested?"

"Oh yes, of course I'm interested. Thank you, Norman. Really, I mean it, thank you. I'll go over the papers and get back to you right away." I am breathless.

"Take your time, Abby." He smiles and places a file on my desk, tapping it once. As he leaves, he pauses in the doorway. "Who's Charlie?" I make a small squeak and try to meet his eye.

"No one. Sorry, I don't know where my head was."

When he leaves, I sit back in my chair, thoughts of finishing my brief totally gone. I am a partner in this firm and will be a mother in a few weeks, and I can't help feeling that finally, everything is going my way. I pack up my desk, piling up the unfinished work for tackling first thing in the morning. I should take it home, but who am I kidding? I plan on celebrating tonight, not working. I can't wait to tell Jack.

~⑨

"Jack? I'm home," I yell, lumbering through the doorway. I don't care how many times he tells me I'm beautiful, I feel like a marshmallow. No, wait, those are light and fluffy, and I definitely don't feel light and fluffy. More like pudding, thick and slow moving.

"Hey, Abbs, I'm just changing." I drop my keys and purse and make an effort to hang up my coat. I can hear the couch calling my name as my back and feet scream at me to relax.

"My feet are killing me. This pregnancy gig is hard on the body," I complain half-heartedly as Jack appears on the stairs.

"You look gorgeous to me, babe. How was your day?" he asks as he sits beside me, places my feet in his lap, and rubs them.

"I had a great day, but it just got much better," I say moaning as he kneads the soles of my feet. Is there anything in this world more heavenly than a foot rub?

"So, tell me."

"Charlie made me a partner."

"Abbs, that's awesome news! Congratulations. This is huge." He pushes my legs to the floor and grips me in a hug, as best as he can around my belly. We both jump back when we feel the baby kick. "Oops, I think we're crowding the little one," he says, grinning and rubbing my belly. "This calls for a little celebration. A sip of champagne I'm sure is allowed at a time like this." He dashes off to the kitchen for bubbly and glasses. He's right; surely one sip can't hurt. Jack's phone vibrates on the couch – it must have slipped out of his pocket.

"Hon, your phone is buzzing," I call.

"My hands are full. It's probably Leon at the office. Check it, will you?"

I can hear Jack rummaging in the kitchen. I click on his emails and see two new ones. Neither is from Leon. One is from Marilyn and the other is from Sarah. Well, of course curiosity gets the better of me, and I find myself opening Sarah's first.

Jack, I'm fine, thanks for asking. The baby is growing quickly; you'll soon find out how fast the time flies. Ken travels a lot, so I find it tough to be on my own so much. Even when he is here, it feels pretty lonely. Lord knows how our mothers did it alone! If you have some time, I'd love to catch up over coffee or a drink again soon. Sarah

Again? *Again?* They had coffee or a drink together *already?* My mind is spinning. Jack never mentioned anything to me about running into Sarah, let alone sharing a beverage. I feel a little queasy. Even though I know I shouldn't, I click on Marilyn's email. This one appears to have gone back and forth multiple times. Scrolling down, I catch snatches of what appears to be an argument. Again, something Jack hasn't mentioned to me.

We need to discuss the baby's name further. Jacqueline would be lovely, to play off your name.

Oh no, that queasy feeling is coming on strong. She's trying to make another Jacky Junior. Over my dead body.

I read on.

Mom, thank you for your input, but we have names well in hand. I don't think Jacqueline will fly.

You tell her, Jack. I look toward the kitchen, but there is still no sign of Jack. I keep reading the back-and-forth fighting that continues, until I come to the last entry from Marilyn.

Jack, at the very least, I expect Marilyn to be the middle name. It is my right. After all, I did pay for that child.

It feels as if the air is sucked out of the room. Oh my god, I can't breathe. I do my best to put my head between my knees, but that position is next to impossible with my protruding belly. I can feel myself begin to hyperventilate. She *paid* for the baby? *That's* where the IVF money came from? She owns my baby and she's never going to let us forget it. I can't breathe. *Why is there no air?*

"Abby, what the hell?" Jack comes through the kitchen door and sees me in distress. He dumps the celebratory tray of food and drink onto the dining room table, and I hear the sound of glass breaking. "Shit," he mutters and runs to my side. "What's wrong?" I can feel air slowly reach my lungs, but I can't trust myself to speak. Thrusting the phone at him, I glare in his direction. Taken aback by my face, he looks down at his phone and pales.

"Are you kidding me? When were you going to tell me?" I screech. "I'm not even sure where to begin. Oh let's see, my husband has been sneaking around with 'The One That Got Away.'" I make quotation marks with my hands in the air for emphasis. "And they are going to schedule another illicit date."

"No, Abby, it's not like that." Jack tries to defend himself, but I've only just begun.

"Oh please, that chick wants you back, and she's been working on it with your mother for the last year. But really, if that wasn't bad enough, let's talk about that lovely mother of yours. She wants the naming rights to her grandchild. *Why*, one might ask? Because she owns it! You let your mother pay for our child. Are you out of your mind? On what planet might that be a good idea?"

"Hey, your family offered to help us out too, don't forget."

"They offered us a loan, Jack. They weren't expecting to name the baby. If I had known you were taking money from your mother, there is *no way* I would have agreed. This—" I gesture at his phone. "This is exactly the reason. Your mother would never let us, or this poor child, ever forget it. We would spend the rest of her life thanking her and bending to her. Don't shake your head at me. This just proves it. The kid isn't even here yet and she's already staked her claim." I am up now and stomping from end to end in the living room, fists clenched at my sides.

"Just calm down, Abby," he starts.

"Don't 'just calm down Abby' me. You know what the worst part of this is? You lied to me. You've been hiding things from me and lying to my face."

"Abby!" Jack shouts. "I didn't take Mom's money. Yes, she gave it to me, but I didn't take it."

"Well, your mother is pretty sure she owns our child. Explain that," I yell back.

"I didn't cash the check. I told her we didn't need it. She insisted. I'm sorry. I'll give it back, I'll rip it up."

"So where did the money come from?" I was so busy trying everything to get pregnant, I let Jack take over as the money guy and was for once pretty clueless about our financial situation.

"I had enough left over from the bonus. I saved a little on the side and managed to scrape enough together. Dr. Greenberg let me pay in instalments." Again, this is news to me.

"Jack, I want to believe you, I really do." I take a deep breath. "What about Sarah?"

Jack runs his hands through his hair and looks at the floor. "Look, she's been having a rough time, that's all."

"What? *She's* been having a rough time? I'm sorry, what we've been going through for the last two years, has that been a cakewalk? Poor Sarah, she can't get what she wants – and how pathetic of you to fall for it. I am *your* wife. I am carrying *your* child. Remember, the child we tried so hard to have together."

"I remember, Abby. It wasn't all roses for me either, you know."

"Oh right, because it was so difficult and painful to spluge in a cup. I'm sorry; I forgot how much you suffered!" I scream.

"That's not fair."

"Don't even get me started on what's fair. This isn't fair. All of this: your mother owning our child, meeting your ex on the sly, and me, feeling big as a house and being lied to by my husband."

"I'm done. I can't take this anymore." Jack grabs for his coat.

"Are you kidding me? You can't *take* this anymore? What can't you take: your wife? Your baby? Are you telling me you don't want this? What about all of the shit I have to put up with?" I throw my arms up.

Jack snatches his keys from the table and storms out, slamming the door hard enough to turn the artwork askew. I collapse on the couch in shock. When everything was going so well, how did it go so badly so quickly?

∽

"Abby, is that you? Are you okay? Did something happen to the baby?" Jules's concern is palpable, but hard to hear over my sobs.

"He, he, he left," I stutter.

"What? Who left? What the hell is going on?"

"Jack. We got in a big fight and he left. He just walked out. Oh, Jules, what am I going to do?" I wail, clutching the phone in one hand and holding my huge belly with the other.

"Abby, tell me what happened." I sniffle and rub my runny nose on my sleeve and try to explain the last two hours.

"Everything was fine, you know. We were about to celebrate. Oh, I didn't tell you, I made partner."

"Honey, that's terrific, congratulations. That is huge news," Jules interrupts my story. Somehow her enthusiasm over my promotion brings fresh tears to my eyes.

"Anyway, I was relaxing and Jack was getting some champagne and his phone buzzed. He was waiting for an important work email, so he asked me to read it to him." I sniffle a little more, the torrent of tears at bay for the time being. "There were two emails waiting, one from Marilyn and one from Sarah." I hear Jules's quick intake of breath.

"What did they say?"

"Sarah's was mostly news about her life and the new kid. You didn't have to read between the lines to see she wants Jack back. She complains about her husband and then asks if she and Jack can meet. *Again*." I pause before "again," to add the emphasis.

"No. Oh, Jack, you idiot," is Jules's reply.

"That's not the worst part, although it's pretty bad. Marilyn's is worse. She is insisting on naming the baby."

"What? How is that possible? Don't tell me Jack agreed?" Jules sounds shocked.

"No, he was fighting her on it. But her last line was how it's her right, considering she's the one who paid for the baby," I cry.

"Oh shit. Jack never said anything to you?"

"I didn't even know she'd offered us money. Jules, I would never have taken it, knowing Marilyn would hold it over us and the baby forever."

"What did Jack say?"

"Oh, you know, he says his mom lent him the money, but he never cashed the check. He had a little left over from his bonus and he managed to scrape the rest together. It all just kind of blew up from there, with his mom, and Sarah. I don't think I've ever seen him so mad. He yelled that he can't take it anymore and stormed out. Oh, Jules, I'm so alone."

"Abby, honey, listen to me. You are not alone. I'm here, everyone is here for you. Get yourself up, pack a bag, and go check into a hotel for the night. Order room service, watch a movie, have a small glass of wine, just relax. I promise you, things will look better in the morning." Jules, the voice of reason again. What I wouldn't give for a hug from her right now.

I hang up and immediately call for a cab. I grab a few things and shove them in a bag, still sobbing, and blow my nose and grab my coat. The taxi is parked out front as I pause at the door and look around.

The house feels empty and sad. In the cab I mumble the name of a downtown hotel, and the cabby sets off. My neighborhood is a blur as we leave, not because we're going fast, but because the tears make it hazy. Before I know it, we pull up in front of the hotel.

"Um, miss. We're here," says my cabbie. He's probably had his fair share of weeping women and crazy people in his taxi before. I'm sure he's trying to figure out if I'm one of the certifiable ones. I nod to him and look up at the hotel, and it suddenly hits me: I don't want to be alone. But where can I go? If only Jules lived closer ... I take a second to consider going out to the airport and flying to see her. That would be the perfect solution, except I have no idea if there are any flights out tonight, I'm hugely pregnant and probably wouldn't be allowed to fly, and I'm an emotional disaster. The cabbie is still looking expectantly at me. I surprise myself when I finally answer.

"Sorry, I've changed my mind. We'll go to this address." I give him a location and sit back in stunned silence.

27

CASSIE ANSWERS THE door, and I can't tell if she's more surprised to see me on her steps, unannounced, or by the crying and wrecked face I must present.

"Abby, what's wrong?" she asks, leaving me on the doorstep. I motion with my hand at the door. "Oh sorry, come in." She ushers me inside, helping me out of my coat, which doesn't zip up over my swelling belly. I drop my purse and collapse on Cassie's couch.

"I'm sorry, Cassie. I know I should have called. I just didn't have anywhere else to go." Fresh tears spring up. Roger appears in the hallway, MJ attached to his bare chest. He nods in my direction and dodges into the kitchen to grab a glass baby bottle from the pot of water on the stove. When he ducks back into the bedroom, I've been diverted enough to ask, "Um, Cass, it looked like Roger was…" I pause, not sure how to word my weird thought.

"He's letting MJ suckle." She says it plainly, as if it's the most natural thing in the world. Having a baby seems to have cracked them up.

"MJ is sucking Roger's nipple?" I have to say it out loud to digest it. "You all know he doesn't make milk, right?"

"I've been reading about this tribe in Africa. While the women hunt, the men suckle the babies to soothe them." I'm seriously beginning to reconsider my decision to come here. Being alone in a hotel room might be depressing, but at least there would be wine, chick flicks, and a comfy bed. Here, I'm probably in for a lot of tofu, coconut water, and a straw mat. "What's going on, Abby?"

"I'm sorry to just show up here. Jack and I had a huge fight. It was terrible." I take a shaky breath before I continue. "He left." My shoulders slump as my own words sink in.

"He left? I can't believe it; that doesn't seem like Jack. He adores you." Cassie passes me a box of tissues and rubs my back.

"Yeah, well, it seems I play second fiddle to Marilyn and even Sarah these days." I can taste the bitterness in my mouth.

"Sarah? What does she have to do with anything?" Cassie looks confused. I tell her about the email and how Sarah has re-entered our lives through the ever-so-helpful Marilyn. Then I tell her about Marilyn's money and how she thinks she's purchased our baby. We both hear MJ crying from the bedroom. She smiles tiredly and motions me to continue.

"That woman drives me insane. The problem is that her antics don't surprise me anymore. What hurts the most is that Jack can't seem to cut the cord. She has this hold over him, and he does her bidding. For once, I'd like to know he has my back. All of this went on behind it, and now he's gone." I break down in fresh tears.

"Abby, I'm sure he's not gone. He probably just went somewhere to cool off." Cassie stops when we both notice Roger peeking out from the bedroom door, to the symphony of screams. She squeezes my arm and heads to the bedroom. I grab a few tissues to try to mop up my face, and pull out my phone. My message box is empty. Cassie returns, rolling her eyes at me. I look at her questioningly.

"Don't get me started. MJ is really fussy these days, and Roger seems totally unable to cope. Honestly, I do everything around here, and it kills me that I can't sit out here with my sister who needs me, without being interrupted." She yells the last part in the direction of the door. "If you weren't so upset right now, I'd probably tell you that you're lucky to be missing a husband. Having a baby is really hard work and guys make it worse by being *incapable*," she hollers. "Sorry," she says to me quietly.

I am stunned. I've never heard my sister raise her voice, ever. She and Roger are usually so in tune with each other.

"You're finding motherhood hard? But Cass, you always seem so peaceful and, I don't know, earthy. You've flourished as a mom." Cassie's made it look so easy, but oh no – what if it is terribly hard? It's been so difficult getting to this point, I don't know if I can handle anything harder.

Cassie and I sit up until the wee hours of the morning talking. Every few hours MJ wakes up for food and Cassie changes, feeds, and burps her, then bundles her back into the crib. I'm certainly no parenting expert, but for a six-month-old, she seems to get up in the night a lot. I guess I've got a lot to learn.

I wake up to the smell of coffee and a sizzling sound from the kitchen. Cassie and I have fallen asleep together at opposite ends of the couch, our feet intertwined under a knitted blanket. Used tissues, cold cups of herbal tea, and empty chocolate bar wrappers litter the floor. Sometime in the night I had a craving for something chocolaty, and to my surprise, Cassie pulled out a box of hidden treats and we gorged like teenagers.

Roger is in the kitchen making coffee, toast, and eggs, tiptoeing around, making murmuring noises to MJ, who is strapped to his front. I watch him as he organizes a bottle for the baby and shoves a frittata in the oven for the rest of us.

"Morning, Roger. Something smells great." I smile at him and touch MJ's head.

"You girls had a late one. Breakfast is almost ready." He pulls out cutlery and plates and sets the table. I whisper my thanks and head to the bathroom to clean up. I know I won't be pretty, but my reflection in the mirror shocks me. I'm a disaster. I have makeup smeared under my eyes, which are red and puffy, and something that must be chocolate beside my mouth. My hair is dishevelled and I have a kink in my neck from sleeping on the couch. A hot shower would be heavenly right now, but the thought of putting yesterday's clothes back on changes my mind.

I slowly take out my phone to see if Jack has called. Damn, the stupid thing is dead. In my rush to get out of the house, I never thought to grab the charger. Fifteen minutes later I emerge from the bathroom, mostly clean. My stomach growls loudly when the smell of Roger's breakfast hits me. I see

Cassie and Roger sitting at the table, heads bent together, whispering to each other. Cassie strokes his arm and Roger returns by kissing her gently on the lips. Given the arguing that went on last night, it looks like a beautiful moment. I wonder if Jack and I will find that peace again. Cassie sees me in the hall and gets up to greet me.

"Are you okay?"

"I'm a little stiff from sleeping on the couch, but I'm fine. Something smells wonderful, and this little one," I point to my belly, "is ready for food." I sit down at the table and tuck into my frittata. It is wonderful and I applaud Roger.

"I make it with organic vegetables, free-range eggs, and tofu," he says, smiling in my direction. I usually avoid tofu, but this is really good. We all look up, startled, at a sudden pounding on the front door.

"Cassie, its Jack," comes a muffled voice from outside. "It's an emergency." He sounds panicked. I sit still, feeling frozen, while Roger and Cassie open the door as a united front.

"What do you want, Jack?" Cassie's voice is icy. I can't quite see the door, but I can tell they are standing as a barricade.

"Cassie, this is serious. I can't find Abby anywhere. I've been all over and she's not answering her phone. We had a huge fight last night and I can't find her. I'm so worried. What if something awful has happened to her? Oh god, I should call the hospitals." Jack sounds terrified. Part of me wants to run and soothe him, but I stay in my chair, rooted in place. "It's all my fault, Cassie. I know my mom isn't always the nicest to Abby, but I'm all she's got. I couldn't handle... Oh god, I walked out. I just needed to cool off, but when I got back, she was gone. She must have thought I'd left her. In the heat of the moment I probably wasn't making sense. Cassie, you have to help me."

"Maybe she doesn't want to be found, Jack. Your mother has been a bitch to Abby and you haven't done a thing about it. Abby and the baby are your family now, and your mother is going to have to suck it up."

Jack sounds wounded when he speaks next. "I know, Cassie. I told my mom that last night. I told her that if she didn't stop meddling, I wouldn't have her in my life anymore."

Jack's voice sounds so final and heavy with those words –
I'm sure it was the hardest thing he's ever done. Finally I
speak up.

"You really said that?" Cassie and Roger part, and Jack
steps over the threshold with a look of disbelief. He runs to me
and drops to his knees to hug me.

"Oh thank goodness you're okay. Abby, I was so worried. I
was such a jerk. I love you, I'm sorry. Please forgive me." I
don't think I've ever seen Jack so scared. "I've been looking
everywhere for you. I never thought to look here." He grimaces
and turns toward Cassie. "No offense, Cassie." She nods at him
and smiles at me.

"You really told your mother off?" I'm still not sure I believe
it. Cassie and Roger disappear down the hall, giving us privacy.

"I did. After I left our house–" we both wince at the word
'left,' "–I grabbed a beer and tried to cool off. I know I'm all
Mom's got, but you're all *I've* got, Abbs. I'm sorry I've let her
get in the middle. I promise you, things will be different from
now on." He looks at me eagerly.

"What about Sarah?" I whisper.

"There is nothing going on between me and Sarah. I swear.
I've told her to stop emailing me. I know I've been an ass, but I
love only you."

I'm betting this will not be the last I hear of Sarah, and I'm
sure Marilyn will still cause major problems down the road, but
maybe, just maybe, Jack and I will handle them as a team. I am
ever hopeful.

Roger materializes in the kitchen, refills the coffee pot, and
refreshes our tea. Cassie joins us and we all sit around the
table, MJ attached to my sister's breast. When it's time to go,
Cassie presses a bamboo container containing Roger's frittata
into my hands. Tofu to go, and I'm happy to take it. It's
amazing how much life can change in twenty-four hours.

28

I CAN HEAR the train doors closing as I head down the subway stairs. A year ago, it would have been a mad dash down the steps, desperately jumping through the doors as they closed, but now, thirty-four weeks pregnant, I have to take my time. I feel my phone vibrate in my purse, but I leave it, not even bothering to check who it might be, another shift from my ordinary. I've changed through this whole pregnancy process, and I'm tired of rushing through life. Knowing my impending motherhood is weeks away, I want to savor the time Jack and I have together as only a couple, and then I don't want to miss a minute of this kid's life.

"Jack? Are you home?" I yell as I open the front door and strip off my coat, which offers me little warmth against the early October chill. Thankfully I'm always hot these days, so that kind of balances out the temperature extremes. I kick off my shoes, which are killing my swollen feet. I see the red light on my phone flashing, but drop my purse on the table without a further glance.

"In here, Abbs. I've got a surprise for you." Jack pokes his head out from behind the kitchen door, using his body to shield whatever is waiting for me in the kitchen. He carefully closes the door behind him and meets me near the front door. "Did you have a good day?"

"It was fine. What's going on? What's the surprise?" I just hope it's a good surprise – good in my books might be different from good in his.

"Look, after what happened the other day and everything that we've been going through, and then with your big news, I wanted to surprise you with a proper celebration." He prods me toward the kitchen. "Go ahead."

Before I open the door, I turn to search Jack's face. He looks giddy and proud of himself. I silently pray I won't find Marilyn inside. I push the door and my mouth drops open in amazement. Three glasses of champagne greet me, and there, standing in the middle of my kitchen, is Jules.

"Congratulations on making partner, honey," she says.

"Jules." I rush forward to hug my best friend.

"And congrats on becoming a mom." I grip her tighter, and as the surging pregnancy hormones overtake me, I cry with joy.

"I'll just leave you two alone for a while," Jack says, backing out of the room as the waterworks continue, flowing freely from both of us now.

"When did you–? How long are you–?"

"It's a quick trip. Jack invited me, and I wanted to make sure you guys were okay." She examines my face. "Plus, it's high time we celebrated your partnership." She reaches for the champagne glasses and passes me mine. We clink glasses and smile. "Congratulations."

"Thanks. I'm good. Jack and I, we're good now." I take a tiny sip, feeling the bubbles burst on my tongue. "So, how's Victoria? How's Liam? If it's a quick trip, you'd better get talking." I grab her hand and drag her to the living room and the couch. "Jack," I call up the stairs. "Do you want to join us?"

"Sit around and gab all night with you two? I don't think so. Before the marathon begins, come check this out," he hollers down.

"When did you get in? You should have called me. I could have picked you up at the airport." I'm still holding Jules's hand, afraid she'll vanish if I let her go. We put down our glasses and walk to the stairs.

"Jack picked me up a few hours ago," she says as we climb the stairs. Jack is standing in front of the baby's room, beaming. When I turn to Jules, her clothing catches my eye – she's wearing paint-covered jeans and a baggy sweatshirt.

"You guys did it? You finished the baby's room?" I'm stunned and touched.

"Scott popped by a little while ago with the finishing touches. Tell us what you think." Jack opens the door. I had wondered why Scott had disappeared this afternoon.

As I enter the room, Jack flips on the light switch, and my breath catches in my throat. It is the most beautiful room I've ever seen. True to Scott's vision, the room is chocolate brown and dusty rose. My feet sink into a plush pink carpet with brown trim, and the walls are painted a very pale shade of dusty rose. An espresso-colored crib stands against the wall to my right, with light pink bedding and a mobile of dancing bears. A matching dresser with a change-tabletop occupies the opposite wall. In front of the window is a gliding chair, and I can easily picture myself nursing our baby and rocking her to sleep. The wall surrounding the window has been stencilled with butterflies and flowers. I smile toward Jules, knowing this is her special touch.

"So? What do you think?" Jack asks.

"It's perfect," I whisper, rubbing my belly.

"Thankfully your husband is handy, and putting the crib together wasn't nearly the catastrophe Liam encountered," Jules chuckles. She and Jack exchange amused glances, so I can only imagine it wasn't as easy as she says.

"You guys are the best." I pull each of them to me for a group hug. We stand together, imagining a little girl running around this room.

Hours later, Jules and I are firmly ensconced on the couch. Jack has cleared away the take-out boxes and cleaned up the kitchen. He plants a kiss on the top of my head.

"Don't stay up too late, you two."

"Okay, Dad." Jules rolls her eyes. I refill her wine glass and then cup my mug of tea, warming my hands.

"So, you guys are okay? I mean, really okay?" she asks, taking a sip of wine.

"We are now. Honestly, I really wasn't sure. It was awful, Jules, but we're okay now. He told his mom off, which is nothing short of a miracle, and she's been keeping a pretty low profile. Lord knows how long that will last. I'm sure Marilyn will revert to her usual self and Jack will be hard-pressed to do anything about it. Shame on me, I guess – I mean, I knew he was like this with his mom when we were dating."

"And Sarah?"

"That's over too. I mean, there wasn't really anything going on, but he isn't going to be her shoulder to cry on again." We lapse into a short silence until, "Jules? I know you talked to Jack a lot that night. Thank you."

"I wouldn't say 'talked'; more like chewed his ass out. And you're welcome. You gave us all a good scare when we couldn't find you. I never thought you'd hide out at Cassie's place."

"It's funny, but Cassie and I are getting closer. This whole motherhood thing has sort of leveled the playing field, I think. It's nice to know our kids will be close in age and hopefully good friends. She can still drive me nuts with all of her Internet-doctoring and tofu this-and-that, but she's kind of mellowing. I guess I am too."

"I still can't believe her in-laws aren't freaking about the name. With an old-money name like Ashfield, Moonjava is totally out there."

"I know, but it kind of grows on you, and they seem to be adopting the initials, which is probably best for everyone, including little MJ." I shift uncomfortably as the baby kicks a field goal into my ribs. "I've been pretty good at being patient with this kid, but honestly, she could come out any time."

"You know, Abby, the whole baby room thing, that's Jack's way of saying sorry. Guys suck at apologies."

"No kidding. But seriously, the room is magnificent. Thank you for being here and helping Jack. But I do have a bone to pick with you. You promised me a horny pregnancy stage and it never happened. I went from feeling crappy to feeling slightly less crappy – no burst of energy in the second trimester, and my libido completely abandoned me."

"That's too bad. I was an animal. It was a little embarrassing, even now. I hit on my doctor, the grocery bag boy, and there was a cute dog walker in our neighborhood who still goes past our house every day – I can barely make eye contact with him." Jules's face flushes and she cups her red cheeks.

"How do you do it, Jules?"

"Do what?"

"All of it – a great job, raise a wonderful daughter, run the PTA, and keep it all together? You make it seem effortless. I lie awake at night worrying I won't be able to handle it." Articulating it for the first time loosens the worry-knot in my stomach a little.

"Trust me, it's far from effortless. It's hard work, Abby, but it's great. Liam and I work together, balancing our crazy schedules and chauffeuring Victoria everywhere. You and Jack will figure it out. You won't be perfect at everything. That was the hardest part for me."

"Thanks for coming." I hug her fiercely.

"I'll be back to see the baby, I promise. You're going to be great."

29

"HOT OFF THE presses, Madame Partner." Scott bows and hands me my new business cards. I've been feeling a little melancholy since Jules's visit two weeks ago, but Scott's enthusiasm is infectious and I feel like a kid on Christmas morning as I snatch the box from his hand. I carefully untie the red bow, lift the lid, and catch my breath. "Abigail Nichols, Partner," is gleaming up at me in embossed gold. "What do you think?" Scott asks, smiling.

"Wow. They look great. Wo-ow, ow ow," I say. Either the baby just kicked me or my lunch is repeating on me. I inhale deeply and exhale slowly.

"Abby, what's going on, are you okay?"

Scott looks panicked as he rushes around the desk and pulls my chair out to peer into my face. He's the company safety officer, and if I'm not careful he'll try out his first aid skills on me. I wave him off and am opening my mouth to speak when suddenly I feel a gush of fluid. Scott shrieks and jumps back. We stare at the puddle darkening my pants, my chair, and the floor. All I can think is, *I hope I can get a new chair*. Scott, on the other hand, springs into action. He grabs my desk phone and punches the office intercom button. I hear his voice echo through the halls.

"Attention everyone, the baby is coming. I repeat: the baby is coming. Assume your positions. Get me hot water and blankets, pronto. Prepare the birthing room. I repeat: prepare the birthing room."

"Shut up, Scott!" I yell, hearing my voice on the overhead speaker. I push the release button on the phone, and the infernal intercom stops. "Hot water and blankets? *A birthing room?* Are you *high*? Call Jack and tell him my waters broke. I don't think I should move too much. In the prenatal class, they told us to expect more than one rush of water. Damn, I loved this chair." Scott punches Jack's number into the phone as I email our Procurement department and request a new chair.

"Oh my god, Jack, its coming, the baby is coming!" Scott screams into the phone.

"Give me that," I hiss, and wrench the phone away from my hysterical assistant.

"Abbs, what's going on, are you in labor?"

"Well, funny story actually, I had a contraction and my waters just broke. So, I guess it's time. Can you come and get me? Scott is about to call for an ambulance." As I finish, another contraction hits me. *Holy Mother of God, this hurts.*

"Abbs? Abbs? Can you hear me?" I hear Jack's voice and feel Scott take the phone from my hand, but all I can focus on is the intense pain.

"Jack says you have to breathe, Abby." Scott sounds as if he's a million miles away. "Breathe, Abby, that's it. He's on his way. Are you sure you don't want an ambulance?"

"You just want to see a cute guy in uniform," I pant, attempting a joke to get my mind off of my reality. "I thought firemen were cuter."

"Well, I can hardly set you on fire, can I? Your chair is certainly not flammable now. Firemen are of course the cutest, then the EMTs, and then police. Actually, I think park rangers are higher than the cops," Scott says, warming to the topic.

"You live in downtown Toronto. When have you ever seen a park ranger?"

"Well, if they are anything like the lifeguards at the swimming pool, trust me, they're hot." I catch Scott watching the clock. I'm sure he's praying for Jack to arrive.

"Do you keep a hotness scale?" I have no idea why I'm having this conversation; I just know it helps to get my mind off what's coming next. I also have no concept of time. It feels as if hours have passed since Scott phoned Jack. I only hope it hasn't been seconds.

"Whoa, here comes another one," I cry out, and I grip the handles of my soiled chair. Scott puffs with me, holding my hands. As the pain subsides, I hear a ruckus in the hallway, and then Jack barrels through the office door just as the head of our Production department appears with a bucket of water and blankets.

"Abbs, I'm here. I ran about four red lights and drove on the sidewalk for a block, but I'm here. Are you okay?" Jack is panting as well, but from racing here, not labor.

"Her contractions are five minutes apart. I could check to see if she's dilated..." Scott tapers off when Jack and I both shoot him daggers with our eyes.

"Over my dead body—" I start, but Jack cuts me off.

"Thank you for taking such good care of my girl, Scott. You've been terrific. Just help me get her to the car." Jack and Scott flank me and take my arms. "Show's over folks," Jack tells the crowd gathering at my door. Jack and Scott heave me upright, and another gush of water spews forth. I hear a volley of "Eww, gross" from the hallway, and I cringe with embarrassment. Just moments ago I was basking in the glow of my partnership title, and now I'm the woman who peed on her chair.

Four more contractions hit me in the car on the way to the hospital. Jack forgoes the parking lot, pulling into the emergency entrance instead. He leaps out of the car and runs to open my door. We leave the car parked at a weird angle, hazard lights flashing, and shuffle into the hospital.

"Oh, Jack, wait," I say, stopping in my tracks and gripping his arm. "We have to call my mom."

"I already did. She knows." He steers me toward the elevator. I barely hear his last line. "I called my mom too."

The elevator takes an eternity to arrive, and I am mentally counting down the seconds until the next big one hits. All I can think about is how badly I want drugs. Jack pushes the button for the fourth floor, just before a woman in her fifties joins us and a guy in his early thirties squeezes past the closing doors. Suddenly my body is wracked with pain and I moan aloud, trying my best to breathe through it. I look up, expecting the older woman to be calm and the young guy to be freaking out. Instead, the woman looks as if she's going to have a stroke, staring at me, eyes bugging out, while the guy nods in my direction and whispers loudly to Jack, "I was there yesterday, mate; hang in." *Hello? Remember me?* The woman writhing in pain? Thankfully the elevator doors open, and Jack helps me to the delivery ward.

As we enter the triage area, another contraction hits me. I know our prenatal instructor worked us hard on the breathing exercises, but honestly, they do fuck-all for the pain. I moan again, louder this time. A nurse appears as I double over, clutching the counter with white knuckles and wet clothes.

"Hi, my wife, Abigail Nichols, is in labor. Can you help her? She's only thirty-six weeks. Is it normal to be so early?" I can hear the rising panic in Jack's voice, but he seems to be holding it together.

"Well, I see someone's water has broken. Let's get you to a room," she says with a big smile. "Don't worry, Mr. Nichols, is it?"

"Williams, Jack Williams, actually."

The nurse turns to me. "Will you want an epidural?" *Will I? Let me count the ways.* I nod emphatically. "Okay, Abigail, come with me. The anesthetist is headed into a C-section, so we'd better grab him now." She strides down the hall and I follow slowly, leaning heavily on Jack, my soaking clothes hampering my effort. She leads us to a tiny delivery room that barely has room for the bed, let alone nurses, doctors, and daddy. Jack raises his eyebrows and I know what he's thinking: this is not the room they show on the prenatal tour. I don't care. I'd happily give birth in the parking lot, as long as someone gives me drugs. I groan again at the pain rushing through me.

"You are moving along quite quickly. Let's get you out of these wet clothes. The epidural should be here in a minute."

"They seem really close together now; is that normal?" asks Jack.

"She's about a minute apart. It just means we're going to have a baby soon. Here, Daddy, why don't you help Abigail?"

"Call me Abby," I mumble through clenched teeth.

"Abby it is." She bustles around the cramped space, opening cupboards and pulling out gowns and booties for me. The two of them handle me like a toddler who can't get dressed. Jack helps me out of my blouse and bends to take off my shoes.

The door to our room flies open and hits Jack squarely between the eyes with a thud. I see him stagger back into the wall and slide down to the floor. My eyes whip from Jack to the doorway. *Marilyn.* My worst nightmare. I'm mostly nude.

"There you are. I've been looking all over this hospital for you. I came as soon as you called, Jacky. Jacky? Are you okay? What on earth happened to you?" Marilyn crouches to check on a semiconscious Jack. Our nurse rushes over to check his vitals, shoving Marilyn out of the way in the process.

"Abigail, cover yourself, you're practically naked. It's really inappropriate, dear," Marilyn hisses in my direction. If I wasn't starting into my next contraction, I might laugh at her absurdity, even at the fact that she barged in and knocked my husband senseless, but humor is not my companion right now. Pain and rage are my BFFs. A contraction ripples through my body. My coach is lying prone on the floor. My only medical assistance is now treating my prostrate husband, and I am left on my own to deal with the pain and with Marilyn.

"Get out!" I scream at full volume. Marilyn's head snaps up, and I see Jack slowly coming around, my shrillness reaching his brain like smelling salts. "Get this woman out of here – now." There is no stopping me. Doctors, nurses, and even some security-looking types materialize at my door, and I hold my blouse over my chest.

"Is this woman bothering you?" says a voice from the crowd. I see Marilyn shaking her head and Jack trying to focus but still looking pretty out of it.

"Yes," I yell. "She is totally bothering me. She is not supposed to be here and I don't want her here." Marilyn looks at me with a shocked expression.

"You'll have to come with us, ma'am," one of the security guys says. Marilyn looks undecided. I know she hates being called "ma'am"; she complained to Jack and me once that it made her feel old. I let out a guttural moan, with the next contraction riding on the back of the previous one, and that seems to change her mind.

"I actually have a few things to do, so I'll just check back later." She is holding her head high, as if it's her decision to leave. "Really, I don't know what all the fuss is about, Abigail—" Before she can try to turn the situation into one in which I take the blame, our nurse nods at the security guards and closes the door firmly in Marilyn's face.

"Thank you," I say to her as the pain eases momentarily.

"Wow, she's a piece of work," she says as she helps Jack to a chair and then turns back to me to help me slip on a hospital gown. I wiggle out of my pants and underwear and sigh.

"You don't know the half of it," I say, and tense as the door opens again. A masked man in scrubs enters the room.

"Ah, here he is. Abby, this man here is going to make you feel a lot better." The nurse helps me sit on the edge of the bed, and I half listen to the warnings and side effects of an epidural. The whole accidental-paralyzing part doesn't remotely worry me. Feeling nothing from the waist down would be a dream right now. I nod my assent, and the nurse tells me to hunch over and curve my spine. Oh sure, I'll just hunch over with a watermelon pressed to my body. It's next to impossible to get myself in the right position. My nurse is so patient and cheers me on as I do my best to hold the proper posture for what seems like an hour.

"Hold very still, Abby," the nurse whispers in my ear. I try my hardest, and just when I think I can't take one more second, I hear the anesthetist.

"Okay, we have it in place. You should feel a warm sensation, and then you should feel not much of anything." He cleans up his supplies and checks the clock on the wall. I'm sure they are waiting for him in the operating room. Within seconds, I feel the warmth he described moving from my toes to my belly. My legs tingle a little, and then everything feels heavy. I try to move, but nothing happens. He lowers his mask and smiles at me. I smile very contentedly back at him. I like this guy. He talks quietly to the nurse and then departs.

Our nurse helps me lie back on the bed and covers my lower body with a blanket, pulling up my gown to expose my huge belly. She straps two belts around my middle, explaining that one monitors the baby and the other monitors my vitals. Another woman clad in scrubs appears, doing a double-take when she sees Jack groggy on the chair. She rolls her eyes and smiles at me. If she hasn't heard about the commotion, she probably thinks Jack is one of those men who pass out when his partner is in labor.

"Hi, Abigail, I'm Dr. White. I'm the doctor on call for deliveries today. It's nice to meet you." She is calm and authoritative, and between her and the nurse, I feel I'm in good hands. "I'd like to take a look and see how far along you are." I nod my assent, and they help move my legs to allow for a full-frontal view. Dr. White places one hand on my knee and the other disappears. I can feel pressure, but thankfully no pain. "Okay," she says and both hands are visible again as she strips off her gloves. "You're about three centimeters dilated. We have a ways to go still. Just lie back and relax. I'll be back in a little bit." She confers quietly with the nurse, shoots a glance at Jack, and then departs.

"What hit me?" Jack asks from the chair, trying to rise slowly.

"You walked into the door. It happens a lot in these small rooms," says our nurse, winking in my direction.

"I'm sorry, I didn't catch your name," I ask, when she finishes pointing out how the monitor works and how I can self-administer my pain drugs.

"Joy," she says with a smile. The banisher of Marilyn and the bringer of drugs. Joy is a perfect name – and one to remember.

30

"HERE COMES ANOTHER one." Jack loves watching the monitor and seeing the red line build up with each coming contraction. "You really can't feel it?" He's sitting beside me, wedged between my bed and the wall on a hard-backed gray metal chair. The egg on his forehead is diminishing, but a Technicolor bruise is appearing. He periodically rubs my belly and holds my hand.

"No. I mean, I know something is happening, but I can't feel it. Wow, look at them go." We both watch as each contraction hypnotically peaks and then dives off, only to peak again. I hold the magic wand of drugs in my hand and keep an eye on the red light. I can't go crazy with my epidural; it's on a time sensor. I don't push the button every time the light changes, but hold it close in case I need a top-up.

"Have you given any more thought to a name for our little one?" I ask.

Joy bursts into the room, followed closely by Dr. White and two other people dressed in scrubs. Tension follows them like a cloud of thick smoke. Jack and I instantly freeze and look wide-eyed at them. Joy bustles around me, pushing buttons on the monitor and readjusting the straps across my belly. Dr. White and the other two stand alert at the foot of my bed. No one seems to be breathing. Jack and I exchange worried glances, and I feel him squeeze my hand painfully.

"Is everything all right?" I slowly enunciate each word. Jack is applying quite a bit of pressure to my hand. I can feel that, at least. No one answers. "Joy?" I ask again.

Suddenly we hear the sound of the baby's heart beat and the room lets out a communal breath. I see Joy's shoulders relax, and the two scrubs smile and walk out. The room suddenly has oxygen again.

"We lost the heartbeat for a minute. I think your belt slipped a little. Just to be on the safe side, we're going to attach a monitor to the top of the baby's skull. That way we'll have a direct line to her," Joy says, pulling on latex gloves. The two scrubs reappear, pulling a cart behind them.

"How exactly do you attach it to the skull?" Jack asks, the engineer in him wanting to understand how things work.

"We basically screw it into the top of the head," one scrub pipes up.

"Excuse me? You screw something into my baby's head?" I ask, in disbelief. "Are you joking?"

"Abby, it's perfectly safe. We need to keep track of the baby's heartbeat. I promise it won't hurt her. We also need to see how dilated you are now. It's been a few hours since Dr. White checked, and your contractions are very close together." Joy's voice calms my fears as she gently bends my legs, placing my feet together, and lets gravity pull my knees to the side. Dr. White leans in to feel the diameter of my cervix, and I see the other two scrubs lean in close. Jack shifts in his seat, uncomfortable with so many people checking out his wife's nether regions, but the time spent in Dr. Greenberg's office and the parade of interns and techs who saw me naked or violated me has made me pretty immune.

"Ten centimeters. Good job, Abigail." Dr. White looks up and gives me an encouraging smile. "Head is engaged, but she's turned. Dr. Walling, thoughts?" Dr. White looks back at the scrubs. Joy sees the look of confusion between Jack and me.

"The baby should be coming out face down. It appears your little one is sunny-side up," she explains.

"Is that bad?" we ask simultaneously.

"It's not bad, just not ideal." Joy is cut off as the interns bounce ideas off Dr. White. I miss most of the back and forth, but pay attention as they agree on a game plan.

"Okay, Abigail, here's what we're going to do. I'm going to manually turn the baby, and then we'll have you push a little. I'm hoping that will re-engage the head, and then she'll be facing the right way. Okay?" Dr. White asks.

"Sure," I say hesitantly.

Jack holds one hand and Joy takes the other while Dr. White almost disappears between my legs. I didn't think ten centimeters was a very big measurement, but it looks as if she's going to climb right inside. I feel a ton of pressure, poking and prodding, and am so grateful for the epidural. I'm sure I'd be screaming bloody murder without it. How Cassie did this drug-free is beyond me.

"Okay, Abigail, give me a big push." Dr. White's voice seems to float up from inside my vagina. A big push; I can do that. I screw up my face and attempt to push with all of my might. Nothing happens. Actually, something might have happened, but I can't feel anything, so I have no idea if I even pushed at all. What a weird non-sensation.

"Good, that's really good. There, she should stay there." Dr. White reappears and takes off her gloves. The interns look pleased with themselves, and Joy pats my hand.

"It won't be long now, Abby," Joy says.

When the room clears out, Jack runs his hands through his hair and stifles a yawn. "What time is it?" I ask. It's as if the passage of time doesn't exist in this vacuum.

"Ten o'clock," he says, yawning again. Our prenatal class taught us to have a bag packed in advance. I had it all picked out and the printed list of required items on my dresser, but my water breaking this early means I didn't have it ready. Poor Jack. I had snacks, music, and a change of clothes for him on the list.

"You haven't eaten all day; you should probably go get something downstairs," I say. "I'm fine, you go ahead."

"Oh shit, I forgot all about the car," Jack exclaims, jumping out of his chair. "Christ, they've probably towed it by now." He fumbles in his pockets for the keys and blows me a kiss as he runs out the door.

I lie back and close my eyes. I listen to the monitor softly beep out the heartbeats of my little girl. I hold a hand to my belly and whisper, "I can't wait to meet you, little one."

I hear a soft tap on the door and I open my eyes, praying Marilyn hasn't sneaked past security, but no. "Mom," I breathe, and tears fill my eyes.

"Hi honey, is everything going okay?" My mom breezes into the room, her gauzy dress flowing behind her. She kisses my forehead and takes Jack's seat beside me. I catch a subtle smell of incense, but it feels reassuring for once, and I clutch her hand.

"It all happened so fast, I didn't get a chance to call you." I know Jack and I decided to have the labor room to ourselves, but it feels nice having my mom here.

"It's okay. Jack called me when he was on his way to pick you up. He sounded quite panicked. I know you two want to do this alone, but I thought I'd sneak in and check on my baby girl."

"I'm okay, Mom, just kind of scared and freaked out. Marilyn came barging in like she owned the place and knocked Jack out cold with the door. I didn't have any drugs yet, so I started screaming and they had to call security. That isn't exactly how I planned it. I don't know that I'm ready for this." I wipe away tears with the back of my hand.

"Abby, you have to remember that when it comes to babies, and even children for that matter, life rarely goes according to plan. You have to give up some control, which I know you hate to do. Trust me, things have a way of working out, but they might not go along with *your* plan. You might not be ready, but this little girl is ready to make her appearance today." She smiles at me and kisses my forehead again. "You're going to be a wonderful mother. Look at all you and Jack have been through. This is the easy part."

"I don't know, Mom. I don't know what to do."

"I am so proud of you and I love you so much. You can do this. You are the toughest person I know."

"Really?"

"Really. Now, I should go. I don't want Marilyn to see me if she's lurking in the halls." I laugh out loud for the first time all day. "That woman is very strange, but being a mother makes you do strange things sometimes. I don't know how you put up with her, Abby. I would have decked her by now – although having her taken away by security was a nice touch." I laugh at the mental image of my peace-loving mother slugging Marilyn. "Good luck, sweetheart; you're going to be great."

"I love you, Mom," I say, squeezing her hand three times the way my nana used to.

"I love you, too, baby girl," and she leaves as quietly as she came.

I dry my eyes and lie back, both hands over my belly. "Come out soon, baby girl. I love you," I whisper.

31

"IT'S TIME, ABIGAIL." My eyes open, and I find Joy at my head and Dr. White and her shadows by my feet.

"Jack should be back any minute," I say, willing him to materialize.

"It will take us a few moments to get ready. Don't worry, he won't miss it," Joy reassures me. Activity happens all around me while I lie still, taking it all in. Joy reaches for the magic wand of drugs, but I clutch it to my breast like a safety line. "Abby, we need you to be able to feel the pushing to get the baby out. If the pain gets too intense, I'll top you up again." She's talking to me as if she's a cop disarming a suspect. I hand it over, hesitantly. Jack arrives at the door looking flushed.

"Whew, thankfully the car was still there–" He stops in his tracks when he sees everyone in the room. "Oh no, did I miss it?"

"Good timing, Daddy, we're ready to go."

Jack perks up at being called Daddy. I have to admit, it has a wonderful ring to it. "We'll need Dad on one side and Joy on the other," Dr. White continues. "Abigail, they're going to hold your legs. Each time a contraction comes, you are going to take a deep breath and push. You might be able to push a few times during each contraction. Are you ready?" On one hand, I'm totally ready; on the other, I'm completely terrified.

Joy senses my hesitation. "You can do this, Abby, I know you can." This woman should be sainted. They should use her to defuse the conflict in the Middle East. I'm sure she could bring about world peace. Her tone, her smile – she exudes calm and safety. I nod, knowing that because Joy says so, I can do this.

"Here comes one," an intern shouts enthusiastically. Dr. White gives him a stern look. We all look at the monitor and see the peak forming, which means a contraction is coming.

"Push, Abby, push," Jack and Joy say in stereo on either side of my head. And I do. I take a deep breath, scrunch up my face, and bear down as hard as I can.

"Good, good," I hear Dr. White say. I pause for another big inhale. "Again, push again, Abigail." So I do. The cycle seems endless. At the beginning of each contraction, I take a deep breath and push with all of my might, take a quick breath, and do it again. Between contractions, Jack offers me chips of ice to suck on while Joy mops my forehead with a cool cloth. I'm covered in sweat from my efforts.

"Okay, let's take a little break. Abigail, you're doing great." Dr. White stands and stretches. "You've got a stubborn one here," she says lightheartedly. "I've got another woman to check in on. You can try a few more pushes, but it doesn't seem like we're making much progress here. I'd like to suggest using forceps." I can see the new intern rubbing his hands together with glee. I shudder at the thought of large tongs being used to grab hold of my baby's head and wrench her from my body. No thanks. Joy is carefully watching my face. She rubs my arm.

"Let's see what we can do. It will be fine," she says reassuringly. As Dr. White and her shadows open the door to leave, I can hear the sound of someone in pain. The door closes behind them, sheltering us from the yelling and beeping of the delivery ward.

"I don't want forceps," I say as soon as they've gone.

"Well, if we really get stuck, we might not have another option," Joy says calmly. Tears spring to my eyes, exhaustion weighing me down.

"I'm not sure I can do this."

"You can do this, baby." Jack kisses my cheek and strokes my hair. "I wish I was half as strong as you are," he whispers in my ear, his voice thick with emotion.

"I just can't," I cry.

Joy squeezes my hand, and I can almost feel a transfer of her energy into me. I blow my nose and nod at both of them, and we start the cycle again.

"Come on, Abbs, push," Jack chants.

"She's made good progress, Abby; we're getting close," Joy says, as she continually bustles around me, doing things.

"You're doing great, Abbs. I'm so proud of you," Jack says, eyes shining. He kisses the tip of my nose, probably the only spot that isn't sweaty. I instantly get a lump in my throat.

"Samantha," I whisper.

"Samantha – Sam – I like that." Jack smiles at me.

There's a knock on our door, and Dr. White returns with her interns, one carrying a metal tray. Oh no, the dreaded forceps. Just looking at the tray makes me squirm.

"So how are we doing in here?" Before I can answer, Joy comes to my rescue, again.

"We've made some amazing progress. I was actually about to call you. Abby has done tremendously well. I think we're almost there." She pats my knee.

"Great, let's take a look." Dr. White gloves up while I keep an eye on the guy with the tray. "Abigail, do you want to try again?" *Hell yeah,* I think, nodding. *Just keep those tongs away from my kid and my crotch.*

We all resume our positions, and I push like crazy throughout the next contraction. I slump back afterwards and signal Jack for ice chips, to quench the desert-like conditions in my mouth. I catch an exchange of glances between Joy and the doctor and worry, until Joy beams in my direction.

"Abby, we're almost there. I need you to push really hard on the next contraction," she says. *What do you think I've been doing for the past few hours?* I nod. Jack leans toward me and our foreheads touch.

"Here we go, babe. You've got this. It's all you." I appreciate his effort, but I feel more like a quarterback than a woman in labor. He's obviously digging deep into his pep-talk repertoire. I see one intern pointing toward the monitor, and I know from the tensing in my gut that it's show time. From somewhere inside the depths of my body, I call on every last ounce of strength I possibly have and … push.

I inhale quickly to try another push before the contraction ends, but I realize Jack and Joy have released my legs. Then I notice everyone standing around looking shocked. I look between my legs, and there is a baby girl on the table, flailing around on her back.

"Oh my God," I yell, and that seems to break the trance. Joy and Dr. White scoop up the baby, and I hear a wonderfully angry cry. It is the most beautiful sound in the world.

"You did it, Abby. She's here." Jack kisses me and strokes my cheek.

"Daddy?" Dr. White turns to Jack. "Would you like to cut the cord?" I lie back and close my eyes, exhausted and elated all at the same time. I've been up for hours, maybe even days at this point, and I'm physically spent, but I know sleep will not come, nor do I want it to. I have a feeling that this is my last moment of peace for a very long time, and my brain is urging my body to take it. I can hear everyone bustling around, checking the baby, weighing her. Joy leaves her with the group of doctors and turns her attention to me, wrapping blankets around me to keep me warm.

"Well done, Abby. Sunny-side up and all in one push. You have a stubborn little girl there who wanted to check out the world as she entered. She arrived like a champagne cork popping. I like her style."

"Holy cow, Abbs, if she wasn't attached to the cord, she would have shot across the room." Jack is shaking his head in amazement. I close my eyes again, relaxing.

"Abbs?" I open my eyes at Jack's voice. My breath catches in my throat. What a picture: Jack is standing beside me, holding the tiniest little bundle. This is my family.

"Do you want to hold her?" he asks quietly. All I can do is nod and open my arms. Jack, with some help from the nimble hands of Joy, settles the baby on my chest. She is so small and helpless, and she is the most beautiful creature I've ever seen. Our baby: I like the sound of that.

I barely notice that Dr. White has returned and is working intently on my ravaged nether regions. Jack and I are too enraptured by our baby to care.

"So," Joy says quietly, "does this little girl have a name?"

"Samantha," we say in unison.

"Samantha Joy," I finish, looking to Jack for confirmation. We hadn't discussed a middle name, but this feels right. He nods at me in agreement.

"That's wonderful," Joy says, sounding choked up. "Thank you."

"No, thank you. We couldn't have done this without you." Jack pulls out the camera to take a picture of Mommy, Samantha, and her middle-namesake.

When Joy leaves, Jack, Samantha, and I enjoy our first quiet moments together. I make my first attempt at breast-feeding and am overjoyed when we have a successful latch.

Once I've been stitched up, Joy wheels us over to the maternity ward. Since she's a delivery nurse, her work is finished, and saying good-bye is like losing a best friend. We promise to keep in touch, exchanging email addresses and contact details. She hugs me one last time, and I try to imagine the emotional roller coaster she must ride every day if she gets this attached to all of her patients.

Thanks to Marco's questionable lifestyle, Axis has a great health insurance plan and we are fortunate to get a private room. Jack stands at the end of the bed and stares at me and Samantha.

"I can't believe it, Abbs. You were incredible. This ... this whole thing is unbelievable. I'm so happy." I tear up again, surprised I can still make tears, and then our maternity ward nurse arrives, wheeling in what looks like a clear plastic box. Turns out it's a bassinet for the baby – gone are the days when babies went to the nursery so new mothers could get some rest. She carefully places Samantha, fully swaddled, in the bassinet. Jack stretches out on the vinyl chair and drops off to sleep immediately, snoring softly. I know this is my chance to sleep too, but instead, I find myself staring at Samantha, talking to her softly as she sleeps.

"I love you, baby girl. We wanted you so badly. Someday I'll tell you all about it. Here you are, finally, after all that waiting. Sam."

I whisper to her through the rest of the night until the sun peeks through the blinds, signaling daybreak. Even without sleep, I feel rested. Today feels like the first day of my life, as if everything till now was just practice for the real thing.

There's a soft knock at the door and our nurse reappears. As the door opens, I hear the sounds of the hospital and the cries of babies not as well behaved as ours. She helps me to the bathroom, eager to record any business on my part. When I emerge, having washed my face and brushed my teeth, I hobble back to bed.

I watch Jack working with the nurse. She is coaching him on how to change a diaper, how to swaddle, and how to carefully cradle Samantha's head. Once I get settled back on the bed, it's time to feed again. I'm not nearly as graceful or swift as Cassie, but somehow Sam and I figure out how to make it work. I watch her cheeks work in the effort to drink.

Outside our room there are loud voices, and I know that our cocoon of warmth and safety is about to be breached.

"Auntie Scott is here," he sings as he pushes through the door with a magnificent bouquet of flowers, balloons, and a huge pink teddy bear. He envelops Jack in a huge hug, letting the balloons float to the ceiling. "I brought the most adorable outfit; where is the little one?" Scott kisses me on the forehead, admires Sam, and in a mock whisper says, "So, any cute doctors?"

Someone clears their throat and I look toward the door, hoping Scott hasn't dragged Marco along with him to see my boobs hanging out, but instead of Marco, there is a nervous-looking Marilyn in the doorway, holding a small suitcase. She looks unsure.

"I hope you don't mind, but I let myself into your house. I figured you could both do with a change of clothes." She is still hovering in the doorway.

Maybe it's because I've just become a mother, maybe it's hormones, but either way, my heart goes out to her.

"Thank you, Marilyn. That is so sweet of you. Come and meet your granddaughter." I pat the bed beside me, making room for her to join us. Marilyn's face is all the thanks I need. She pecks Jack on the cheek and brushes past Scott to sit with me.

"Oh, Abby," she starts.

Abby? Wow, that's a change. Jack raises his eyebrows – he heard it too.

"She's absolutely gorgeous. She looks just like you."

"Would you like to hold her?" I ask.

"I'd love to." I carefully hand over Sam and try to rearrange my gown, tucking my breasts inside it. I watch as Marilyn gazes at our daughter.

"Mom, her name is Samantha Joy. We're going to call her Sam." Jack takes a picture of Marilyn looking radiant, cradling Sam.

Scott leans over to whisper in my ear, "I think you've finally tamed the beast," and I suspect that's the case.

Over the next several hours, doctors and nurses appear to check, measure, chart, and test. Scott heads back to the office with digital photos and baby stories to share. Marilyn reluctantly heads home with promises to see us the next day, Cassie arrives with my mother, and Jack sneaks home to have a quick shower and check in at the office.

"Open it, sweetheart," says my mom, handing me a pink package. As she walks around the room, bouncing Sam in her arms, I open the box to find a mini version of Nana's quilt, the perfect size for a little girl.

"Do you like it?" Mom asks, smiling at me.

I bite my lower lip. "It's gorgeous, Mom. How did you–? Where did you get it?"

"Mom's been taking a quilting class," Cassie says.

"Your sister gave me the idea. I didn't realize you still had Nana's quilt."

"I love it. It's perfect. Thank you." I stroke my mother's handiwork.

∽

By late afternoon, Jack, Sam, and I are finally alone, just the three of us. Sam wants to eat every two hours, and in the short time we've had together, I am becoming more adept at the whole breast-feeding thing. Our nurse arrives and quietly makes another check of Sam.

"Okay, I think you're ready," she states, clapping her hands together softly. Jack looks at me and I shake my head. I have no idea what she's talking about.

"Ready for what?" Jack asks.

"To go home, of course."

"We're going home? *Now?*" Are these people insane? I just had a baby. My mom was in hospital for a week when she gave birth. It's only been, like, twenty-four hours.

"You're fine, dear. Samantha is the picture of health. It's time." She sounds so final. I can feel the walls closing in on me and I struggle to breathe.

How can they send me home? I don't have a clue what to do with a baby. I want to stay here, with the doctors and nurses, to tell me when to feed and help change diapers and give baths. *Breathe Abby, breathe.* I've read every possible book on how to get pregnant, and what do to when pregnant, but we were having such trouble conceiving, I didn't want to jinx us by reading the baby books. So, I haven't read a single thing about babies. I can feel myself hyperventilating. Jack grips my arm, and I stare up at him in a wild panic.

"Abbs." His voice is calm. "Abbs, we can do this."

"I don't know what to do. How do you know the bath is the right temperature? How do you know which cry means food and which means a wet diaper? What happens if she gets sick? How do I know if she's getting enough milk? Oh Jack, we can't do this? We're not equipped!" I can hear the hysteria in my voice.

"Abbs, we'll have lots of help. Jules is available by phone, and there are two very excited grandmothers waiting in the wings. I think it's time we let them loose. You're going to be an awesome mom."

"Really? You really think we can do this?" I still don't know, but Jack sounds so sure.

"Let's go home."

Acknowledgments

My parents told me getting pregnant would be no problem –
apparently our folk are from fertile stock. So it was a total
shock to me when, month after month, nothing happened.
Struggling with infertility is a very sad and isolating state.
We found it easy to wallow in our despair, but tried our
hardest to find something lighthearted on our quest. Talking
with friends over a glass of wine, my husband and I would
highly exaggerate our clinic visits to the point of hilarity,
mostly as a coping mechanism. After one such wine-soaked
evening, a friend suggested I start writing it all down. And
here we are.

Thank you to my early readers, including Jo Ann Cole,
Jennifer Bradley-Reid, Ashley Audrain, Y.J. Oh, Michelle
Askew, Carol Morawetz, Joanna Sugar, Kate Greenhouse, and
Melanie Evans, for offering up comments and suggestions, and
for cheerleading.

Thank you to Michelle MacAleese, my wonderful editor;
Two Dots Design for my fabulous cover and website; and
Anna Prior Photography, who made me look my best.

Thank you to Jenny Govier and Meghan Behse at Tryst
Books, for bringing *Ms. Conception* to life. We have been on a
terrific journey together.

Thank you to my parents, who might have been slightly
off-base on the fertility advice early on, but who have given me
their unconditional love and support throughout my life. My

mother, father, step-mother, and mother-in-law make up a quartet of fantastic grandparents, and I am ever grateful.

Thank you to my sister, Joanna, for your advice and support on my pregnancy journey and on my writing adventure. You are a brilliant naturopath, a great sister, and a wonderful mother.

Thank you to my kids, Sydney and Travis, who wake me up earlier than I'd like every morning, but make me smile each day. This journey started because of you.

Thank you to my husband, Tom, for riding the crazy infertility roller coaster with me. You knew when to hug me, open the big bottle of wine, or duck. I wouldn't have wanted anyone else by my side – although I think you may have derived a little too much pleasure in giving me needles every day. Thank you for making me smile when I didn't think I could and for challenging me to write this book and see it through.

CPSIA information can be obtained at www.ICGtesting.com
Printed in the USA
LVOW10s0317100415

433968LV00003B/119/P